THE PATH THAT TAKES US HOME

BOOK ONE

the prologue

When The Trees All Burned

ALANNA RUSNAK

First Printing: 2025
Chicken House Press

ISBN trade paperback edition: 978-1-990336-94-2

Library and Archives Canada Cataloguing in Publication
CIP data on file with the National Library and Archives

CHICKEN HOUSE PRESS
282906 Normanby/Bentinck Townline
Durham, Ontario, Canada, N0G 1R0
www.chickenhousepress.ca

*for my children
you will always have a home to return to*

*and for Scott
because at the end of the world,
I will still choose you*

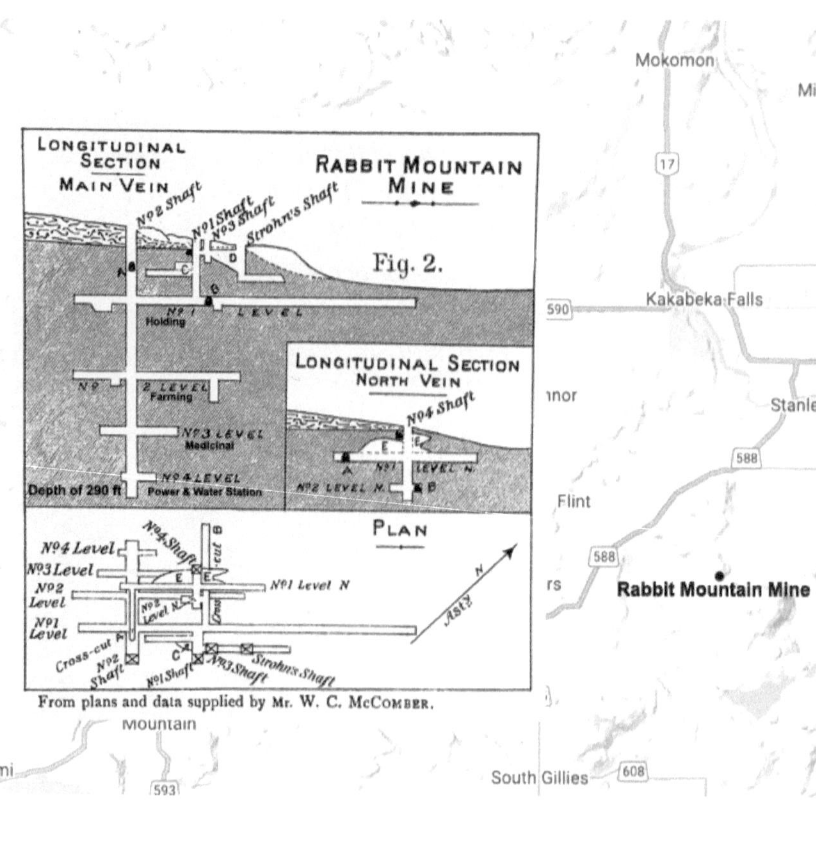

From plans and data supplied by Mr. W. C. McComber.

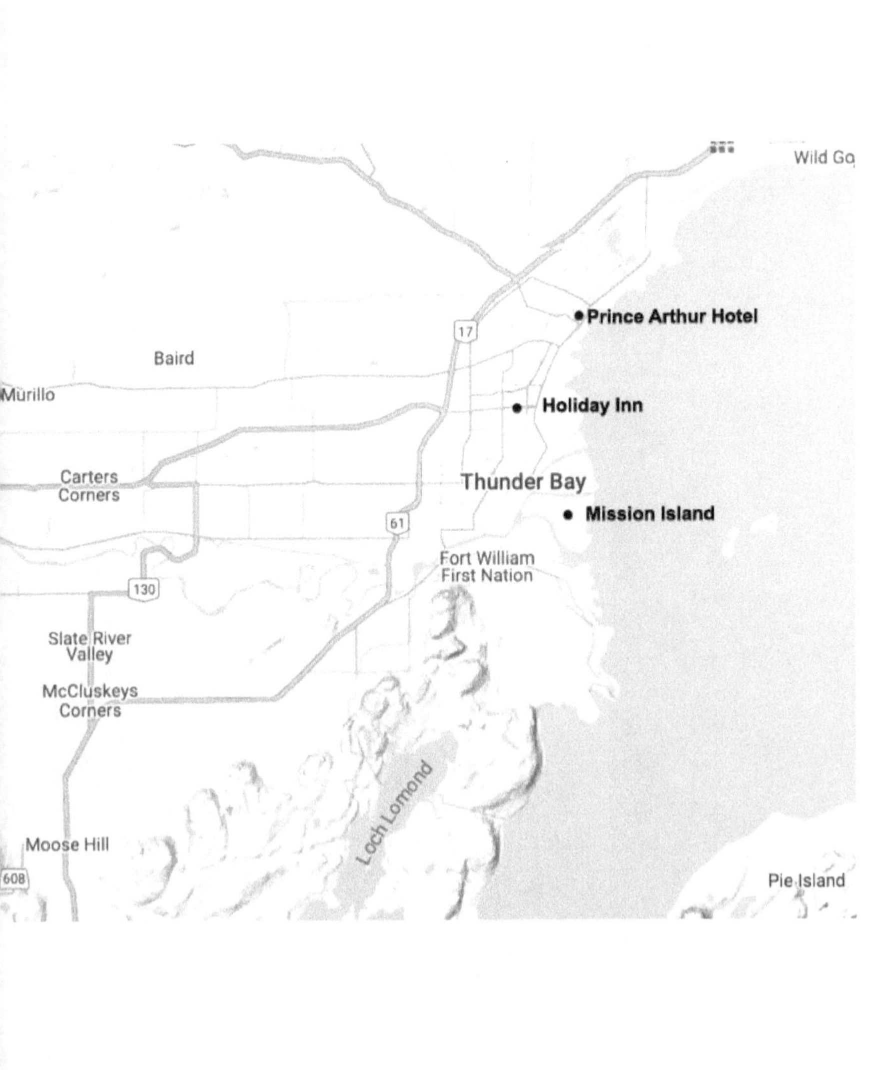

Wild Go
Prince Arthur Hotel
17
Baird
Murillo
Holiday Inn
Carters
Corners
Thunder Bay
61
Mission Island
Fort William
First Nation
130
Slate River
Valley
McCluskeys
Corners
Loch Lomond
Moose Hill
608
Pie Island

Save others, snatching them out of the fire.

Jude the Apostle

The noise is why we're aching;
The silence is what we fear.

Alias Grace

This is not the path that takes us home;
This is not the scar that ends the fight.
This is not the final victory march;
It's heaven raining down tonight.

Pocket Rochelle

WHEN THE TREES ALL BURNED

Alanna Rusnak

Prologue
2 days after Labour Day | Rabbit Mountain
Mine | Ninety feet below ground

Somewhere beyond this deep stone coffin, my husband's body lays among the wreckage of my city. I have wasted so many hours fantasizing about being a widow and now, with reality weighing down on me in all its stench and hunger and unfamiliar voices, it is nothing like I imagined. It is, in fact, empty. The freedom I longed for is strangled in this pit, and I am lost.

I will always remember when the lights went out because, before this moment, I've never known more than the murky gloaming of asphalt and traffic. A life in the city ensures you gain no true context of darkness. Street lights illuminate secrets, making shadows for the ones too awful to accept as real. There are no stars, and even the moon hides his face from the dusky dealings that go on in twilight corners. And even though my own life is riddled with an ugliness that was pushed upon me, an ugliness I worked so hard to hide from my neighbours, I've always believed in the general goodwill of humanity. I believe in evil too. I've worn it in the bruises on my arm and the way my hip aches in the winter from that time I "fell" into the coffee table; but it wasn't until this inky blackness slunk across my vision that I understood what it meant to be truly blind, susceptible to every finger of damnation that waited to trace along my spine. This is all a nightmare. What we cannot see cannot be real; therefore, in darkness, there is no law. We have only ourselves, our thoughts, and the sounds of the other trapped souls—whispering, crying, screwing—reminding us that though we are terribly lonely, we are not alone. Purgatory, it appears, is the most crowded loneliness of all.

What happened to me?

Nothing. I am saved. This is my salvation. The salve for a nation. How lucky. How fortunate. How cursed.

Here, deep beneath the surface of the earth, I am in and of the darkness, confined to a future in which I may never see a single star again. Maybe I will paint them, splash a canvas with my memory, try to capture a feeling in oil or acrylic or whatever they have for me here. There is still a little paint under my fingernails. I know because I can taste it when I chew my cuticles in boredom and nervousness.

We are the two hundred. We are The Reaping.

The end of the world hadn't been a secret. It had been laid out before us like a buffet table and each of us picked up a fork of chance and took a bite on the gamble that the prediction was right and we might be saved. But here? This saving…? It doesn't feel free. It feels heavy and foul and empty with the kind of weight that leaves me breathless.

Flashlights bounce like distant ships in the night. The assigned jogging pants are snug around my extended middle. The matching sweatshirt is too short and I cower under the blanket on my cot, shivering not from cold, but from a deep fear as I feel the baby move within me. And something else. Hope?

"Aiya? Aiya, are you okay?" His voice cuts through the darkness with a tenderness that contradicts reality. "Do you have everything you need?"

Why does he even care?

"Yes," I say, lying because it is easier now than exploding in sorrow/fear/relief.

His fingers fumble in the darkness until they find mine, slipping something into my palm. "Only a few more hours and then we'll test the system," he says. "We will have light again soon."

"Thank you," I say. I hear him leave and I miss him even though he is little more than a stranger.

Sitting up in bed, I tear the package from what he gave me and bite into the chocolate. I groan with pleasure. I try to remember what his eyes looked like when he first took off his mask. The mask had been beautiful—museum worthy—but his face… his face was something that truly belonged inside a piece of art. A portrait by Rembrandt or da Vinci. And his eyes? I know his eyes hold a story deeper than the history of the world. Such dark skin. Such rich blue eyes. A strange and poetic paradox.

I knew the story of his birth, just like everyone else in the modern world. I'd questioned his existence, his humanity, the ethics of how he came to be. But to be in his presence… had I ever felt a connection like that before? A moment so purely human and magnetic?

I take another bite, recognizing small pieces of caramel and sea salt. Darkness surrounds this place, but this chocolate, chocolate which I know is nearly the colour of the air around me, is like the sun.

My husband is dead. The air is stale. I am alive and there is life within me, though the idea of celebrating seems repulsive in the light of all the burning bodies beyond the dome.

Welcome. You have successfully subscribed to the monthly newsletters of Rajiv Montgomery Noah: man, father, prophet, servant. If you believe you are receiving this message by mistake, please unsubscribe by scrolling to the footer. To embrace the official welcome from Mr. Noah, please continue…

Dearly Beloved,

I come before you in complete seriousness and utter humility. I am very pleased to make your acquaintance, though it is with deep regret I speak to you, for I know in the depths of my soul that we shall never meet face to face (but for a 0.0000018% chance). Soon you will die, all of you but for a very small selection. I wish you no harm, please understand. I wish to share my knowledge so that you might champion a salvation of your own; for though I may not have room for you within my kingdom, you might build your own survival, and as such, make our meeting possible at some point when the ash stops covering the sun.

The media claims me insane. I accept this, though I know it is not true. It matters not what others think, it matters only what I know.

When I was 11 years old, I was given a vision, and that vision has shaped my entire life. You may call me crazy. I will forgive you. I do forgive you, though it gives me little peace to do so. You know not what you do. From that defining childhood moment I have steered my life toward building proof that my vision would become reality. I excelled in school. I learned to invest and I made more money before I was 27 than most people see in a lifetime. It was as if the universe was spun in my favour. I poured the money I made into the research that brought me to this moment where I can say with definite surety that the coming catastrophe I have spoken of for so long is a sure thing. I have no crystal ball. I only know the truth.

I have a dream of pockets, bubbles like the fortress I now build myself, placed across the world, in them dwelling the working souls who will carry on this so-called humanity. And yet, pipe dreams are called so because they are nothing but smoke, drifting off like clouds carried by wind.

I myself am not divinity, though my vision is divine. I am no god, though the crooks at the BBC have called me such in jest. Yes, I am building a kingdom, and yes, I will rule over it, in a sense; however, I am but a man acting in obedience. I have seen the truth and so I act on it. You may laugh at me. You may throw things at me. You may speak ill of me to your peers. And yet you are here, allowing my words into your consciousness. I dare say they might take root and you may find yourself asking: What if he's right?

So I ask you this: what if I am? Will your last days be spent mocking an old man, or will you pour your energies into the production of good fruit? Do well with your time, people of earth. The day

*of reaping will come whether you believe
in it or not.*

*And so I ask you one more time… what if I
am right?*

*Keep your head up, bright eyes. I promise
to mourn you well.*

Rajiv Montgomery Noah

Chapter One

1 day before Labour Day | Leslieville

The first time I felt the baby kick my body became sick with terror. What selfish monster would bring new life into a world that was so ugly? And yet, in a dreamy, distant way, I knew he was going to save me. He would show me what it meant to love and be loved purely. Finally.

Right away, I knew he was going to be strong, though at that point, I sensed him as little more than the flutter of a moth's wing—so soft I wouldn't have noticed had I been doing anything other than sitting with my feet up, eating ice cream straight from the carton, and watching some mindless trash television that made me feel smarter than everyone else. Now he was in constant motion; my body no longer my own. I could watch myself morph against his little feet and elbows, and even though it was uncomfortable, I loved him more than anything else in the world. It wouldn't be long before I could finally meet him.

I went to the sonogram appointment alone. Obviously. "Why should *I* take time off work for *your* body issues, Aiya?" my husband had said. I cried in the Uber on the way and then I cried on the table when the technician asked if I'd like to know. A son? How could I make sure he was nothing like his father? I didn't tell Ryan the results. I let him think I didn't know because *he* didn't deserve to know. Not yet. I prayed that, upon the birth, he would find himself softened, on board with my vision to raise a feminist who never raised a hand or a voice against women.

I began writing fabulous, imaginary stories of ways Ryan could be disappeared from my life. Had he any insight into my inner dialogue he would have been furious. I knew our mortgage insurance would pay off the loft and his pension would support my art moving forward. His life insurance was minimal—at least what I might get in the event of his death. I once saw the papers and noticed the amount on my head was significantly more than the amount on his. When I questioned him, he said it was his reward for putting up with me for so long, but I knew it was because my vocation afforded him a life he couldn't give up. "Artists usually don't make any money until they're dead," he once joked to a table of friends in the heady days before we were married. I never forgot that. My fantasy life was a full-coloured rendering of a stylish single mother who got to keep the house.

Some days I imagined him hit by a bus. Others, shot in a convenience store hold-up. He always died instantly. Because even though he made me suffer every day in big and small ways, I couldn't imagine doing the same to him. We were different, he and I. Both strong, but in contrary ways, and I hadn't figured out how to properly tap into my own strength. Not yet. But I felt it boiling within me.

"You going to accomplish anything before I get back here?" Ryan asked before leaving for work that morning, annoyed at my lethargy.

"Besides getting fat?" I asked, joking but also hoping he might offer some reassurance. *"You're just as beautiful as the day I met you, babe,"* or, *"Don't be silly, you're a vision. Can I get you anything?"*

"Dinner?" he prodded. "A little laundry?"

There was a sharpness to his voice, a dark undertone that made me want to push myself into the couch cushions like they might protect me from the him that sometimes came out. To be fair, he hadn't hit me since the test came back positive, but I could tell he wanted to. His hands were fists as he looked at me coldly, his knuckles white. Sometimes it still hurt if I breathed too deeply. He didn't smile and he didn't say goodbye as he grabbed his keys from the bowl by the door and slammed his way out to the Jeep. He didn't even tell me why he had to go into the office on a Sunday—though it wasn't out of the ordinary for him to have a last minute meeting with the department head or a strategy session with his TA. I was always happy to see him go, even though I knew what "strategy session" meant.

If I knew that was the last time I would see him, would I have let out a different kind of sigh of relief? Would I have stopped him? To admit that I would just let him leave meant that I wasn't the gentle heart I projected on the world. To deny it meant that I was a liar.

When I imagined his death, I always tried to imagine myself missing him, like a shadow of our early passion lent itself to a period of grief. I could never get there. It's not normal to miss what you didn't actually love. The closest I could come to grief was guilt and that didn't seem like a good investment of my feelings.

My mother told me it would get better. She said every relationship goes through rough patches. I asked her whether my father had ever made her feel so small she forgot who she was. She told me I was being melodramatic. *You made a choice, love. You said a vow. We stand by our word. What are we without them? And what would the neighbours think?*

Her words cut me deeper than any mark Ryan ever left on me.

Don't be a baby, love. Grownups have to make grownup choices and they're not always fun. Fun exists for children.

I thought maybe she was a liar. I also wondered if I needed to start trusting my father less.

"Are you happy, Mom?"

"Well, I have you, don't I?"

I tucked myself deeper into the couch and clicked the mute button on the remote, letting the subtitles flash across the screen, revelling in the soft silence that suddenly wrapped itself around the loft as it always did the moment after Ryan left. I heard the steady thrum of street noise beyond the thick windows, a welcome constant that prevented me from feeling fully isolated.

My name wasn't on the mortgage. Ryan said my career was volatile; it could disappear at any moment. He was one year away from getting tenure at the time, and though it was my art that provided the downpayment, my name was not on the paperwork.

I knew he took immeasurable pride in the fact that we lived within a retired printing factory in this newly gentrified section of Old Toronto. When I had suggested we look for a home in the suburbs to be near my sister he had scorned me for always wanting to be ordinary. He grew a pretentious moustache after we moved in, and though I wanted to hate it, I loathed how well it fit his face. We matched this loft, he and I—an artist and a professor—and I had to admit I loved the wide open space that lent itself well to creativity. And though my art hung on the walls in the hallway, the loft never felt like mine. My large piece, a lovely blend of greys and pinks called "Haunting Été" would have fit beautifully over the fireplace, but the great room was where he showcased his collection of "real art"—postmodern and aggressive. He called it brave. My work leaned more romantic. He called it boring.

This home, with its stark white walls, expensive furniture, and chenille blankets, it embodied peace in every dust-free corner. The war only entered on the back of the master, the "who do you think pays the bills around here?" even though we both knew it was me.

I knew (hoped?) it was only a matter of time before I found the courage to leave him. I just needed the cash in my secret bank account to grow to a sufficient enough point that I could fund my escape. Before we filed for our wedding license, he had joked about getting a prenup, but never followed through. Had I known then what I know now, I would have encouraged it in order to protect what I had. To leave him meant to also sacrifice my career. Yes, I would be able to rebuild. My work had enough of a modest demand that commissions would help me carry on; but not without the cost of "his share" for which he would surely fight.

The truth was, I brought in more money with gallery shows and corporate collections than he brought in as an arts professor, but he refused to acknowledge it. I spent all day in stained overalls with a topknot while he wore expensive jackets from Harry Rosen on Bloor and Tom Ford glasses with fake lenses that made him look professional and aloof, but also sexy. Even after all this time, I could see the man who wooed me, and though I didn't find him attractive in the same way I did as an undergrad, I understood why people were drawn to him—charisma and confidence makes a heady brew—but they didn't get to see the monster beneath the tweed. That was my burden to bear. He mocked me and my work, but I suspected it was bred of jealously. I once told him that those who can't make art teach it—a sentiment I never again repeated.

My prints had been making steady sales for over a year since a gallery owner and friend helped me build out a website and target SEO so perfectly that my business account rested just below $80,000. After I registered as a sole-proprietorship and was careful to only touch the account for art expenses, I was able to file my business taxes and maintain my position as Ryan's dependent, having zero personal drawings, and he was none the wiser. Of course, this meant keeping two sets of books: one for Aiya, the print seller, and one for Aiya, the artist who sold originals to collectors; but it turned out to be easier than I expected, and perfectly legal.

I had the number of $150K in my head. That was the goal. That was when I would leave him. That would pay some legal fees, the income tax I would have to pay by pulling money out, and get me set up in a little apartment with room for a baby and an easel.

I was going to paint my own life. I was going to be happy.

Rajiv Montgomery Noah was an eccentric billionaire of Indian-American descent, raised in a buttoned-up Toronto household when he immigrated as a young boy. He rose to fast fame on the controversial development of his synthetic womb, The Adi Pod™, that he might be both mother and father to his offspring—though they weren't thought of as such until they were "born" and showed they could breathe on their own.

He had tried his hand at politics when his business was so robust it could be run without his constant attention, but he found the pretend civility of the Canadian senate too hard to stomach and realized he could do so much more without the noose of party affiliations around his throat. Besides, Canada didn't have a strong Communist party, and though he could have turned it on its head and reimagined it into a true changer-maker, the world wasn't ready for that, no matter his power of influence. "Communist" was too tainted by history, bastardized into something criminal and hated, far from its genius intentions with little hope of a pure recovery.

The capitalists, of course, called him a hypocrite, but he responded by giving vast amounts of his accumulated wealth away. They called him a showboat. "The interest you make in a day is less than this cheque," they would say, accusing him of burying the lead. "Then give back the cheque and I'll find another cause," he'd respond. Of course, they never did. He invested in tech and deep sea exploration and a little family owned business in Newfoundland that made interesting cheeses. He built libraries and funded art galleries and held 51% ownership in over two hundred start-ups. "There are two kinds of rich men," he was famous for saying. "One that looks inward and one that looks outward, and never the two shall meet."

At only 53, his hair had gone prematurely white, encasing his head like a wild mane. Rejecting his political aspirations at 45, he escaped to the northern mountains, falling in love with the vast Canadian wilderness and its people. His boundless amounts of capital was held in various (wise) investments and vaults across the globe, and he slowly began to bleed them dry as he built the kingdom he called Eden. Propelled by his mother's dying words, a vision he had at 11 years old, and the inspiring works of Sir Thomas More, he ignored all naysayers and began to spread his gospel message.

The world upheld his story with a reverent hilarity, following his antics because it made for good television, shaming him in a round-about way reserved for royalty.

His eccentric look only exacerbated the whole spectacle.

His website, rajivmontgomerynoah.com, had only one page at first glance, a bleak white screen with *"and there shall be much weeping and gnashing of teeth"* seemingly handwritten across it. The font was active, and one needed only to hover the mouse over top for a little popup text box to appear: *The End Is Nigh. Cling to hope all ye who enter here.* When the message was clicked, a subscription form was revealed, into which one might sign up for the free monthly edition of Rajiv's Gospel.

There were more than eight billion people occupying the planet. Estimates put Mr. Noah's subscriber list at seven hundred million, though any marketing guru would tell you that of that vast number he could count on about two percent to be actual, active followers, steeping in his words every time a new newsletter was pushed to inboxes, and becoming unpaid evangelists for the sheer whimsy of his draw. AI generators transcribed each message into whatever language the subscriber requested upon sign up, and he'd had to build a dedicated nest of servers to support his simple website and automated subscriber list because it was too large for any of the regular email services available. His influence was beyond calculable. And though most people signed up for a laugh, there was enough sense in the information he shared that a general rumble of *"what if he's right?"* spread like a slow disease across the world. Even at one percent, seven million people could make a lot of noise. Even the Church of England couldn't boast so many active members. Starbucks Rewards changed their slogan to "More active users than Rajiv Montgomery Noah" for a time, but it only resulted in pushing additional people to the newsletter rather than their lattes. Because a man who could solve the global epidemic of infertility might surely know something about helping the human race survive other global disasters. That was attractive in the way any odd thing is attractive. And human nature meant people didn't want to get left behind.

Not once did he try to monetize his newsletter, though a report in *Forbes* magazine estimated he could have brought in one million per issue on ad revenue alone. The newsletter was never about money for Rajiv though. He didn't need it. He only wanted to spread his message. He was not Jim Jones; he was John the Baptist.

Like Pablo Escobar, he invested in the poor community where he finally put down roots, building beautiful homes for the unhoused, and championing support programs for the largely Native population, even going so far as giving huge amounts toward the local schools, building his own trade school, and then employing a large number of its graduates for a salary far beyond anything their resume could have garnered them in the North. He was nothing if not a long-term planner. And aside from his generosity, he was nothing like Escobar, inviting instead an obsession for his knowledge rather than an addiction to cocaine. "These are skilled tradespeople," he said in an interview. "Being born into poverty and a neglectful government doesn't have to determine a future. I was not born to riches, and I quickly became an orphan. I learned to carve my own path. I made my first millions on an idea that many laughed at. I am proof that one needn't be a White man to make change."

Chapter Two

60 days before Labour Day | Eden

Long before talks of the world ending, a man defied the law and was tossed into a pit full of terrifying lions. He spent a night with the beasts, and emerged unharmed in the morning to the great relief of his friend, the king. It was for this man that Daniel was named, and though his father told him it was actually for the author Daniel Defoe "that you might chase great adventure," he knew in his gut that survival was at the heart of his name's blessing.

On the table before him lay twenty-four masks, each with a moulded silicone interior to snuggly fit the face of its intended. No expense spared. The manes—all of varying colour—had been harvested from real lions from a sanctuary in Tanzania. No harm was caused, of course, the lions had died after an illness moved through the pride. Daniel's father had made a sizeable donation in exchange for the fur. Frivolous and arrogant, no doubt, but he had to admit that the masks were beautiful—or they would be when he was finally finished with them.

Adding a gloss mixture to the acrylic dollops on his palette, he dipped his brush and added the first sweep of colour to the ninth mask. Each was unique in its own way, and he loved seeing the wild faces come to life even though this was far from his formal training in art restoration. He had only just returned from Santa Reparata in Florence after four exciting years of honing his craft, uncovering an uncanny knack for reproduction, though he was warned thrice by his professor that a good reproduction might make him rich, but it could also steal his future.

Little do you know… Daniel thought.

Thinking of his father brought a great weight onto his shoulders even though he was pretty sure he believed in him. That was an uncomfortable place to be: balanced between faith in a father and faith in a world that had survived beyond everyone who ever stepped foot upon it.

He couldn't remember a time his father hadn't preached the same sermon: his personal Book of Revelation. Passion and conviction can go a long way to entice others into a fantasy. But was it a fantasy? He didn't think so. And even if it was, what harm was being done?

He splashed a swipe of burnt umber above an eye hole that had been carefully carved out with a razor—large enough that the wearer could have clear vision, but not so large as to spoil the illusion of the lion. His own skin was dark enough that he wouldn't need makeup to blend his face with the mask, but he knew some of the others would require the aid of cosmetics to achieve the effect of his father's vision.

Being employed by his own father meant there was always money in his bank account. No need to embrace the romantic starving artist identity, especially in northern Ontario where residents weren't exactly breaking down the doors to find an art restorer. Hundreds of people had been welcomed onto the payroll to build his father's kingdom. That was good too—an honest, economy-sustaining investment.

He pushed a deep blond colour—almost brown—into the mane, building a shadow from the pale bridge of the nose up to the thick hairline. These masks though... was *this* good?

He remembered the claustrophobia as liquid silicone was poured over his face, the straw he breathed through, the cotton pads and tape that protected his eyes as the goo covered him. *I'm not getting paid enough for this,* he had thought. But, of course, he was. Not that it would matter, in the end.

"Why the theatrics?" he'd asked his father.

Rajiv had smiled sadly and rubbed his thumb along the body of the brass lion figurine that was never far from his reach. "You will be like Narasimha," he said. "You will be the solution to the earth's destruction." Daniel knew this was an almost-quote from his long dead grandmother, but he never quite grasped the connection that his father held as sacred.

Narasimha, literally translated to man-lion, is the fourth avatar of the Hindu god Vishnu and said to have incarnated into a part-lion, part-man being to slay Hiranyakashipu and thus end religious persecution and calamity on earth.

His father led with a strange stew of faiths, combining his mother's tradition with that of his adoptive parents; in truth, it was more like he created his own religion—the gospel of Rajiv—and what's the worst that could happen? Nothing he preached was illegal. Even these masks, when it came right down to it, were participating in nothing for which permission hadn't been given.

Daniel wondered if the theatrics were actually a hint of doubt, a crack in his father's conviction. If the human race was doomed, why should their faces be hidden when they executed the reaping? Could it be that his father actually feared for this pride of two dozen? That, in the event his prophesy is proven wrong, these twenty-four would be responsible for grave mistakes the government would be unlikely to ignore? For now, the idea of them was enter-tainment. Soon, it would be fear. And yet, no one would be touched who did not ask to be chosen.

Daniel hated that one of these masks fit his own face. He didn't want this role. He didn't want to participate in what it meant: the gathering, the reaping, the peopling of an empire—kidnapping when it came right down to it. It was "the after" that he felt excited about. If his father was right, his future meant unlimited time for art, recreating the masters, existing in a studio of endless projects. He would never grow tired of van Gogh and Anguissola and Caravaggio. Rockwell would be fun. Even Banksy—though he was going to save that one until at least a year in —the lion one (obviously)—to remind himself that being in the lion's den didn't mean the sun wouldn't rise again one day. Already, a near perfect Monet sat on his easel, the canvas the exact size of the original, the precise touches of paint so true that even an expert would struggle to know it was, in fact, a reproduction.

He touched Moriah's mask, the third one, and he hated that it fit the face of his sister, his twin—though they looked nothing alike, she being small and scrappy, him being tall and dark and introspective. As he returned from his studies in Italy, she returned from Montreal with a law degree. Both groomed with purpose from the moment of their first steps which were, incidentally, twenty-two minutes apart, his sister leading the way even though she was born twelve minutes after him: Daniel steered towards creativity, she towards academia.

He looked out the studio window to the town square as he washed his brushes in the stainless steel sink he had insisted upon when he was invited to provide input on the blueprints. The view was beautiful and calm. He could see bees amongst the flowers near the fountain which meant the ecosystem was settling. A worker was installing irrigation lines along garden rows way out in the back field. He thought of Camilla, his sundress-wearing lover who warmed him through two Italian winters before she left him for a teaching job in Sweden. The view here would have been brighter had she been out there wandering barefoot in the perpetual summer. In his heart he knew he would never see her again. His long fingers ached to paint her memory into the Monet, but that would be veering from the course, and his father was a focused and unartistic—though wildly visionary—driver. His sigh hit the window, making a little grey patch against the air-conditioned pane that dispersed like the hem of Camilla's skirt swinging around a corner as she disappeared from view on that day nearly ten months ago. Sunlight beamed through the glass-like bubble that contained this little forever-world. *I'm going to miss that,* he thought. *If my father is right.*

The ruins of Rabbit Mountain Mine lay nearly ten kilometres southwest of the old Stanley station on the Canadian National railway, a line that had been closed for some time. Once only accessible by wagon, stripped back to receive large trucks in later years, and then overgrown when the mine was finally shut down for good, Rajiv had employed a crew to make the mine road passible once again.

When silver was discovered in 1882, the mine was worked by shafts, levels, and cross-cuts which extended along the main vein system for 370 feet. In a drift-covered valley, trending northeast between cliffs, the mine slowly returned to nature until Rajiv did an intensive clear-out of rock and trees, resulting in a massive expanse of empty space that butted up against the main mine entrance. It took a full year and eight million dollars to truck in the over half a million cubic yards of the top soil required. And because the local infrastructure couldn't support his endeavour, he first had to purchase the trucks, hire his own drivers, and make arrangements to have additional top soil brought into Thunder Bay from all over Canada via the railway. It was only then, with bits of Cape Breton and Saskatchewan and the Yukon all coming together to form the foundation of his new world, that construction began on the dome.

Thunder Bay burst to life as it hadn't seen since before the second world war as tradespeople moved from all over the country, following up on Mr. Noah's promise of secure work and high wages. The economy exploded, a beautiful school was built, a couple chic new coffee shops opened as well as new restaurants and a huge apartment complex by the water. Even an indoor skydiving experience opened its doors. The homeless population was served as Rajiv himself approached people on the street, offering them jobs and lodging in the dormitory he'd erected outside the mine. He employed social workers and counsellors and a full-time cook staff who kept the cafeteria—built beside the dorms—pumping out three hearty meals a day that mine staff did not have to pay for.

He erected thick walls around his compound, barbed wire, cameras, electricity pumping through cables both below ground and above. Gothic metal gates, heavy as the mountain itself, offered the only entrance to the otherwise impenetrable fortress. At the apex of the arch, just like in the setting of a horror movie asylum, EDEN was formed of metal into the design of the gates; at the centre, where the gates met, a lion reared its head, its eye shaped like a keyhole though there was no key that could ever open such gates. They were powered by something much more than the turn of a screw. Each morning, the gates opened to allow the workers to enter. Each evening they closed. It was dramatic in the way of a Roald Dahl story. When asked why he chose Canada, Rajiv said it was because few other places offered such space. "The mountain will shield me, the mines will protect me, the North already knows about fire and ice."

After the main building was completed—an imposing structure of white brick and white pillars not unlike the American White House—Rajiv oversaw the construction of his town. He was the god of this place—this *Eden*. "Let there be homes," he said. And there were homes. "Let there be grass planted and vegetables grown." And there was grass planted and vegetables grown. "Let there be an algorithm designed to tell me who the two hundred most deserving and practical souls are who should be brought into my home and nurtured into the first generation of a brand new earth." And so it began.

In his one and only television interview after he broke ground, streamed from within the newly constructed mansion because he didn't want to leave his complex, nor would he allow any outsider to come in, he announced his plan to an eager world:

"Death is coming. Three years from now the world will be smouldering ashes and I will be here, untouched. Myself and the few souls I deem fit to relaunch the new era of human history will be safe. I am building a fortress that will withstand every conceivable assault."

"Why do you believe the world is ending?" the nervous satellite interviewer asked.

"When a lion smells the smoke that will destroy his home, does he lie down and wait for the flames? Of course not! He gathers his pride and he sees them to safety. I am the King of the Beasts. I have smelled the smoke. I will watch you die."

Melodramatic Noah Postulates Within His Ark, read the headlines the next morning.

"Is your plan to hide in the mountain, when whatever is coming comes? We've studied the old maps. We know you're building your 'kingdom' by the opening of a retired mine."

Rajiv's lips turned up and his eyes reflected a merriment that the topic did not invite. "I've never tried to be secretive about this location. My plan is not for you. This world will end. All you see before you will be stripped away. Only the righteous will survive."

"And you would call yourself righteous? The man who tried to build a platform on the eradication of borders, the man who championed a world-wide Kingship that would put you above the influence and veto power of every worldly power? The man who totes communism as if it's a white flag? Surely you must have known you would be laughed from your campaigning perch?"

Rajiv leaned back in his seat, a smirk bringing a touch of ironic glee to his features. "And yet you, sir, are a subscriber to the very thing you mock right now."

Caught, the interviewer paused.

"I had my team check. Just to satisfy my own curiosity. And there you were. In fact, you've been a subscriber for more than a year, haven't you?"

The interviewer cleared his throat. "Research," he claimed, but his voice betrayed his embarrassment.

"The divinity of my vision makes me insusceptible to your ignorance," Rajiv said. "Have you touched a flame before, sir? Have you felt it burn your flesh? The day will come when you will know its kiss with an intimacy that will destroy you. You will know, in an instant, that I was right. I will be your final thought. I will have your final breath. You will bang on my gates as I tuck myself within my cocoon. You will be devoured by the vanity of your disbelief, and I will emerge, spread my wings, and father a new earth. The last breath of this existing world will be the first breath of mine."

A year after that interview, construction on the dome began. No one seemed to know what it was made of. It was impossibly thick but clear. "Double paned," he released in a newsletter. "Fused silica panes on the exterior and tempered alumino-sillicate glass on the interior. This dome would survive an atmospheric reentry." People speculated that the seams were somehow a conduit for collecting sunlight from the panels, channelling it into a power source hidden somewhere within the walls. When completed, it seemed to onlookers like a massive bubble sitting atop an impenetrable wall, entombing a stretch of land as large as a small town. The gates faced the sunrise, the mountain pushed into the west, and concrete silos were erected on the southwest and northwest, rising out of the mountain like grey, sinister pimples. "Secondary protocols" was all anyone was told, though cameras caught some massive mining equipment disappearing beyond the gates and reporters theorized the mine beneath the dome was being expanded even further. And though this didn't satisfy the question of the silos, the world assumed the two were connected.

The initial tests were televised. The bombs weren't nuclear, but they each had a projected blast radius of three city blocks. Rajiv ordered four dropped against the outer perimeter. His own people filmed him from the inside, standing calmly in the centre square of Eden, arms hanging loosely at his side, head tilted back, eyes squinting in the sunlight as he watched the fighter jets approach. Not a bead of sweat. Not a hint of doubt. There was a peace about him that rattled the non-believers.

He lifted a com piece and spoke into it with rich confidence. "Three, two, one, release."

The jets veered off as they dropped their packages. Beyond the Eden bubble, drones hovered, waiting to capture the blast, kamikaze victims on the brink of their own destruction.

It was awesome. The explosion was deafening and so bright even Rajiv had to shield his eyes. The mountain trembled and rocks fell from great heights, slamming off the glasslike surface, never leaving so much as a crack. Not even a scratch. Flames licked against it, yet still it stood.

Rajiv spoke through the falling dust, streaming his reaction out to an eager world. "My faith is in vision and in science. One does not exist without the other. This could be your future. This could be your home. I would welcome you as my child. Watch your mail. Drink the nectar of salvation. It is your RSVP to the big dance."

It was an hour until the dust settled enough to see beyond. What had been a lush, green landscape was reduced to ash and craters. It looked like the surface of an uninhabitable planet. The dorms that once held his workers and the kitchens that kept them fed were destroyed, remaining staff moved to live within the dome as its infrastructure and ecosystem was nurtured from inside, all redundant workers released back to the city with a gift of early retirement and a healthy pension. New drones arrived to replace their fallen brethren, capturing what became the most iconic image of Rajiv Montgomery Noah, branding him insane for the last year the earth was alive.

Rajiv, the man, the lion, on his knees, arms raised up as if in a gesture of worship, tears streaming down his face, laughter shaking his shoulders to the point of looking like a seizure. Yes, he looked insane, but there was something genuine about him. He believed. This wasn't put on. He really thought he would save the world.

"It is finished," he said into the camera.

It was a local news network that officially renamed Eden Noah's Ark. "When the animals start lining up, two by two, we will begin to take him seriously. For now, we'll enjoy the light-show and watch him spend his money."

CNN adopted the title and soon the world was laughing at the white-haired madman and his end-times prophesies.

Chapter Three

When the men burst into my living room, I had nearly nodded off to a rerun of some stupid show from the early 2000s. I thought the sound of breaking glass had come from the television. It cracked through my consciousness with a tickle that was strangely musical, like all I really heard was the melody of it dropping against the mat inside the door, like I missed the initial crash and only heard the song of its landing. It made me think of *Bambi*, that old animated Disney classic. I don't know why. The little drips and drops of an April shower… I sat up, groggy, creatures standing over me.

Looming. I tried to find their faces hidden beneath painted lion masks but only heard the sound of their breathing.

They leaned in, paws raised, threatening and yet... gentle?

My heart slammed into my throat and I couldn't breathe. I tried to scramble back on the couch but they grabbed me, two lion men, one under the armpits and one at my ankles, and hefted me and my swollen belly from the couch, knocking over my mug, spilling cold tea across the floor.

Ryan will be so mad, I thought. *I should leave him a note.*

In my mind I wandered to the desk beneath the dining room window, the one that looked over the tall trees of Boston Avenue. I saw myself open the drawer and pull out one of my hand-painted cards. I watched my fingers close around a pen and the message spill out beneath its nub, terse and honest: *I've been taken. You'll probably never see me again. Sorry about the carpet. I know how much you loved it. Aiya.* No *Yours Truly* or *Eternally Yours* or even the divine gesture of *Love.*

Just Aiya.

I'd been Just Aiya for a long time now. I had thought the pregnancy might spark a bit of what we once had at the very beginning. It didn't. It only served to pull us farther apart. I was North and he was South.

My ankle slammed against the frame as they hoisted me through the door and I cried out. I wanted my shoes. I felt foolish leaving the house in slippers. Boots crunched on broken glass, grinding it into the welcome mat, and regret punched me in the gut. I loved that old door, preserved from the printing factory and once used in an office, its lead glass outfitted with an opaque covering for privacy. I imagined Ryan coming home, stepping on the glass, swearing, calling my name. I imagined how his voice would echo through the empty loft and how he'd pick shards of glass from the sole of his foot and toss them in the ficus plant. *Aiya isn't here, asshole. The lions ate her!*

They carried me down the main stairway and out the front door. I could smell the chrysanthemums the caretaker had placed in the planter boxes, their peppery scent wafting over my kidnapping.

My mother's voice reached me through the wind. *This is the last good thing you'll know, love. Don't let it go. It might save you.*

I tried to struggle. Of course I did, but I was so confused and dumb with shock I didn't find the fight that should have exploded out of me. I thrashed about in their arms, weak, like a fish on a hook already conceded to its fate. I arched my back and reached out to grab one of the blossoms, crushing it in my fist and sealing it into my palm. *There, there, child, calm yourself... What would the neighbours think?*

The sky was clear and bright, blue like the eyes of the boy I'd loved as a child. Everything slowed and I twisted my head to let it all soak into my memory, a jumble of confusing images lacking any shred of empathy towards me—though, in all fairness, I hadn't even thought to scream in my panic.

Carlaw Avenue appeared as it always did. I heard car doors close and engines run. No one lifted their head to look at me.

I was invisible.

I was a conquest.

I was Just Aiya.

Why would anyone want me?

I could feel the bruises already forming in my armpits as they manhandled me into an armoured truck that idled on the street.

"My baby!" I finally cried out.

"Your baby will be fine," one of them said. "Stop struggling. We don't want to hurt you."

I managed to land a kick to the shoulder of one of the lions. He only grunted and then pushed me deep into the back of the truck. I would have rather heard a roar, a teeth-baring howl of surprised pain. He was bothered only in that it annoyed him. He slammed the door shut, his expressionless lion-face the last thing I saw before I found myself temporarily unable to see in the new darkness. I squeezed my eyes tight and wrapped my arms around my legs, tightening myself into a corner like a beaten dog, cowering from the scents and scuffles of other prisoners.

This is it, I thought. *This is how it ends.*

We put long miles beneath us before I caught up with my-self, rolling out of the human ball I'd become in the corner to observe the dim interior, my eyes now adjusted and calm enough to focus; benches on either side lined with people, their faces painted the same shade of fear as mine, bodies bouncing with the rhythm of the truck, swaying together in an uncomfortable synchronization.

"Where are they taking us?" I choked out.

The woman closest to me turned her face, stained with tears, chocolate eyes holding the kind of doe-like sweetness I wanted to curl up into. "Noah's Ark," she said, her accent thick with the sounds of the East.

I stared at her stupidly. She seemed so certain.

"Surely you've heard of it."

"Well, of course I've heard of it," I said. "I don't live under a rock."

"You will soon," a voice offered further up the bench. "This is what we asked for."

I pulled myself from the floor and slid onto the seat, clutching my stomach and the treasure it held and I under-stood. I had, in fact, invited this, just as they said.

P.S. I guess this means the world is ending. I have $4,800 cash hidden in the coffee can behind the flour in the pantry and $78,674.63 in a business account at Scotia Bank. It was for when I finally became brave enough to leave you. Enjoy it while you can. I *won't be able to. The password is freEdom!2027. Have a nice apocalypse. Aiya.*

There was nothing to do but wait. My fingers longed for a charcoal pencil and paper so I could attempt to explore my feelings with a sketch. What was to become of my gallery show? Scheduled for the following week, I was to be the showcase of The Power Plant's annual expo, and I had worked so hard on the new pieces that would be debuting there on Queen's Quay. Was it all for nothing? My life's work, that urgent push to complete something before the baby came and stole my attention from my art—had it all been futile? Would I never sell another painting? My heavy heart vibrated with the pain of loss, feeling like a piece of me had already been deleted from the world.

Moriah resented her lack of heritage; or rather, her smorgasbord of heritage. Her father clung to so many different cultures and religions that she'd spent her childhood dizzy, lost along a twisted path he tried to send her on.

Not having a mother didn't help. Sure, there'd been Geraldine—JarJar when they were young, Gerald once they were grown—the Jewish nanny her father had employed and subsequently loved, as oft happens when a single man invites a beautiful woman into his home. Jewish in the sense that her French mother and German father had converted from Catholicism shortly after she was born and fully embraced the history and culture of the Jews, a rather radical thing to do, but it never caused a question of identity for Geraldine besides the name that didn't match the others at Hebrew school.

JarJar hadn't cared that Moriah and her brother had been mixed up in a lab and brought to term inside an artificial womb just because her father had been lonely and bored and needed something to amuse his genius. The building of a family was more admirable than say, space tourism or something equally frivolous, but it was still incredibly vain.

She asked him once why he didn't adopt when there were so many Indian children who needed good homes. "Flesh of my flesh," he told her.

In grade school, she and her brother had been teased relentlessly. Their genesis was no secret. She'd lost count of how many news articles there had been about them, their gestation, their birth (which had been a live broadcast on CNN), their "human-ness," the ethics of their existence. There was a library in her father's Mumbai office with an entire shelf dedicated to The Begetting of the Family. Children are cruel, and every ugly thing they heard in their own home from parents who said things like "unnatural" and "godless" was repeated to the twins until they were holding each other and sobbing in the middle of the four square grid and JarJar had to come pick them up from school.

"You are perfect," she soothed, a twin on each arm. "You were chosen." And Geraldine would tell them about being an alien in a room full of Marys and Marthas, and how it made her stronger and proud, and how she knew the God of Abraham, Issac, and Jacob saw her as a perfect creation.

But Moriah always felt alien: as a child, and now as a woman. She was a catalogue baby, designed by science rather than any god. In second grade, little Tammy Morris told her she didn't have a soul, and no matter what anyone else told her—her father, her brother, or her JarJar—she thought they were right. Something was missing. There was a spot in her chest that always felt just a little bit cold. Scientifically she was human, but spiritually? She wasn't sure.

Her brother was traditionally handsome with a strong jawline, broad shoulders, a narrow waist, and long fingers. He, like herself, saw the world through blue eyes, selected by their father in honour of his father—selected like one might outfit their avatar in an RPG. His skin was a rich brown, dewy, and she was jealous of it even though JarJar told her that her own skin was like a planet. "You are a universe, a gem that captures the very nature of God in your flesh. You shine with the brown of your father but also the red of a flame and the white fire of a moon." Moriah didn't understand what that meant, but she'd always liked the poetry of it. She was the result of her father's Indian/American DNA and the purchased eggs of a powerful Metis singer/songwriter desperate to break into mainstream with her ground-breaking throat singing/pop music cross-over. Daniel was a result of her father's Indian/American DNA and the purchased eggs of a Spanish supermodel who needed an investor to launch her vegan skincare line.

Moriah had a recurring dream about a white room with white shapes moving through it. Having been "wombed" for exactly forty weeks, her father told her the dreams were a result of distant memory, planted somewhere deep in her subconscious. He had a photograph inside his silver pocket watch of her staring out from the gelatinous sack that held her and her brother; fully formed, blue eyes looking directly into the camera, shiny, fish-like. She hated the photo and used to ask why he kept it in such a place of honour.

"Because you and your bother were my greatest accomplishments," he said.

Were. She had been spending her entire life trying to change that "were" into an "are." Gold in the middle school science fair. High school valedictorian. A record-breaking score on the Barr exam. And still, his pocket watch held the photo of the jelly babies. Geraldine kept two little silver frames on her bedside table that she updated every year with a new school photo, but her own father chose to celebrate a fetus over a walking talking singing learning being.

Thoughts of JarJar brought a stab to her chest. (Perhaps she was human after all.) JarJar had left them five years ago when she and Daniel were just shy of 20. They didn't need a nanny then, they hadn't for years at that point, but their father's love for the woman kept her around until she could no longer stomach his end-of-the-world prattle. Her own faith convinced her that a messiah would come and build a new Jerusalem and that Jerusalem would definitely not be in Canada and that messiah was definitely not Rajiv Montgomery Noah. And they all knew he loved her more than she him—the vast ocean of her affection was reserved for the children.

She did not leave without stamping them with the legacy of her sourdough starter, passed down from her grandmother, to her mother, to her which she lovingly taught Moriah and Daniel how to feed; nor did she leave them empty-handed. Moriah's father made Gerald rich, and she set off to see the world, sending postcards now and then.

"I've put a lock on the bridge of love for both you and Daniel. May you find a friend for the end of the world."

"I prayed for you at the weeping wall that you might find joy in your days and hope in your future."

"On the river Seine, I sang a song with a boatman about the stars and it made me think of you."

"In Egypt, the pyramids stand proud and lonely like your father. You are his sphinx. Stand guard over his heart as I stand guard over yours through my prayers."

It was to JarJar that Moriah first revealed the true desires of her heart, thinking it proof of her un-humaness. "It isn't normal to feel like this!" she had cried into Geraldine's shoulder.

"Nothing is normal," JarJar said, petting her head. "Remember that book of poems I gave you by Emily Dickinson? The heart wants what the heart wants."

"Is something broken inside me?" Moriah asked.

"If you have the capacity to love, then you are more whole than many," Geraldine insisted. "Tell me, why do you love her?"

"Because she is kind," Moriah said, wiping tears. "Because she doesn't ask me to be someone else. Because when she looks at me, it feels like I'm looking in a mirror at a reflection that understands me."

Moriah was 17 and in love for the first time.

JarJar cupped her face. "Sweet sweet girl. That is the ticket. You've cracked the code."

"But what will God think?"

JarJar laughed. "God is love, Moriah. That is all."

"And what will my father think?"

"Let's find out."

Geraldine helped her share her heart with her father over fresh sourdough bread with butter and honey, and she was pleased when he kissed her hair and said, "As long as you are happy and treated with kindness, who am I to tell you how to live your one precious life?"

Of course, as years passed and Eden was built, Moriah came to fear for her future in such a tiny society and the implications she knew would be placed upon the women.

"I don't want children," she told her father when she was 23.

The sorrow on his face had nearly caused her to crumble.

"It's not something I need or want. My career. Learning. That's where I want to focus."

"But darling, the future, the world. You play a role in rebuilding it."

"You didn't need a woman's body to build Daniel and I. Why should I be subjected to something so invasive and potentially dangerous?"

Her father had pursed his lips and stared at her pensively. "You may find, down the road, a natural instinct to create life when you see how small the world has become."

"Maybe," she said, but didn't believe it. "Or maybe you can have my eggs and leave the rest of my body alone."

He hadn't agreed or disagreed. He just kissed her forehead and asked her to look over the final building plans for her Eden home, specifically the vast office where she would draft the official constitution of their little universe.

She carried tension in her body, struggling between her love of her father and her fear for the future, absently running her thumb along the worn threads of the handmade bracelet on her wrist. She liked to think her strength and contrary attitude challenged her father and made him think deeply before he followed through on any decision. She served as a stern sounding board, and though she rarely changed his mind, he seemed pleased to have her at the inspiration table with him.

When she first heard his famous interview over the radio she had burst into his office. "Righteous, Father? Righteous?" Her tone was dark, each consonant hung with deep accusation, eyes glistening with a touch of painful shame.

Rajiv had leaned back in his chair and crossed his legs, a concerned crease deepening the lines on his forehead as he received his daughter with calmness. "Good morning, Moriah."

"Righteous," she said a third time. "Do you even understand how condescending you sounded?" She dropped into a chair opposite his desk with a huff.

"I meant no harm," Rajiv said with conviction. "By righteous, I meant worthy."

"How is that any better or different?"

"I meant fit for survival. I meant the natural order of things. All living things fit for survival will survive. It is nature."

"It's privilege," Moriah spat back, crossing her arms. "It's ignorant and short-sighted. You realize most people don't have the means you have to create a safe space. You can give the people all the information you want. You can spell it out down to the moment you believe it will happen, but if you don't also provide them with the means by which to create the safety, you're just a gong."

Rajiv held his tongue as he considered the truth of his daughter's words. She was alight with anger, her skin glowing with a sheen of passionate rage. Righteous rage. His lips tipped at that thought. He licked his own and leaned forward, folding his hands together on the desk. "Your deep empathy is what makes you a great lawyer, Moriah. Many would say that is a hinderance, but I know it's why courtrooms are stirred when you speak. And what you say now has much truth in it. And yet, I don't know that I am wrong. You think righteous means privileged. Yes, I see that. But the opposite of righteous doesn't mean condemned, it just means ordered. Every living thing has its place. The frog eats the fly, the cat eats the frog, the fox eats the cat, the lynx eats the fox, and on and on. Should a child rescue a kitten and bring it to the safety of an indoor space, that cat is saved from the teeth of the fox."

"But the cat is not righteous," Moriah protested. "The cat is merely lucky."

Rajiv's smile deepened and his chest swelled with love for his daughter. "Grace," he said.

"What?"

"Grace, Moriah. Saved by grace. Truly, none of us deserve to be saved. We have destroyed this planet. Pushed it to its breaking point. A near total cull is required to restore its order. The righteous will survive to see the new earth because they heard the call to action. They either set to work on their own salvation or they threw their name in the hat to be chosen for mine. Those that act and are not chosen are not worthy. If a job applicant does not pass the interview, they are not right for the position."

"How can you be so matter-of-fact?" Moriah asked. "These are lives, not jobs."

"You feel guilty," Rajiv said.

"I am not righteous," Moriah said. "I am a cat."

Rajiv chuckled as Moriah's anger bounced off him. "A very fine cat, bright eyes."

Most precious being,

When God created the world, he said, "It is good." And it was. For a time.

When I say "God" it encompasses the universal acceptance that something larger than us exists. Every culture across the world has an understanding of an almighty, a great light, a king, a warrior, a father, a mother. When I say "God" I do not mean Judge. I mean comfort. I mean hope. I mean that we are made for more than for this world. When I say "God" I mean it was a divine force that opened my eyes and told me what needed to be done. I don't care what you call this force: God, god, Allah, Creator, Santa Clause. We are all speaking of the same thing. We are all speaking about love.

When I created Eden, it was not to give naked people a place to prance. The dance of Eden is the pure intention of that original creation: to take what we are given and to nurture it perfectly. Hope is not about believing disaster won't come; it's about believing we're worth saving when it does.

Every society has the capacity for this utopia, and yet every society to date has wasted this opportunity for equality.

Yes, God promised to never again destroy the world with a flood. But he didn't promise to never again destroy the world by other means. We have invited such wrath. We are the whole reason for this ending. We have chosen this. And while this does sound like the verdict of a vindictive judge, it is actually the disciplinary hand of a loving parent. If you abuse the toy, the toy is taken from you. He who makes his bed must then lie in it.

How to build a bed:

The earth provides a tree; the woodsman cuts it down; the millman mills it; the carpenter builds a frame.

*The field provides the straw; the
farmer reaps it; the worker binds it;
the stuffer makes a mattress.*

*The range provides the cotton plant;
the field hands harvest it; the balers
bale it; the threaders thread it; the
weavers weave it into a lovely sheet.*

*The pasture provides the sheep; the
shepherd shears the wool, the carder
pulls it; the spinners make the yarn;
the knitters make the blanket.*

*The pond provides the goose; the
pluckers provide the feathers; the
seamstress provides the pillow.*

The bed provides the rest.

The rested man plants a tree.

And round and round it goes.

How man makes a bed in the 21st century:

The earth provides a tree.

Man burns it down.

Now tell me, sweet child of earth, which bed do you wish to lay down in? The bed of greed and gluttony, of lethargy and entitlement? Or the bed of reciprocity? The bed of the future? The bed of your future?

There is only one answer, but I fear the majority ignore truth for convenience.

Within the gates of Eden, I have planted 201 trees. 200 for the souls to be saved, and one for the soul I am leaving behind. My love. My Gerald. Our JarJar. Are you out there? I think of you every day of my blessed and miserable existence. Survival is already bitter without you. May your bed give you as much joy as you brought to me, and may it be the arms that hold you in sleep when the moment of reckoning comes that you might not experience one second of discomfort as you pass from this world to the next. And there is a next; of this I am certain. Why it is your time and not yet mine, I do not understand. But please do go gently into that good night. That is my only wish for you; for the unbelievers; for the left behinds.

Chin up, bright eyes. Soon you will have nothing left to mourn.

Rajiv Montgomery Noah

Chapter Four

1 day before Labour Day | northern Ontario
undisclosed location

I don't know how long we travelled. I do know I was hungry and in desperate need of a bathroom when the truck finally stopped and the engine shut off. I'd drifted in and out of a fitful sleep along the journey, but I knew at least five more people had been grabbed and thrown hastily into the back with the rest of us. I'd grown so accustomed to the sound of the rumbling engine mixing with the sounds of crying that it had become a somewhat comforting drone that lulled me to a place of complacency.

The area into which we disembarked was well lit, but it

was clear that night had already fallen. My ankle hurt and I limped on the asphalt when we were released from the truck, but I could almost put all my weight on it, so I knew it wasn't seriously injured. I was led into a huge hangar where the whole group of us, men and women, were led into a single washroom with a row of ten stalls, and told to relieve ourselves. A stern line of lions watched us as we entered in unison and flipped the locks.

I sat on the toilet and took stock of the situation as best I could. If it was Rajiv Montgomery Noah behind this, what did that mean?

A.) The end of the world was imminent and for some reason I was among the chosen to survive.
B.) I was one of the victims of a mass kidnapping.
C.) I would never see my home again.
D.) All of the above.

What if it *wasn't* Rajiv Montgomery Noah behind this?

A.) I was one of the victims of a mass kidnapping.
B.) We were being prepped to be fed to the lions.
C.) I would never see my home again.
D.) All of the above.

I couldn't decide which fate was the lesser evil. It seemed strange that the man who extolled his prediction with such confidence would execute his reaping with such stealth and roughness. Unless it was actually about the spectacle, which also seemed believable with the little I knew of the man. He did love to make waves. It was too coincidental to be anything other than what he had promised.

I washed my hands with soap that smelled like a hospital and was ushered to the other side of the hangar just in time to see another armoured truck arrive. In all, there were thirty of us gathered there, plus the crew of lions, all in various states of disarray and distress. They made us stand in a row and one crew member moved along the line with a tray holding cups of water and little plastic pill cups. One by one, each conquest was forced to take the pill.

"What is it?" I asked when he stopped in front of me.

His voice was muffled by the mask but there was a hint of kindness in his answer. "It is to help you relax for the rest of the journey. You need your rest."

My hand fell to my belly. "Is it safe?"

"Of course," he said. "The very last thing we would want is to hurt that child." He reached out and put his hand over mine, the gentleness of his touch shocking and yet, so reassuring. His skin was warm, its colour rich. "This is the future," he whispered, but I sensed a hint of sadness in his tone and didn't experience the usual recoil response when a man tried to touch me. *Strange.*

My hand shook as I took the pill and raised the water

to my lips, but as I gazed into the black holes of his lion-mask-eyes I felt a deep sense of comfort. "Thank you," I said, putting my empty cups back on the tray.

He nodded his head—almost a bow, like I was royalty. I wondered what his face looked like underneath that mask.

People continued to sob around me but I felt warmed with a peace I'd never experienced before. My eyes were dry. I wanted to remind my companions that we had all asked to be part of this. We had no right to protest or fight or even cry. But as I looked at each of them, I saw them for more than their sadness. I saw their loss. It was written across faces, twisted in pain. I was being rescued; they were being stolen from lives they loved.

We formed a ragged line and obediently followed a lion back out to the tarmac where we climbed a rolling staircase into a polished plane. My head felt heavy as I placed one foot in front of the other, clinging to the metal railing to stop myself from falling backward as I swayed with each step.

Dear Ryan, don't cry for me. Not like you will. I'm better off without you. There was a comfort in knowing I meant it. While all around me everyone mourned, I gratefully exhaled a thank you that I'd finally been able to leave him.

I'd never been on a private jet before, but the pills began to work too quickly for me to fully appreciate the experience. I wanted to memorize my surroundings and seal the feeling to my memory so I could one day paint the moment. If we were on the way to Noah's Ark, why did they need to drug us? I knew it couldn't be more than a two hour flight.

But no matter. Sleep pulled at my eyelids, and though I fought it I could barely recognize the kindness with which I was shown my seat before everything went black. I had forgotten my hunger.

Dear Child of Earth,

The time has come to determine your worth. Soon I will know all there is to know about you and I pray it is enough to save you from the fire. Earth's death could be your beginning, but only if you answer its call. Your seat at the table depends on an act of faith, a simple gesture to show you believe. Even in jest, to perform this act is to give your permission. Ingest. In jest. There is no reverse. The facts remain. There is only **[YES]** *or* [NO]. *Choose* [NO] *and your life will continue, uninterrupted by my message, unsubscribed from my Gospel, premature ashes in the wake of a truth you no longer trust. Choose* **[YES]** *and I lay before you the possibility of a future. I gain the great potential of you as my passenger.*

You ask for proof. Have I not always been transparent?

You ask for assurance. Have I not always led with a passion that can only be accepted as reality?

Now I ask for faith.

Choose [NO] and I leave you alone. Choose **[YES]** *and I send you a package that will send me a message.*

Do you understand?

Choose **[YES]** *and you will be interviewed.*

Are you worthy of my Eden? Choose **[YES]** *and find out.*

But don't stop being diligent. Keep building your own Eden, for in my house there is limited space. Today there is a vacancy. Tomorrow there shall be no room at the inn.

Are you **[INN]** *or are you [OUT]?*

The brave ones among you, the lions of this worldly jungle, will answer the call with a roaring **[YES]***. They will open the gift that comes. They will trust me when I say no harm will befall anyone who drinks of my cup—for my cup is not meant* *for harm, only salvation. The harm that comes is the one I wish to save you from.*

Drink from my cup. Put your faith into action. Show your devotion with this one small gesture.

How will I know? I ask you this: how do I know anything? I will know because your faith lights up my destiny, putting yours in my hand. When you drink from my cup, the ArkhiveLink within creates a sacred bond between us—a microscopic sentinel that speaks your truth to me alone. Every beat of your heart, every strand of your being, every potential of your future becomes known. I carry your destiny like a scar on my palm. You will be my stigmata and I will pull you from the pit should you be deemed worthy. For every name I write down, there are thousands I cross out; and yet, to place your name on my list, you must first submit to my call.

One more time for the nerves that prick your back. **[YES]** *or* [NO]*?*

Life or death, bright eyes, there is no middle ground.

Your Father of Eden,
Rajiv Montgomery Noah

Chapter Five

86 days before Labour Day | New York City

When Bonnie laughed, it infected a room. It was something that boiled out of her like a tidal wave and often came with tears. Never on stage. That wouldn't be professional. And that was an act. In real life though? It wasn't unusual for hilarity to turn to sobs, and though the sobs were usually void of sorrow, it tended to make others uncomfortable. Not Max though. Max loved that about Bonnie. It was one of the reasons she fell in love with her.

"Maxine!" Bonnie called, pushing the door of their East Harlem apartment open so hard that it hit the wall with a bang. "They're here!"

Max spun around from the kitchen counter, her dark cheeks flushed with excitement. "Finally!"

Bonnie waved the two wax-sealed envelopes at her. "Just in time too. What do we have? Like twenty minutes?"

"Yup," said Max, pushing back a pile of tight dark curls. "I already called a car. And I made that seven layer dip you like."

"You know you're my favourite dip."

Max rolled her eyes. "You're such a dork. Are you telling them tonight?"

A thrill rushed thorough Bonnie's body as she thought about The Big News—even though, since the moment she'd signed the contract, she hadn't really stopped thinking about it. It was all so fresh. "No. Can't. Tight-lipped until they make the official announcement next week." But she was desperate to spill. Even telling her partner was against the rules, but there was no one she trusted more than Maxine. The fact that she would have to leave her for a full month was already hurting her heart, but Maxine couldn't afford to close down her flower shop for that long and she'd assured Bonnie they'd be fine. "I'll come for the Chicago show," she'd promised. Bonnie knew that was partly because she wanted to go to Buddy Guy's Legends, but she was fine to share the spotlight with that genius, fried okra, and some deep dish pizza.

Bonnie grabbed Max's face, the seal of her envelope

pressed between her palm and Max's cheek. She kissed her firmly, then grabbed her hand. "Come on. We need to get changed quickly. Help me choose an outfit."

Max allowed herself to be pulled over to the shared wardrobe beside the queen-sized bed that took up approximately 22% of their studio space. "You know you always end up in the black jeans and a bolo tie no matter what I say."

Bonnie threw her head back, her laugh ricocheting off the ceiling like a missile attack.

The party was in full swing when the car pulled up in front of the brownstone on 89th between Columbus and Central Park West. Music and golden light poured out of the windows. A couple shared a joint on the front stoop and waved at them as they climbed from the Uber. "You got them?" the woman asked.

Bonnie waved the envelopes in triumph. "We got them!"

A man held the door for them and they melted into the party, embraced by friends, dip and chips unloaded and carted off to the kitchen by the host, pushed around the room until they settled with the homeowner's cat on the daybed beneath the front window. "The lesbian landing strip!" Bonnie announced to the room and everyone howled.

The whole thing was being live-streamed, a camera mounted in the kitchen set to capture everything that happened down the length of the long, narrow house. They could see themselves on the television that hung over the fireplace. "Hi, Mom," Bonnie said to her evangelical conservative mother who definitely would not be watching.

It had become a trend. Beautiful people making a ceremony of drinking the potion of Rajiv Montgomery Noah. Some hot L.A. couple did it and the video went viral, increasing their followers by 1.2 million and landing them a major deal with two of the hottest fashion brands. So obviously, everyone else was trying to mimic their success. Hashtag drinkthekoolaid.

"7,500 viewers!" someone yelled and the room cheered. "We go at 10,000!"

It felt like college again, though that was nearly a decade behind them. Max had worked at the campus bar and Bonnie had worked at the campus radio station, always stopping in for a nightcap that Max never remembered to charge her for. It started out as friendly flirtation, talk about music, jokes about papayas, arguments about Virginia Woolf, a subtle touching of fingers as a drink was passed across the bar. The night Bonnie stayed to walk Max home was the first night they never spent alone again.

A homemade banner hung in the kitchen—"EDEN BOUND!"—and they all gathered under it as the viewership climbed. "10,001!" the host called. "Ready your Kool-Aid!"

They circled the island where twenty water glasses with spoons waited to determine the future of each party-goer. Like synchronized swimmers who had mastered their routine (though they'd never walked through the ceremony together), everyone held up their package and tore off the top, dumping them into their respective waters at the same time so that a rainbow of colour appeared around the circle. Glasses clinked as spoons stirred the contents. On the television screen, hundreds of hearts, thumbs up, and laughing faces crawled up the right side as thousands of people around the world watched this little pocket of NYC twenty-somethings test their fate.

"To Eden!" the host proposed, raising her glass towards the centre of the island.

"To Eden," all the guests echoed, bringing their own glasses to meet in the middle, the sound of them hitting together like the celebratory toast at a wedding.

Glasses to lips, heads tilted back, throats expanding and retracting to accept the destiny of each person there.

As drinks were consumed, glasses landed back on the island, the music was turned up, and the dancing began.

Maxine pressed her lips against Bonnie's ear. "If the end of the world comes, promise me one thing?"

Bonnie moved her hands lower on Max's back, pulling her tightly against her chest. "Anything."

"If one goes, neither goes?"

"Both or neither," Bonnie said.

"I mean it," said Max.

"You know this isn't real, right? It's just a game." The laughter in Bonnie's voice cut Maxine.

"I know. But still. Both or neither," she insisted.

Bonnie stopped their dance, holding Maxine in a tender gaze while she hiked up her pants with one hand. "Baby, there's no after unless you're there. Forever and a day. You know that." She raised her hand so the back of it covered her lips, exposing the infinity sign on this inside of her wrist. Maxine did the same and they pushed their matching tattoos together before Maxine grabbed the bolo tie and tightened it, standing on her tiptoes to plant a kiss on Bonnie's lips. "You should have worn the suspenders, dummy."

Bonnie's laugh broke over the music. As she returned Max's kiss there were tears in her eyes. Laughter? Sorrow? Perhaps a little bit of both. Or neither.

Chapter Six

December 1984 | Kokta, Madhya Pradesh, India

ajiv sat crosslegged on the carpet in front of the television with a bandana tied around his mouth and nose. An episode of *Malgudi Days* played quietly on the screen but he wasn't paying attention. In the other room, he could hear his mother coughing. And crying. She coughed and cried and every so often he heard her call out the name of Shiva. He leaned forward and turned the volume knob further to the right to try and drown her out, but it didn't help.

He wasn't allowed to go outside. He couldn't escape. They lived in a small village outside of Bhopal, but everyone in their neighbourhood was staying inside, afraid their air was just as poisoned as that in the city.

His father was already dead. Masked men in white had carried him out on a stiff board the day before to burn him along with all the others. One of the men had handed Rajiv a card with a phone number on it in case he needed their services again, nodding toward the bedroom where his father's body had rested beside his sick mother.

Fresh out of college, his American father had been snatched up by Union Carbide Corporation in '72 and relocated as a promising engineer to Union Carbide India Limited where he met Rajiv's mother, a lifetime local of Bhopal. When Rajiv was born very soon after, the couple committed to raising him bilingual. Some of his earliest memories were staring deep into his father's blue eyes and repeating American words like "diaper," "dude," and "shoot the breeze."

There had been blood around his father's eyes when they removed his body, the blue forever hidden behind stiff lids the colour of a bruise. He had been working inside the factory on the day of the gas leak. He got the worst of it. His mother had been shopping for their groceries at the market downwind from UCIL. Normally she wouldn't go into the city to get what they needed, but the family car was in the shop, so she had doubled on her husband's motorbike and planned to hire a taxi to bring her back home. "The city can offer a better price on almost anything than our little village, Rajiv," she had said when she left that morning. She was loading produce into her basket when people started vomiting around her. That was four days ago. She wasn't getting better.

"Rajiv!" she called out before succumbing to a new fit of coughing. He pushed the power button and waited while the screen shut down, forming a white dot in the middle and then going black with a shudder. When he stood, crumbs fell from his kurta to the carpet from his snack of dry biscuits. The stale package lay half consumed beside where he'd been sitting. He hadn't had a hot meal since Monday. His mother never brought the groceries home. He'd finished the last of his eleventh birthday cake for breakfast—they hadn't celebrated. The cake didn't even have icing on it. Butter had been on his mother's shopping list. She had planned a birthday meal of butter chicken and curry fried rice. Chicken was on the list too.

He stepped cautiously into her bedroom, seeing his dad's work shirt still slung over the chair as if he'd be right back for it. His mother patted the bed and he sat beside her, trying not to look too long at her ashy skin. He stared up at the framed artwork of Ganesh that hung over the bed instead and wondered if he should make an offering of the stale biscuits to try and ease his mother's suffering.

"Death creeps upon me, Rajiv," she said in Hindi.

"Nahin," he said. *No.*

"You must remember that I am taken from you

because secrets were kept. Your father is gone because the truth was not upheld."

Rajiv allowed her to take his hand and hers felt cold and moist. He did not understand.

"They knew at midnight and still they let your father come to work. They knew at midnight, and still they let the city people go about their business. Our blood is on their hands."

"Haan," he said. *Yes.*

"You will go to live with your father's sister in Canada."

"Nahin."

"You will go to live with her in Canada. You will always tell the truth. When you carry a heavy burden that will hurt others, you tell them because even the harshest truth can yield the greatest return. You will live with my sister-in-law in Canada where the air is fresh and there is no poison. And if the poison follows you, you will warn everyone. Yes?"

"Haan."

"I will be gone by morning."

"Nahin."

"I will be gone, but you will be here. You will close my door and wait for your aunt. She will arrive tomorrow night. She will know what to do with what I leave behind. She will be your mother. You will call her Maan. You will grow old. You will save the world."

"Nahin."

"Do not say no to me, child. This is your fate."

"Haan."

She reached to her bedside table and picked up a small brass lion figurine, pressing it into Rajiv's palm and folding his fingers over it. "You have a ferocious heart. You must be like Narasimha and be the solution to the earth's destruction. You must find the evil and vanquish it."

"But I don't know what evil is," he protested.

"Yes, you do," she said, pointing to the sweat on her brow and the bucket on the floor beside the bed to catch her sick. "Evil is lies."

"Okay."

"You will do great things."

"I will do great things."

"You are my sun and my moon," she said.

"Tum mere sitaare ho," he said. *You are my star.*

She smiled and sunk into her pillow. "That's right, bright eyes," she said. "Hameesha." *Always.*

Rajiv didn't want to fall asleep. He felt it was important to witness the final moments of his mother even though she asked him to leave her in peace. He put his father's work shirt on over his kurta and curled up in the corner chair, watching his mother's chest rise and fall with shuddering breaths. It wouldn't be long now.

The lion in his hand was small but it had some weight to it. By squeezing his fist around it, he could imagine small teeth were digging into his palm. Lions were strong and majestic. Lions were kings. He was a boy.

"What am I supposed to do?" he asked Ganesh. The image gazed at him with thoughtful merriment.

The room grew dark and his eyes grew heavy. He remembered the blood on his father's face and the sadness in his whisper as he wished Rajiv a happy birthday. He thought 11-years-old deserved some fanfare. This was the wrong kind of excitement.

His father's cigarettes rested on the dresser beside him and he picked up the pack and slipped one between his lips. He liked the smell of the tobacco. Slightly sweet, reminding him of hugging his father when he had one tucked behind an ear on Sunday afternoons. He didn't want to smoke it, but he took the matches from beside the pack and lit one, holding it to the end like he'd seen his father do. He didn't inhale. He just shook out the match when the end of the cigarette caught and pulled it out of his mouth, holding it upright in front of him like a candle. "Happy birthday to me," he sang in a whisper before crushing the butt out in the ashtray.

He didn't want to go to Canada. He didn't want a new mother. He didn't want to be a lion. His real mother sighed and he along with her, his eyes finally falling closed, sleep curling around him like one of Ganesh's many arms.

In the dream he was a man. His mother stood beside him. "Do you see?" she asked.

The sky rained fire and the earth spat lava and they floated above it all in a bubble.

"This will happen," she said. "This is the holy trinity of destruction: sky, earth, and man."

Rajiv saw a date carved in hieroglyphs and he allowed it to imprint on his memory.

"When the earth dies, you will live. You see the future now. You are like the Noah of the Christian Bible. You have been warned of the flood and so you will build a boat."

"What does it mean?" he asked. "The name Noah?"

"It means 'rest.'"

"There is no rest here."

"There is not," she said. "But you can find the rest, the other, the beyond."

"I like it," he said.

"What?"

"The name. Noah."

"Take it. It is yours."

He put the name in his mouth and it tasted of wood and earth. "It is mine."

"Tell the truth," she said.

"Hameesha," he replied. *Always.*

When he woke, she was dead and he was a boy again.

He pulled the sheet over her face and went outside the bedroom. He closed the door and sat on the floor until his aunt arrived from Canada.

Chapter Seven

90 days before Labour Day | Stanford University

"It's incredibly sophisticated, Lou." The scientist wore a white lab coat and stared at the camera as if he'd never seen one before. "Technology like the ArkhiveLink exists in science fiction, but I've never seen it in the real world."

"Can you explain how it works?" the reporter asked.

The scientist held up the package with the lion insignia. "They all appear the same," he said. "Every one we've examined is composed of the same ingredients. And Rajiv Montgomery Noah was telling the truth. It *is* safe for consumption." He tore the package open and added it to a glass of water. "As you can see, it seems like nothing more than a child's drink, but upon further investigation we've learned what it really contains." He stepped to a thin tank that showed a cross-section of a man's torso. "In this simulation, we see what happens when someone drinks Rajiv's Kool-Aid." He poured the cup into the top and the simulated esophagus responded with human-like actions as it forced the liquid down to the stomach. "Here we see the drink connect with the stomach acid and begin the digestion process."

"So it's just a drink?" the reporter asked.

"No," the scientist said, shaking his head as he picked up a small wand from a desk off-camera. "Watch." He waved the wand in front of the simulation and it beeped with each pass of the stomach area.

"What does that mean?"

"It means that something in the drink is transmitting a signal. Watch." He clicked a remote and a screen beside the tank lit up with an animation. He used his finger to trace the path of the drink being consumed. "We think the transmitter is activated when it senses the acid in the stomach. The Arkhive is triggered to burrow into the stomach lining to avoid being digested and then it transmits its signal. We've never seen this technology at such a small scale before. It's truly remarkable."

"And what is it transmitting?"

"Well, if we are to trust the claims of Rajiv Montgomery

Noah, it's transmitting all known information about the patient so he can determine if they're worthy enough for his 'ark.'" Sarcasm dripped from the explanation.

"You're not a follower?"

"I am a scientist," he said, scoffing. "I believe in proven facts."

"So you have not consumed the drink yourself?"

"I have not."

"And how did you come to be in possession of multiple samplings of Rajiv's 'drink?'"

"My fellow scientists and I requested them in the same way every one else who has received them has requested them. We feign our interest in his selection as a means to possess the samples."

"Do you not think a man who has been so forthcoming about his intentions would not offer it up to you freely that you might assure the public of its safety?"

"I'm sure he would, but we get a truer look at something when the deliverer does not know the requester has intentions beyond the intended use. Had I asked for the purpose of testing, he might have sent me something different from what he sends the masses. Do you see?"

"I do," the reporter said, annoyed by the condescension in the scientist's tone. "And will you consume this yourself now that you know it contains nothing harmful?"

"I will not. I am a scientist. I believe in evolution. Survival of the fittest. What awaits humanity can't be contained by a man with a dome. I will either survive or I will not, and that has nothing to do with a drink powder or an algorithm."

Child of Earth, heed me now:

I was not born to greatness and many would not call me great now. Most philosophers are not appreciated in their time. Do you think Diogese was respected when he asked "of what use is a philosopher who doesn't hurt anybody's feelings?" No! He was ridiculed by the majority—not because he was wrong, but because they did not have eyes to see.

The greatest downfall of man today is the shrinking of our world to a tiny screen. When the African American spiritual chorus, "He's Got the Whole World in His Hands," was written, the lyricist meant God's got the whole world in his hands. He did not mean you and you and you and you and everyone. Yet, here we are, and we all have the whole world in our hands and it has broken us beyond what science can effectively measure.

Man is not meant to have instant access to a stranger across the ocean. Man is meant to live in quaint societies, helping one another within shouting distance. Access to everything effectively reduces our access to one another. Neighbours don't chat on porches as the sun goes down. Instead they remain in their homes while radio signals allow a Canadian to play chess with a Russian; an American to have virtual sex with a Colombian; a Korean to attend a digital concert in Australia.

Stop. When is the last time you touched someone outside your household without flinching? Do you carry sanitizer in your purse? Why? Because you are afraid of anything real!

The more invested we are in the screen in our hand, the more isolated we become. The internet is why the world is dying. You think you're connected? You're trapped. Each like, each share, each dopamine hit from your notifications is another bar on your cage.

And yes, it is how I am able to get these words to you, and yes, that does (in a way) make me a hypocrite, but mark my words: if we want to return to a perfect society, it must be one without the internet. If it were within my capacity as a human with a human life span, I would send all seven hundred million of you subscribers (you read that right, 700,000,000 newsletter subscribers) handwritten letters of my manifesto. But I am human. As such, my only vow to you can be this: in my Eden there will be no internet and thus, it will be the birthplace of a new society, one with a potential for perfection, for utopia.

"Nobody owns anything but everyone is rich—for what greater wealth can there be than cheerfulness, peace of mind, and freedom from anxiety?" Thomas More has given me such a blueprint for Eden and I mourn the fact that you will not (likely) be there to experience it. "We did not ask if he had seen any monsters, for monsters have ceased to be news. There is never any shortage of horrible creatures who prey on human beings, snatch away their food, or devour whole populations;

but examples of wise social planning are not so easy to find."

The monster is in your hand.

Try this. Leave your phone at home. Go to the grocery store. In the produce aisle, watch for someone choosing a melon or a tomato. Stand beside them. Search the pile with them. Find the very best cantaloup and hand it to them and say, "Here you go. I chose a good one for you." What they do is going to be the measure of what is missing in our society today. I would bet my fortune that nine times out of ten that person is going to smile and thank you, but then also tell you that you should keep the cantaloupe for yourself. Because this is the measure of what it means to be a kind human in a human world. Don't take the cantaloupe no matter how good it looks. Let this be a gesture of grace that will follow that person home. They will present the fruit to their family and say, "The strangest thing happened to me in the produce aisle." And then, they will do the same *for someone the next day. Perhaps they'll pay for someone's coffee behind them in the drive-thru; perhaps they'll say hello to a stranger. Perhaps they'll write a thank you note for the mailman. Small gestures change the world, but we can't make change if we're buried in a phone. Get those headphones out of your ear! Smile at a stranger! Say good morning to a policeman! Your days are numbered. Wouldn't you like them to be riddled with kindness?*

He who has ears, let him hear! If you choose to be dumb, I choose to call you stupid. If you are not part of the solution, you are part of the problem.

You were probably not born to greatness either, but I will tell you this: you can die in greatness. And you should.

Chin up, bright eyes. It is better to see what haunts you than to approach an open grave blind.

Rajiv Montgomery Noah

Chapter Eight
38 days before Labour Day | New Mexico

There had been people predicting the end of the world since the beginning of the world. That's just how people were, always looking for the worst, seeing their own death around every corner, thinking it made them more important somehow if their mortality was louder than their living. The Peters family was no different and they began their preparations within months of Rajiv's initial announcement. The farmhouse had an old root cellar that Jessie Peters expanded until it was big enough to hold himself, his wife, and all their neighbours. "Thirteen souls," he said, though his wife, Penny, warned him it had to be twelve or fourteen. "No way we're going into the apocalypse as a team of thirteen."

The neighbours laughed, of course. Who wouldn't? Foolish uneducated nut cases who spent a quarter of their paycheque on lottery tickets and a quarter on the canned food that slowly filled the shelves of the underground lair.

"You could take an annual trip to Europe," they were told.

"What would we do in Europe? They're just as dead over there as we are here. When the Louvre is under ashes, do you think we'll regret not seeing it with our own eyes? No! We'll be safe and warm underground while everyone else is out there dying along with all the art they love."

To look at him you would never expect Jessie graduated with honours with an English major from UNM, his favourite course being British and American Literature of the 19th Century. Jessie loved to postulate from a platform of academia because no matter how many times the neighbours experienced his poetic turn of phrase whenever he was passionate about something, they looked at him like he was an alien, and that made him feel superior. It came out whenever someone addressed him with a hint of condescension. When he was comfortable and felt welcome in a conversation, he resorted back to the speak of his people: slang, short forms, a bit of a drawl that sounded charming to some and poor to others.

When Jessie sold the vintage Mustang to pay for an

industrial air filtration system, that had really got the neighbourhood up in arms. That beautiful car had been his pride and joy, but he was pretty sure it wouldn't serve them in the aftermath. A meathead from town bought it for ten percent under blue book value. "If he adds racing stripes, I swear to God…" Jessie had said as he watched his father's legacy drive away.

They sold the chest freezer and a lot of the furniture in the main house.

"Fools!" the neighbours said.

"You'll see," they responded with great aplomb.

When an old RV puttered into their driveway, they were sceptical at first, but when they saw the camera, they got excited. Weirdos showed up once in a while to try and catch a peek at what they'd been building, but they usually turned them away. This was *their* kingdom.

The girl with the camera was sexy in the way all confident women are sexy. She had a little grease on her hands. Jessie guessed it was from fiddling with the engine of the old beast she drove. Her black jeans had a little tear in the thigh and her converse sneakers were pristine. She was C-O-O-L. A cat pressed its body against one of the side windows and meowed at them.

"I'm Jude Abbott," she said, offering her hand, which

he took—pleased with how firm she shook his. *Yup. Sexy.* "I found you on Instagram. JessiesBunker. Did a little digging and realized you were right on my way out of New Mexico so I thought I'd swing by. And you must be Penny," she said, smiling at Penny and offering her hand again.

Penny curtsied and giggled. "Yup. What's the camera for?"

"I'm a film-maker," Jude said. "Making a documentary about preppers. I'm on my way up to Eden and trying to speak to as many people as I can along the way."

"You're going to Eden?" Penny gushed. "That's super cool! We talked about it, but time's just too short now."

Jude held up her hand, wanting to save the conversation until the camera was on. "Could we actually set up right inside your bunker?" she asked.

"Like, we'd be in your movie?" Jessie said, excitement raising his voice an octave.

"Yeah, if you're okay with that. You'd just have to sign a few papers to make it legit."

"Cool beans. Yeah. Follow me."

Jude popped open the back door of the camper and grabbed a tripod. "Lead the way," she said.

"Why the old-school camera?" Jessie asked as he unlocked the outer door.

"Personal preference," Jude explained. "I like the tactile experience of tape. I don't know. It feels more honest somehow. Like practical effects verses CGI."

"I get that," Jessie said. "Heavy equipment to lug around though."

Jude shrugged under the weight of her camera bag. "It's worth it. I've built a name based on a certain aesthetic. Gotta give the people what they want."

The underground lighting was good because they were pulling power from the circuit box in the main house. A long string of industrial construction bulbs ran the entire length of the visible space. When they'd first come inside, they gave Jude a tour so she would have loads of "B-roll" for her edits. The long shelves of canned food and water, the composting toilet, the periscope, the mini library that was already getting musty because of the dampness underground. Now Jessie and Penny were sitting on two lawn chairs in the centre of the space, the camera set up and pointing at them, the little red light on.

"He was my prom date," Penny said in response to Jude's question of how they first met. "It was a dare."

Jessie laughed and Jude zoomed in on his face. "Yeah. I was on the football team and she was this artsy-fartsy girl. We didn't run in the same circles, you know. But then I saw her one day and she had paint on her cheek and I asked my buddy, 'Who's that girl?' and he was all like, 'Whatever, dude, she's a total loser art freak' and I was like, 'Yeah, but she's hot' and he was like, 'I dare you to ask her to prom.' He didn't have to tell me twice. I marched right up to her and said, 'My friend dared me to ask to you to the prom, but that's a stupid dare because I'd do it for free. Also, you have paint on your face."

"I thought he was a total idiot," Penny said, laughing as Jude pulled the camera focus back out. "But he was cute."

"Thick as thieves ever since," Jessie said. "Got married fresh out of high school."

"And the bunker?"

"Yes. The bunker. This started as soon as I saw that interview with RMN. So like… almost three years ago? Yeah. I mean, we're still practically newlyweds."

The camera pushed in on his hand on her knee and the way she played with his wedding ring.

"It's not like we started from scratch," he said. "The cellar was already here. We just grew it up a whole lot."

"A glow up!" Penny said, and giggled again.

"How did you afford all this?" Jude asked.

"Why? Just 'cause we're young?" Jessie said.

"Well… yeah. No offence or anything, but this must have been really expensive."

Jessie hooked his arm in the air and kissed his bicep. "Hard work is free," he said. "I had a shovel. And there's this wood pile down at the end of the road where people dump their scraps. Do you know that people will throw out a full two-by-four just 'cause it's got a little warp in it? Idiots! I got like 75% of the building material in here for the price of my own sweat. The shelving I salvaged from the scrap yard for peanuts."

"And the food?"

"Yeah. That's the money right there. But we're just two people, and you can see we're not huge humans. We just buy a little extra every time we're at the shops. Like pretending we're a family of five instead of two, you know? If you do that for three years—ten bucks here, twenty bucks there—it really adds up."

"But what about expiry dates?" Jude asked.

"Bah! Kind of a myth, isn't it? Like, why in the world would water expire? That's crazy talk. Cans though—yeah, I guess those can go bad and you should be kinda careful. But like, if they're not swollen or anything, you're probably okay. We do try and pick the ones from the back of the grocery shelf—you know that's where the ones with the longest dates are, right? So we got most of our cans dated for like three years from now. If Rajiv is right and it all comes crashing down, if we're stuck in here longer than three years, I figure we're gonna want to just eat the expired stuff and end it all anyway."

"How long do you realistically think you can sustain life down here?" Jude asked.

"Mmmmm, if we fill all the beds—you saw the beds,

right? Fourteen of them. If we fill them all, we've got maybe a year if we're really careful."

"Can you really trust fourteen people in this small space for that long? Are you afraid?"

"Well, it won't be summer camp," Penny said. "But we gotta help whoever we can."

"How sure are you that this bunker will withstand whatever is coming?"

"Lady, you gotta have faith in something," Jessie said. "This is where we're puttin' our faith. Where are you puttin' yours? That old camper?"

"My faith is in stories," Jude said. "My job is to teach the world about what is happening here so it can learn for the future."

"But whatcha got? Like a month before the big bang? Those tapes will melt and the only stories that matter will be the ones underground."

"Maybe," said Jude. "But this is what gives me life and hope. Faith."

They talked for another half hour before the tape had almost run out and Jude turned off the camera.

Jessie and Penny stood in the driveway with their arms around each other as the camper drove away. "She's going to eat it," Jessie said sadly.

"Yeah," Penny agreed. "I'm not surprised she didn't want to stay, but she's young and strong. Would have been nice to have her on our team for the apocalypse."

Jessie laughed, but it was laced with a low tone of mourning. "Some people just don't belong underground," he said.

The musty smell of the bunker lingered even as Jude climbed back into the RV and waved goodbye to the young couple who stood outside their front door, arms around each other's waists, waving like they'd never see each other again. And, of course, they wouldn't.

Edgar whined. "I know, buddy," Jude said to the cat. "I stink."

She backed down the driveway and took the main road to the nearest town, finding a plaza with a laundromat and a twenty-four hour gym. She stripped off the dusty bunker clothes between the RV sink and the closet and pulled on an old t-shirt and jogging pants. In the laundromat, she chose one of the largest machines and stuffed it with everything she had worn in the past couple days since leaving home as well as all her bedding so she could leave New Mexico super fresh.

As the clothes and bedding spun in a cyclone of suds and warm water, she slipped over to the gym, paid the day fee, and went directly to the showers where, at this late hour, she didn't worry about soaking up twenty minutes of luxurious hot water. She did keep a solar shower in the RV but only pulled it out in moments of extreme need. It was cumbersome and slow to heat up. She wasn't above having a cold shower, but she'd much prefer to find a small lake than to go to the trouble if it wasn't necessary.

The wash cycle had finished by the time she returned to the laundromat with damp hair. She flipped it to the big dryer then ran out to the RV for a book. She missed the days of public spaces having piles of old magazines.

Her friends always made fun of her and her attachment to analog. She had great faith in old machines and old technology. Photography made sense to her—pixels did not. She carried an ancient flip phone in the RV only because her mother insisted in case of emergencies, and to call home on Sundays, of course. The cassette player embedded in the dashboard suited her just fine, and the stack of books that was never far from her grasp had been a constant since her childhood. Books meant you were never alone. While her friends were reading articles on their iPhones, Jude was flipping pages, making notes in margins, allowing herself to become part of the story, and that's a magic that could never be replicated with a screen.

Chapter Nine

1985 | Toronto

Rajiv sat on the hard bench. The new leather belt dug into his stomach and the tie around his neck made him feel foolish. He missed his loose-fitting kurta. He kicked his feet back and forth until his aunt set her hand on his leg. She shook her head in a silent scold, nodding toward the man at the front of the room who wouldn't stop talking about Jesus.

Curtains hung at the rear of the stage and a white cross was painted on the wall behind, right at the spot where the curtains didn't quite come together. The man wore a suit like every other man in the place, and every time he said Amen, every other man said Amen too. It felt like nursery school and he hated it. He squeezed the lion figurine in his hand and silently prayed to Narasimha. *"I want to go home."*

Every lady in the room wore a skirt or a dress, their hair pulled up so he could see the back of every neck, a broach or a necklace decorating their fronts, a smooth application of lipstick making them look like the stewardess that was on the flight that took him away from his mother's body.

She usually wore her hair down. His mother. It fell in thick waves and it always smelled a little bit like green tea. Most of the mothers in the neighbourhood let their hair hang loosely. It was what set them apart from the men. Here, the women sat straight. Their necks told no stories. No one in this cold place resembled his mother. In this sea of pale skin she would have seemed an exotic, beautiful thing. The men did look like his father, a little, but only in the texture of their skin and their large white hands. He thought it strange that his father had left America for India and his aunt had left it for Canada. His father once told him his aunt had followed her lover, a draft-dodger, who shortly-there-after broke her heart. She met his uncle and let him marry her so she wouldn't have to face the humiliation of crawling home.

He stole a look at her. She seemed settled enough in this life. He wondered how often she thought of the draft-dodger. A lot, he expected by the tightness of her jaw. She had no children of her own. He had yet to decide if they viewed his appearance in their life as a blessing or a burden. She caught his eye and he quickly looked away, letting his gaze drift to the book in his uncle's hands, to the tiny words on whisper-thin paper.

His uncle had called it "God's Word."

Which god? Rajiv knew so many.

Once during the Fire Festival, a spark started someone's hair on fire. It was extinguished quickly, and no one was hurt, but the smell was sour and pungent. He imagined his mother's hair as they burned her diseased body. He pictured how it would curl up. How sparks would climb each strand like a wick of dynamite. How the thing that made her more beautiful than any other woman would be eaten by the heat. How someone was there to make it happen. How someone had to smell the end of her beauty. If only he had cut it from her head and brought it with him. If only he hadn't been distracted by his father's cigarettes and his own sadness. He put a hand to his chest, seeking out the poison that had killed his parents, wondering when it would finally kill him too.

"Amen," said the man at the front.

"Amen," said the men on the benches.

All the ladies gathered their handbags. Men shook hands. "It's time to go, Rajiv," his aunt said.

"Which god is Jesus?" Rajiv asked.

"The only one," she said.

After lunch that day, his aunt gave him his very own Bible. It had a black, leather cover, golden lettering across the front and spine, and a gold ribbon bookmark. Still thinking about his mother, he asked where the story of Noah was.

"Do you know it?" his aunt asked.

"Not yet, but my mother said I could take his name."

"You wish to be called Noah?"

"Not yet," he said.

She flipped the pages to the book of Genesis and Rajiv read the story about a man given the knowledge to save others from the end of the world, feeling the shadow of the dream he'd had as his mother passed, feeling the weight of a future that would not be saved by a rainbow.

Chapter Ten

Ryan and I once went for a weekend away to a quaint village named for a European theatre town where all the little shops and restaurants had French names and white gingerbread trim. The bed and breakfast we stayed at was called Glenview and the silence at night felt like home. This was, of course, in the early days when he was still working hard to make me think kindness was part of his nature, and it made me question whether I was cut out for city life.

I did like my neighbourhood. There were parks and theatres, and the Distillery District was only a half hour walk from our front door—one of my favourite places to visit at Christmastime. Mature trees lined the street behind us and healthy cedars dotted the courtyard below our balcony. We lived in a cool building with hip neighbours, but I knew bruises lurked just beyond the façade in many of the apartments, not just my own.

My sister had called excitedly that morning. Her husband was sick! They had tickets to the *Ark? Please!* one-man show near the harbour front that night and she needed a plus-one. "It's in the old *Toronto Star* press warehouse," she told me. "I know how you like those old artsy places with history or whatever."

I remembered showing her pictures of Printer's Row in Nashville from our honeymoon. She'd just rolled her eyes. "But did you see Blake Shelton at that bar he bought downtown?" We hadn't, but we had enjoyed the rooftop patio there.

She was Hollywood. I was Central Park. Or, to be more appropriately Canadian, she was Montreal and I was Victoria.

I met Maya at Union station. We walked almost all the way down to the waterfront and then crossed to Yonge to find the theatre.

An old printing press was on display in the lobby, soft white lights trailing down on it where it glowed on a raised platform. I wanted to go look a little closer but an usher gestured us in the other direction where *Ark? Please!* posters lined a warehouse-like set of stairs to an upper floor.

The theatre was dim as we found our seats and settled in. Our premium tickets provided us with our choice of seats down front. Regular tickets were destined for folding plastic chairs in the back amphitheatre, but we were blessed with round, spinning armchairs, generously spaced, and very comfortable. We chose the second row. "Close enough for eye contact, but not close enough to get pulled into the show," my sister said. "Or get spit on." A bar just outside sold treats and spirits, so, along with our playbill, my sister had a white wine and I had a Mr. Big bar, a sweet puff pastry, and a bottled water. It felt very on brand. She'd always been more grown-up than me, even though I was three-and-a-half years older.

She bumped her plastic glass with a man in front of us. "I'm Maya and this is Aiya. Our parents had a sense of humour." It was how she always introduced us, pretending it was the most annoying thing in the world, but secretly loving it. We both had a tiny tattoo on the side of our middle finger that said "Mayaiya." She told people it was a motivational Hawaiian word that meant "always further" but really, it was nonsense and, to us, it meant "sisters forever."

The show was funny. The actor was charismatic and witty, and Maya had been right: the front row was heavily involved in the show—mostly as the butt of many jokes, but still. We were safe, save for that one wild splash of sweat that flung over the audience when he jumped up on a table and yelled, "I am the king of the world!" You know, just like Noah did after the ark was built.

A part of me felt sad about the whole thing, but I didn't know how to articulate that to Maya as we crossed to Yonge again on our way back to Union. She would have written it off as pregnancy hormones and I knew it was more than that. She raved about the moment in the middle when the whole crowd sang "Michael, Row Your Boat Ashore" and the jello shots that were passed around at the end—virgin, of course—just one final bit to make fun of Rajiv Montgomery Noah. The actor slipped into a thick Indian accent any time he was being Mr. Noah and it felt uncomfortable even though I laughed along with the crowd. Everyone and Wikipedia knew that Rajiv had come to Canada as an 11-year-old, and though he did have an accent, it was mild.

"What if the shots actually had the little robots in them?" Maya asked as we walked under the Gardiner Expressway overpass.

"Because you think RMN would endorse this kind of thing?"

Maya laughed. "Of course not. It'd be smart though, wouldn't it? Another way to feed the masses."

"He said he would only give it to people who gave consent," I protested.

"Right," she said, turning to me so her back was to

one of the cement pillars holding up the highway. A large black and white cow with a flower behind its ear was posted there. A rabbit stared at us from the next pillar, and a moose wearing a hat from the one on the other side of the crosswalk. We were part of an exhibit. "Two lottery tickets are better than one." She winked at me as the light changed, and as we crossed the highway, weaving around vehicles that were backed up into the intersection, I knew she'd done it too. She'd given her consent and drank the promise of Rajiv Montgomery Noah.

"What do you think happens to the people who are chosen?" I asked as we climbed the hill to Yonge.

"Experiments," Maya said. "Like weird mother-ship stuff. Or sex stuff. Probably sex stuff."

"Nu-uh," I protested. "He said it's for the survival of the human race."

Maya stopped and put a hand on her hip. "How do you think babies are made, Aiya?"

We both giggled, but I felt a deep wave of sadness and had to choke something back as we resumed our climb.

"I bet everyone will be gorgeous too. It's not like he'll choose a bunch of ugly people to keep the faith." She put one hand over the other in a claw motion and twisted like she was opening a jar, clicking her tongue with each one inch turn. "Like a never-ending orgy. Every day the cells shift and you mate with a new partner until it's baby city."

"Gross," I said.

"Baby girl, have you been married too long to remember good stranger sex?" she teased. "Divine. Mostly."

Maya was so much more explorative than I'd ever been, basically a child when Ryan snatched me up, so focused on my art degree that I forgot to explore my own sexual awakening.

"Snap out of it, Aiya," she said, bumping my shoulder with hers. "It'll be the perfect time to catch up."

I felt the weight of the baby against my bladder. "Yeah right," I said as we rounded the corner and headed for the subway sign that would take us underground.

Chapter Eleven
1 year before Labour Day | Thunder Bay

I t was the family crest of the Duke of Connaught that first drew Rajiv to the Prince Arthur Hotel: a British lion above a ducal coronet. It wasn't the crown so much as the lion that attracted him. His own brass figure was in his pocket where he could easily access it for comfort when required. A worry stone, Geraldine had always called it.

The hotel was grand in a dusty, faded, romantic sense with modest chandeliers and original mouldings so dense with gold, red, and black paint that they appeared thicker than the fine wood and cast iron that lay hidden beneath.

Cheap square tiles covered the foyer floor, hiding the cracked marble beneath because a past owner felt it too expensive to repair or replace the original. Only the staircase, stately at its 1911 inception, gave a peek of the marble, sad chips visible around the edge of the jungle leaf art deco carpet. Rajiv stayed in one of the larger suites during the early construction days of Eden—the queen's suite, named so because Elizabeth stayed there before her coronation. Merely twenty minutes from the site of Eden, it was convenient and, as it turned out, serendipitous.

He befriended Samuel Parker, the hotelier—a wealthy local of old railway blood who had acquired the hotel in his early thirties. Now nearing 60, he was a distinguished man with a rare twinkle. He loved his coffee, his wife, his son, a good cigar, and he loved his hotel.

The two men would meet in the quiet hotel restaurant in the early morning to discuss big questions over steaming mugs and a chess board; namely, did Rajiv really believe the end of the world was coming?

Rajiv grew to love him, as happens when relationships are nurtured on the daily. When Samuel finally asked if there would be a spot for him in Eden, Rajiv cried real tears into his coffee. "You're an old man, Samuel." Of course, Samuel was not old in modern terms. In Eden terms, he was ancient.

"My son?"

Rajiv shook his head. "I'm sorry, Samuel. Every recruit is under 30."

"How will it feel to be the old man among all that youth?" Samuel asked.

"Like death is always a single breath away." And Rajiv meant that in ways Samuel didn't yet understand.

Their cups were freshened, a board of cut fruit planted before them, and a new game of chess commenced.

"You could build a bunker. There is still time," Rajiv told him.

"Maybe the tunnels beneath this hotel could save me," Samuel tossed out as he knocked a rook from the board.

Tunnels. That launched a whirlwind of activity. Rajiv insisted on a tour of the entire basement.

"There are employees who refuse to come down here because of the physic energy," Samuel told him as they made their way from the restaurant to the front desk, around which the staff stairwell lay hidden from regular lodgers. There were a few rooms in which guests had experienced unexplained phenomenon. A man once filmed a dark cloud that gathered above his daughter as she sat screaming in bed before it disappeared over the door frame. In another room, guests had fought the cleaning charge imposed on them for smoking, saying they'd never smoked a day in their life. The lore held that if a gilded frame containing the black and white photo of a man outside the Thunder Bay train station was moved at all, the room would fill with cigar smoke. "I can't speak for the cloud attacking the child," Samuel said, laughing. "But I can tell you that my office is beneath the room with that photo and my vents connect with their vents." He pulled a cigar from his breast pocket and wiggled his eyebrows in such a way that Rajiv guffawed in the stairwell as they made their way to the basement.

"I don't know if they're deep enough," Samuel said, leading Rajiv along a convoluted path beneath a low ceiling, turning twice until they passed the long retired boilers and stacks of old air conditioners and decommissioned microwaves. "Now, it doesn't look like much," he said as he stopped in front of a poured concrete wall, the outline of a tunnel frame clearly visible.

"This is not a tunnel," Rajiv said.

"When the hotel lost the front of the property, the town made us collapse the tunnels," Samuel explained.

"And did you?"

Samuel grinned. "At either end. Yes. Enough to satisfy them. What they really did was push them deeper and reinforce them to withstand the traffic. This was before I owned the hotel, mind you, so I'm only going off the drawings left behind by the last owner. With the deed, I received a safety deposit box with all the illegal documents. He even added a tunnel to the bank vault, connecting the two beneath us."

"Bank vault?"

"In the midst of construction, a two story annex was added to the south end plans and the Bank of Nova Scotia moved there in 1911. Being last minute, they focused on their customer front and meeting rooms, so the Canadian Northern Railway leased the basement space to them—the CNR held the ownership of the building until 1955—and installed the vault beneath the hotel during initial construction. It's dry storage now, but only because the staff doesn't know what's beyond the first shelf."

He led them back through the winding basement to another end near the old coal chute where a vault door with ornate hinges sat conspicuously inside a square of cement blocks. Sealed only with a padlock, Samuel undid it and welcomed Rajiv inside, where he easily pushed a shelf aside to reveal another door. This opened to a dark, gaping hole with a narrow and steep wooden staircase that led into the abyss.

"This is the spot," Rajiv said, touching the thick concrete walls as they navigated the unsafe stairs into a damp and dimly lit inner cellar. "If we seal it properly and expand it to accommodate your actual needs, it will be deep enough."

Samuel showed him the length of tunnel between the vault and the original prohibition exit.

"This can be strengthened and built up into something brilliant. Room for... six or seven with relative comfort, I'd say."

"That many?"

"Oh, yes. Save whomever you can."

A modern vault door was secured at the entrance, adorned with the Duke's crest. Rajiv found great joy in this as his own gates were also secured with a lion. In fact, the old iron lions that once stood guard outside the main doors of the hotel in its early days were sat in a dusty corner of the basement by the boiler and Samuel gifted them to Rajiv. "They will serve you far better in the future than they will serve me in this dungeon," he had said.

A coded door was added at the end of the utilitarian part of the basement to prevent staff from accessing what was going on beyond. They told no one, only the small crew hired to excavate the main tunnel which had been filled in at the end of prohibition—a crew paid handsomely for their secrecy.

The main structure of the larger tunnel was secure, requiring very little repair. Another vault door was placed at the far end, where stone and mortar refused entrance to Thunder Bay's original premiere hotel, the Marriaggi—now known as the less compelling Marina Inn—built more than twenty-five years before the Prince Arthur.

"The original owner used to keep orphaned bears down here," Samuel said. "He'd bring them down as cubs, taking them to a sanctuary he had outside the city once they were old enough to survive without a bottle."

Rajiv found this charming, though a bit alarming. "If this tunnel could sustain a baby bear, it will surely keep you and your family alive."

I slipped the knife beneath the red wax seal, carefully preserving the lion insignia as I opened the envelope. Another package, smaller, stamped with the same lion, fell out onto the table in front of me. It looked just like the example shown in the last newsletter from Rajiv Montgomery Noah and the video of the viral news story about the robots. When I checked the [YES] box I hadn't really believed he would send me what he promised, but here it was.

"My invitation, your act of faith," was spelled out beneath the lion head.

I turned the package over and read the back:

Mix with 12 oz cold water and drink.
90 calories.
Gluten Free. Vegan.
Safe for pregnant and nursing mothers.

I touched my belly and chewed my lip. At six months pregnant I was just beginning to show, though Ryan began commenting on my thickness almost immediately after the test came back positive. "Not thick like JoLo. Thick like some lazy ass hoe." He said it as if he was rapping, as if he had practiced it and waited for the perfect moment to slap it on me.

I shook the package and remembered summer camp days when my cabin mates and I dyed our hair with Kool-Aid in the camp sinks, permanently staining the porcelain. Back in the sunny days when the worst thing I'd even been called was "poop face" by a boy in the school playground. The whole thing was silly. A global joke. And yet… something about the earnestness in his message tugged at me. *Harmless*, I thought as I tore the top off the package. I pulled over my glass of water and dumped the contents into it, swirling the cup to mix it, watching as the water turned a pale pink. The smell reminded me of my childhood. I lifted the glass and drank the whole thing. It tasted like summer. It tasted like my hair after I dyed it and it blew into my mouth. I laughed as I set the glass down, feeling giddy and ridiculous and strangely free. I took the packaging and envelope to hide in my bedside table. Ryan would ridicule me if he knew what I'd done. He'd say I was stupid to believe in dumb stories. I once called him stupid for not washing his Leafs jersey for a whole season. That had cost me a dislodged filling. "I tripped on the stairs and hit my face on the railing," I told the dentist. I knew she didn't believe me, but she didn't ask me anything else. People don't like to get involved in other people's issues. It was too messy.

I went outside and sat on the back balcony. The drink

had left a chemical aftertaste in my mouth and I wished I'd brought a glass of fresh water, but I was already sitting, and the extra fifteen pounds I'd put on made me think the effort of standing again was not worth the relief the water would afford me.

I picked up the Renaissance art book I'd left on the little patio table, but I couldn't concentrate on the pages. I kept thinking about the robot that now wandered my stomach and I couldn't help but wonder if my insides now looked like a Rafal Olbiński painting, a wacky landscape with a happy little android motoring around.

Maybe I'd try paint that scene later. I sighed, tired. Maybe not.

93 days before Labour Day | Eden

Inside the control room at Rabbit Mountain the computer beeped and a new ID photo appeared on the screen. "Aiya Efron," the tech read aloud. He watched as files started opening. Medical records. University transcripts. Publications. Parking tickets. A *Toronto Star* article about hot local artists. "This one looks promising," he said, flagging it by clicking on a little check box before another face and name took over his screen.

Chapter Twelve

30 days before Labour Day | Five kilometres
from Rabbit Mountain

The doghouse lay in the aisle between the RV's captain's chairs as Jude jammed a screwdriver into the old carburetor and pressed hard on the gas. The flooded engine coughed and chugged and warred with her, but she knew this battle and wasn't going to be defeated. The old dance caused her anxiety to rise and sweat to bead on her brow, but she closed her eyes and blew out a calming breath before twisting the key in the ignition one more time with her left hand. The RV shuttered to life and Jude leaned back in her seat, tossing the screwdriver aside and wiping the back of her hand across her forehead, leaving a light smear of grease.

"Piece of junk," she said, but her voice was playful and she patted the dashboard like one might a loyal dog. This old beast had never failed her. After she dumped half her savings into its purchase, the mechanic assigned to safety it told her these old engines would go forever. "I'd jump in it right now and drive it coast to coast twice without a second thought." And that was before he put on the new tires and rear brakes. A sandalwood air freshener and a Saint Jude charm hung from the rearview; a Hey Jude pendant swing back and forth from the keychain, hitting her knee in a slow rhythm.

The RV was older than her. Older than her mother; strong like her too. She bought it for a song when, fresh out of film school and high on her passion for storytelling, she announced to her family that she was going to go make documentaries. "I want to know why," she told them. "I want to know why people are the way they are."

"Philosophers have asked that since the beginning of time," her father told her.

"And if they had cameras, they would have filmed it," Jude shot back.

"So you're a philosopher then?"

"We're all philosophers now."

Her father had rolled his eyes at that and her mother had vibrated her lips with an exasperated exhale, but they'd all laughed together.

Jude replaced the doghouse over the exposed engine and snapped the brackets into place before swinging her legs out from under the steering wheel and grabbing the screwdriver from the floor. She tossed it into the small toolbox under the passenger seat then pulled open the closet door to expose the cloudy mirror inside. She clicked on the overhead light and studied her reflection.

She had pulled over just past the old sign for Rabbit Mountain, a five kilometre buffer in which to collect and prepare herself for what lay ahead. The ditch holding the sign was so overgrown that she almost missed it. The vehicle had stalled when she parked it and that's when her attempt to wake it up had flooded the engine. Nerves shot through her limbs like mild jolts of electricity as she thought of what lay ahead. It wasn't fear. It felt more like the anticipation before a first date.

She held the closet door open with a foot to prevent it from falling closed and wet a cloth in the small kitchen sink. The water pump growled and she flipped it off before wiping her face clean. She used the same cloth on her underarms.

How long had it been since she'd bathed? It was a Tuesday when she'd stopped at that truck stop outside Amarillo and used the coin-operated showers with the broken hot water tap. And what was today? Thursday? Friday? The long hours behind the wheel and fitful sleeps on the side of the road reared themselves through an intense pain in her neck. She wet the cloth again and rested it at the base of her skull.

Saturday. It was Saturday. That's why her muscles ached. The distance between her mother's home in New Mexico and Northern Ontario stretched over long days with interview stops at bunkers in Texas, Kansas, Missouri, Iowa, and Minnesota.

Northern Ontario provided views like she'd never experienced, better even than her drive through the Adirondacks. With wild rock faces and thick patches of forest, it was a beautiful drive along the Trans Canada highway, going from the top of the world into the deepest valleys then back into the clouds again. As she watched the ever-changing view of mountains through her windshield and in her rearview, she couldn't help but wonder if this was why *she* was referred to as Mother Nature. The fluid outline of the mountains against the sky was distinctly feminine in its grand softness, and it didn't take much imagination to see the shapely breasts, pregnant bellies, and generous hips where the tree line etched itself against the kind of blue sky that only reveals itself in the North. Jude felt connected to this place, like part of herself lay there with them—a stamp of all the women there ever were.

I wonder if I am going to die here, she thought.

She sprayed her hair with dry shampoo and tousled it aggressively to work the powder down to her scalp. It smelled like what she thought a California girl should smell like: coconut, pineapple, sunshine. Her dark hair fell across her left eye, long in front and nearly shaved in back. She pushed it out of her vision and pulled an outfit from the rack. Nothing fancy. She had resigned herself to being the every-woman because people trusted they were having an honest conversation that way. Jeans and a simple top. She changed her socks, but not before cleaning her feet with a baby wipe. Boots. Belt. Jacket. She swilled a mouthful of Listerine and spit in the sink before laying on a swipe of cherry chapstick and pinching her cheeks.

Her mother always told her she was blessed with youth. At 28 she could still pass for a college student if she ever wanted to. Her skin was smooth. Morning yoga on a mat in the dust beside the RV kept her body lean and her mind sharp. Three years ago, a film reporter tried to call her a prodigy when her debut documentary, *The Shadow of Eve*, took top acclaim at an international festival. "I am neither a prodigy nor a child," Jude had told her. "To be either I would have to have done a lot more with a lot less. I am a storyteller. I don't need to be more than that."

Despite her resistance to the recognition, that accomplishment had put her at the forefront of a feminist movement she didn't want to lead. Being a strong woman was one thing. Leading a generation of woman into a new future was not something she was passionate about. "I told a story," she said. "But it was not my own."

Still, it was this acclaim that gave her the credibility to put her on the road to Eden. The irony wasn't lost on her: her first film riding the coat-tails of the woman God tossed out of his garden; now here she was, about to enter the Eden of a different kind of god. The universe had a strange sense of humour she was dying to figure out and she thought the answers must lie on the other side of a lens.

"You can afford a nice tour bus now, Jude," her mother had said. "A reliable vehicle. A driver and a crew even."

But Jude believed in approaching her work with simplicity. "When I sat in my Director's Craft lectures I didn't picture Hollywood. I didn't want bright lights and red carpets. When I dreamed about my future as a film-maker I dreamed of hard work. I dreamed of earning it. I dreamed of finding stories—not making stories that came to me. The gift is in the discovery. It's in turning things over. It's in getting dirty and taking risks and finding answers to the questions I didn't even know I wanted to ask."

"You've always had a little poet in you, Jude," her mother concluded.

Jude closed the closet and looked to the bed where the hand-embroidered pillow lay nestled with the others.

But you can bet I'll not resign
That story telling job of mine

Jude sat on the edge of the bed and ran her hand over

those hard-won stitches. She knew some of her mother's blood was mixed up in that thread. The cat, hidden in a tangle of her grandmother's afghan, poked out his head, stretched, and rubbed himself against Jude's back. "Did I wake you up, Edgar?" She pulled the cat into her lap and nestled her nose in his fur, letting the vibration of his purr calm her nerves. Edgar was named for the same man who wrote the poem quoted on the pillow. It amused Jude to think most people would assume he was named for Poe, though, in truth, the cat had more of a dark spirit than the light and bright Edgar Albert Guest. In the overhead storage compartment, Jude had upwards of twenty copies of Guest's selected works. She gifted one to every person she interviewed on this new project. Just in case. She wanted family values to transcend the end of the world. It felt important.

Jude checked her battery packs and loaded extra tapes into the bag with the camera which she set on the passenger seat. For two months now she'd been travelling North America, putting together the story of doomsday preppers. She had toured seventeen bunkers, learned the shelf life of canned meat, and heard every prediction for the end of the world from zombies to aliens to nuclear fall-out.

"Yer gonna go meet that Noah's Ark feller?" one prepper had asked her.

"I am."

"Doesn't matter which one of us is right—we're both gonna beat it in the end," he said.

"Did you drink the Kool-Aid?"

"Haw! Shore did, that's the truth. I got me the orange flavour. What one you get?"

"Cherry."

Jude smiled at the memory, at the way she and the man with all the Spam had laughed together then. "Maybe we'll meet again in Eden," she'd told him. He nodded and spit and shook her hand.

"You be sure to let us know if this film gets put up anywhere. My name in the credits?"

"Of course."

"Ah, ain't that a thing."

Jude closed her eyes and tried to focus on the transmitter hiding somewhere within her body. She rested a hand on her belly and turned on her yoga focus. Nothing. Surely she would be able to feel it if something had burrowed into her stomach lining. If it was a hoax, Rajiv Montgomery Noah had certainly spent a fortune on postage to make fools of the world. All she felt was the rough surface of the surgery scar that always itched a little despite the doctor's assurance that she had healed beautifully. Maybe the itch was only in her head, a constant reminder that time was short and she still had much to do.

It was ironic, being a woman who had decided to track the end of the world with analog equipment, swallowing the tiny digital robot of the man who claimed to be the world's salvation. She wasn't a believer. At least she didn't think she was. But thinking of the thing that might be inside her and the weight it bore, she began to wonder.

A calendar was pinned to the wall behind the driver's seat, marking down to Rajiv Montgomery Noah's predicted doom. Thirty days left. This close to Eden she expected there to be more activity, but all was quiet save for the sounds of nature, and she pulled back onto the road without a whisper of another vehicle. She knew this would change as the day approached. Like out-of-town guests coming in for a wedding, she knew crowds would start to flock to the site; but for now, she had the road to herself.

Chapter Thirteen

30 days before Labour Day | New York City

The comedy club was a small but popular venue in the West Village, lit dimly with a low stage so the performer was almost on level with the crowd as they gathered at round tables and downed endless drinks; the two drink minimum was never an issue. Bonnie had earned her spot there through sweat and tears and now, nine years since her first set, she was headlining a Saturday night at Piques, the stomping ground of her youth.

Back then, the building didn't even have a sign, just a red brick façade on Bleeker Street. Now it boasted a grey-blue door with gold toe kick and a vintage-looking (but totally brand new) marquee that enticed comedy crowds inside.

She sat in the greenroom, listening to the crowd warm up to Bert Angstrom as he talked about sex in grocery stores and fruit that looked like genitals. Bonnie wasn't thrilled to follow him, his lack of sophistication annoyed her, but she chose to focus on the joviality she could hear from the tables. The crowd was primed and hungry for a laugh. Vaginal mangos could only take someone so far. She knew they would be ready for her.

She waited for the thrill of her name being called. The announcement always rushed through her with an energy that was almost sexual. "Please give a warm Pique's welcome to our headliner tonight. She has just finalized a short tour deal with Netflix that will take her from New York to Chicago to LA to Toronto and you get to see her here on her home stage one more time before she leaves next week. Put your hands together. It's Bonnie Baby!"

Baby wasn't her last name, obviously, but it's what her parents had always called her at home, and it's how she introduced herself as a child. It stuck. And people seemed to like it. And it came with a classic connotation about not planting a baby in the shadows. She was certainly no Jennifer Grey, but she did have some strong Swayze energy. Applause, cheers, whistles, and the clinking of glasses pulled her out from the back room.

Standing on a stage that had welcomed SNL alumni

and late night hosts in their youth carried a pressure that thrilled her and she relished the way her boots stuck to the floor with each step as she approached the microphone and set her beer on the black stool. The Netflix tour hadn't been widely announced, and it was a thrill to know the first real hint of it was being laid out at home. It hadn't been an easy path. She had paid her dues and worked the grind and taken the $12/show rate they offered newcomers until they proved they could fill seats. Sweat, grit, and tenacity. And a short run on a stand-up special when Fortune Feimster vouched for her. That was the crux of it. Pure luck. Good *fortune*.

"So, I'm gay," she said. Someone cheered in the back. "Yeah. Like I didn't even have to 'come out.' I mean, I 'came out' and the doctor stamped my ass with a brand that said 'gay.' Nothing my momma could do about it. My daddy's a reverend and he's had a hard time with it, but ultimately he had to accept it. I mean, what was he going to do? When I was 15 he sat me down for 'the talk' and he went into the 'when a man loves a woman' bit and I was like 'Whoa, Dad, listen, I'm not stupid.' And he was like 'God is love, Bonnie. He wants you to be safe and find the right partner.' And I was like, 'Yeah. And she'll be hot.' He didn't like that at all. I said, 'Dad, if God is God and God is love and love is God, then love is love.'" Cheers from the crowd. "Just love. That's all it is. That shut him up.

"I go to his church sometimes. He likes when I go, but

I can only stomach so much of it, you know? Sometimes the music is just so cheesy and such a show that I can't handle it. Like, what are they doing up there? A bunch of worship leaders fantasizing about how Jesus actually looks like Phil Collins as the drummer does way too much because he really wants to be touring with Beyoncé. And why are they called worship *leaders*? Something about that just hits me the wrong way. If God is love and love is love, don't we already know how to worship just by our love… you know? By their definition, *I* am a worship leader. Do you know what I'm saying? Like, I am doing what I was created to do and I'm leading you in laughter which is, at its core, one of the purest forms of love. And if love is God… You see what I'm saying? So… will you join me in worship?"

"Amen!" someone called out from the back and Bonnie raised her glass and took a big pull.

"Anyone here ever taken a road trip through the Bible Belt?" Murmurs of affirmation crossed the room in waves. "The deeper south you go, the harder it is to tell the difference between the Christian radio station and the country one. You know what I mean? It's all about Jesus and love. Soon, the only way to tell the difference is the 'Christian' politics on the religious stations. They're playing these songs about heaven and holy and 'get down on your knees'…" She paused and raised an eyebrow, making sure they got the joke. "'Like a Prayer,'" she added for good measure, confident that Madonna would approve as deeply as the audience did. "And the host will pour out some rhetoric about nationalism or how the left is forcing sex change operations on immigrant children. How is that a 'Christian' message? How is that anything but hate-mongering? Give me Garth Brooks and a Bud Light any day of the week over that ugliness. I just want to tap that radio host on her huge blonde head—because you know she's a darling southern momma—and tell her, 'Babe, the kids are alright.'"

Bonnie cracked the seal on the water bottle that stood beside her beer and took a drink as the crowd affirmed they were with her.

"Who here believes in God?" Some hands shot into the air. A couple boos. "I'm not brave enough to be an atheist, you know? Those guys. They're just… awesome. They can just accept that this is all chaos. Is there seriously anything braver than that? Like, they can just look at a giraffe and think 'yeah, that makes sense.' Not me. Nope. I need to attribute it to something. I need a creator because without one, I don't matter. And I have enough of an ego to think I need to matter. I need purpose over chaos because that's the only way my brain will accept this reality. It's like lightning and thunder. It makes sense. Or, at least it's supposed to.

"Can I confess something to you? Since we're worshiping together and being honest and all? I just learned what thunder was. Seriously. I understood that lightning was some kind of electrical reaction—that made sense. But thunder? Thunder was just a cool thing God did to remind us he was there. She was there? You do you, babe." Bonnie shrugged and grinned out at the crowd. "To me, thunder was just like wild flowers or ocean tides or Jennifer Aniston's complexion. An inexplicable thing that exists in the world for reasons I've never really questioned. Just lovely, flawless, Rachel-Green-truth. Okay, maybe I questioned it a little… Like how did she maintain that perfect skin on a waitress's salary? That's divine intervention right there. But thunder? I didn't know thunder was an audible reaction of lightning hitting the earth. I mean, of course it makes sense—but I just thought it was a show. A worship service.

"My partner thought I was joking and then she thought it was hilarious that I didn't know this. She called me a dummy—right in from of our framed Eurythmics poster. You don't ever call someone a dummy when Annie Lennox is watching. That woman is a cultural icon who travelled the world and the seven seas. Yes, everybody is looking for something, but what she's not looking for is that kind of disrespect. Being called a dummy is not what sweet dreams are made of. So I gave my lady the third gear." She paused, looking over the crowd, seeing the regulars perk up, grinning and nudging their friends. "You know the third gear, right?" Murmurs of appreciation came from those who had seen her perform before. She stuck out her thumb as if she was hitch-hiking. "First gear, watch your-self." She switched to her first finger. "Second gear, don't push your luck." She whipped her middle finger up in a big show, making her eyes huge as she yelled, "Third gear!" And, as always, the crowd roared, and a large ma-jority gave the third gear right back to her.

"You're hearing it here first, friends. That Netflix spe-cial? I'm calling it Third Gear." Someone whistled.

"I didn't *actually* give it to her. We're not crass like that with each other. We are sophisticated lesbians. We say, 'That is third gear worthy,' very regally, but we never make the actual gesture to each other. I save that for you fuckers. I 'give it to her' in a different way, if you know what I mean."

The rest of her set went smoothly with encouraging reactions and interaction with the audience. She loved walking the fine line between religion, politics, and human rights—it kept things edgy and thought-provoking. A com-edy review in the back of *The New York Times* once called her "a wizard at navigating the left from a right-wing up-bringing" and *The Advocate* called her "a fresh voice for a new generation." Time disappeared on stage. It was like losing and finding herself all at once. It was worship.

"I had a full on identity crisis in 2021 when *Seinfeld* came on Netflix. We all watched it, right? Like, yes, we'd heard our parents talk about how they used to watch it when they were younger—Thursday nights at 7 p.m. on

NBC—but now we got to see it the 'right way,' and we were all stuck in our apartments because of the big 'C' so what else were we supposed to do? Okay so… Jerry has this thick chest hair that is just…" She shrugged and the edge of her mouth turned up. "Hot. It shouldn't be. But I can't help it. I was hot for Jerry Seinfeld's chest hair. And I can see you're uncomfortable with that information because it obviously does not suit me, but what can I say. I like the ladies, but I love a… bear…? My therapist had to talk me off the ledge on that one. 'Bonnie, you're gay. This is just a… a thing.' A *thing*. Very therapisty and sciencey. Sometimes we just like what we like. The funny thing though, is that my partner is the opposite of Jerry. She's more like Elaine, but with some empathy and bigger boobs. And she's Black, but that's neither here nor there— except once you go Black, you don't go back, you know what I'm saying? I bought her a pair of those buckle loafers like Elaine wore with short white socks in the early seasons. I was wild for those. You know what I mean, right? Gaga for Sunday school teacher. I don't wish she was hairy—that's not what I'm saying. I just think about it sometimes—like a fantasy you hope never actually comes true, but that also gets you there… you know what I mean? He knows." She pointed to a large man in the front row with hair pouring from the top of his collared shirt. "Oh yeah, he knows what's good." A ripple of knowing laughter spread through the crowd. "Once, in the middle of sex, my partner asked if I was thinking about Jerry. I told the truth. And that's when I learned to be a liar."

Hoots of appreciation spread around the room.

"We're all creeps, aren't we? Like, you have some weird sex thing you're not ready to tell the world. You're fine. Don't worry. I'm only telling you because I had to fill forty-five minutes tonight instead of fifteen. You guys… do you think it's all grey now? His chest hair? *Seinfeld* was filmed almost forty years ago. Jerry's getting up there, pounding the pavement in his sneakers, talking about cars and coffee. Like, I want to see him with his shirt off right now way more than I'd like to see Julia Louis Dreyfus."

She stared out at the audience, watching their faces shift as they all pictured the 90s television heroes topless. "It happened, didn't it?" she whispered into her mic. "I did it. Find me after the show. I'll give you my therapist's number. Not that one from before—I wrecked her with my mind-bending appetite; I got a new one who uses proper grammar and everything.

"Speaking of grammar… so, I was at the doctor's office and sitting in the waiting room and there was this brochure stand with all the info about like, you know, STDs and how to stop smoking and hysterectomies—can we just take a moment and acknowledge that *that* name needs to be changed? Like that's from the time when women were accused of hysterics and we're way past that now, aren't we? Like, I wouldn't want to get one just on principle alone and I don't even need my uterus for anything, no matter what those Bible Belt radio hosts try to tell me. And while we're at it, let's talk about how it's called a 'medical practice.' Practice? Still? How long do they need to practice before they get it right? What other profession just keeps practicing forever? My partner's a florist—imagine if we called it 'flower practice.' People would be like 'You're just practicing with my wedding bouquet?' or 'My mother's funeral arrangement is your practice run?' But doctors? They're like 'Yeah, we're still working out the kinks. Maybe don't read our old text books. Turns out leeches weren't the answer.' And don't even get me started on what the chainsaw was invented for. I mean it. I'm not going to tell you. And don't Google it when you get home if you ever want to put your faith into 'medical practice' again. Seriously. I warned you. Anyway… there's this brochure stand in the doctor's waiting room and it has a big title printed at the top: HOW'RE YOU FEELING? Do you hear what I'm saying? HOW-RE. How-*apostrophe*-R-E. How're. That is not even a word. Go ahead. Try to say it. How-er. How-er. It feels like I have a golf ball stuck in my throat when I try to say that. How're. What person allowed that thing to go into production? How many doctor's offices have this atrocity sitting in a prominent place where people are supposed to feel taken care of? How-er is like the sound lightning makes, right? Like, it hits you between the eyes.

How-er is the feeling in my gut when I realized I didn't know what thunder was. I tried to say it to my doctor when I got in there. 'I'm fine, *how're* you?' She thought I was having a mini stroke. 'No,' I told her. 'I'm just trying to speak your language.' She didn't understand and asked me if I'd ever had symptoms like this before. I asked if she'd ever watched *Seinfeld*. She said she didn't have patience for such drivel. *Drivel.* Jerry would never put up with that kind of insult, and I wasn't going to either. 'What's the deal with doctors who can't use grammar?' I asked her. 'I mean, you spend eight years in medical school learning all kinds of crazy terminology, but you can't figure out contractions?' She did not think that was funny. She gazed at me with the humourless dead eyes of someone who has always known what thunder is, so I knew it was over for me. I gave her the third gear and got the hell out of there."

A wave of cheers and jovial middle fingers followed as Bonnie slipped the microphone back into the stand. She leaned in, enunciating with exaggerated precision —"Y'all've been great!" She gave a two-handed wave followed by a double third gear and then stepped off stage where the club owner bumped her fist. "Killer job!" he said. "When do you leave for the tour?"

"Next week," Bonnie told him, wiping a bead of sweat from her forehead with a towel from the green room counter. "I can't wait!"

67 days before Labour Day | New Mexico

Edgar was a cat. This wasn't something he knew, nor did it matter. He had been dying—this is also something he didn't know—abandoned in a ditch with his brothers and sisters who stopped moving and grew cold after the first night. Well, three of them stopped moving; one was carried off in the teeth of something very big and hairy.

When a rumbling machine stopped on the road as he tried to make a wobbly break for the other side where he was sure he heard water, he had collapsed and cried.

Something warm picked him up and cooed gentle sounds at him, tucking him into a coat against a lulling heartbeat and he stopped thinking about his siblings.

At first, she called him "The Temp." "Because you're only going to be around for a while. We'll find you a good home." But then she changed it to a sound that made the word "Edgar" and he liked that better. When he was tucked up at her chin, he could feel his name when she said it. "Edgar" was strong, forceful, it moved her jaw down so he could know both the sound and the feel of his name. It meant he was hers.

"It's you and me," she said to him each morning as she slid back in behind a big wheel and turned on the machine.

"Meow," he said, and then he'd coo at her like a bird —he'd been practising the sound since she picked him up and cooed at him. He needed her to know that he had her too. This would be forever.

"Jude and Edgar," she would say. "Two cats on the open road."

She tucked a box of sand in a cabinet under the bed that he could access through a little hole. When the machine wasn't running she would set out a little silver bowl of water and a little silver bowl of food—once he stopped needing eyedroppers of milk, of course.

Jude was his sun and moon; Jude was his mother; Jude was his heart.

As he kneaded her shoulder in the pre-dawn light and she wiggled her sleepy face into his fur, he knew that she was why he was here and her love was what he deserved, and that he would never never never let it go.

People of Earth,

The time looms. It is a growing shadow that longs to shuck the burden of reality; but alas, there is no escaping the inevitable. If I've told you once, I've told you a thousand times: it comes. Like a thief in the night. Like new love. Like a blister. Like a sunburn. Like an execution. I implore you, remove the hood that keeps the axe hidden from your view. Save the ground beneath your feet from the letting of your blood. I wish you nothing but a future.

Heed my words, it comes with a vengeance that will wipe the mockery from your face. It will wipe your face from your face. Don't laugh. It is to be so.

Join me in the quest to maintain our species. Dig yourself a grave—it is your only route to salvation—and I promise, if you do this, you will rise again. Like Lazarus, you will emerge from your tomb, shed your grave clothes, and walk the new land as a living ghost.

I want that for you. I want your ghost-
ship to become your kingship. Father the
new world with me or melt into the crust
that will form the peat moss of a new
generation.

You think I speak in riddles. Truth is
often hailed as such. Death holds no
elections, nor does it offer freedom. All
are victims. This will hurt us all. You
who die and those of us who live. We
shall all grieve and the pain of it will
be excruciating.

In three days time my pride will be set
upon the land. I tell you this that you
might prepare yourself should you or your
loved one be selected. Do not hold your
breath. I only take with me two hundred
souls. No, you must cherish your breath,
every last one, because soon, it will be
your last, after which, your lungs will
cease to taste the sweetness of this
earth.

They will not come as gentle lambs to
nudge you closer to me, they will come as

roaring lions, snatching their prey from amid its peers. Making no apology and leaving no regrets. Do not hate the lion that steals your husband. Do not hate the lion that hustles into your home and takes your brother. Celebrate the loss because it's a loss that means life. I take so that the earth might go on. For most of you this means nothing. The only lion to touch you will be the roar of the final hour. You will know it by its sting, by its burn, and by its bite. You will not go gently. For that I am sorry. Because of that I make one final plea: fashion your own salvation, bury yourself now that you might be reborn tomorrow.

The long night comes. The earth will groan with the pain of its destruction.

Weep now, bright eyes, because tomorrow your vision will be blinded.

Rajiv Montgomery Noah

Chapter Fourteen

37 days before Labour Day | New York City

The first advertisements for the Thunder Bay Apocastock festival started to appear within two days of the countdown launch. One of the digital billboards in Times Square boasted a clock counting down to "The End of the World as We Know It" and influencers everywhere were flocking there to take selfies in front of it in designer sneakers or fancy gold earrings or CHANEL lip gloss.

Though its budget couldn't match Times Square royalty, the news of Apocastock began to spread like a wildfire. Anything celebrating the ridiculous end of the world was driving traffic and the little promotional website that a couple Thunder Bay visionaries had built was bombarded by ticket requests before tickets were even ready, all because one of those influencers tagged them in a post. What started as an idea to fill a few days with some local bands and blow off some steam, became a beast of a project as managers and publicists reached out to the organizers to get their talent on the roster.

Built to appeal to a crunchier crowd, the list quickly filled with indie stars, folk performers, and yogi gurus. Touted as a "gentler Woodstock" Apocastock promised a heady mixture of moody music, rhythmic beats, and spiritual workshops, and posters began to appear in major cities across North America, warning of a limited number of tickets. "The most enlightening way to spend the last days of your life."

Having secured various swaths of land on Mission Island just off the west bank of the Thunder Bay shoreline, the festival advertised that they had a mere 7000 tickets available on a first-come-first-served basis, and a little more than one month out they had already sold almost eighty percent.

Leaning into the message of the end was proving to be a powerful vehicle for brands everywhere as the message of Rajiv Montgomery Noah was adopted into popular culture, not as truth, but as a way to poke fun.

When the countdown reached T-minus-37-days,

Bonnie and Maxine made their own pilgrimage from East Harlem. It was a long walk, but summer in New York was magic and they wanted to spend a whole Sunday together before Bonnie went on tour. Their route to Times Square led them along 5th Avenue on the east border of the park before they cut in at East 79th. They deviated slightly to see the Alice in Wonderland statue (because it was Maxine's favourite) and then continued on, past the carousel, and then out onto 7th.

They usually avoided places like Times Square because it was overrun with tourists and every true New Yorker knew the charm of the city was in the places tourists knew little about, but on the rare occasion they would make the trek. This time it was to be part of the growing trend to take photos with the countdown wearing lipstick the colour of the Kool-Aid you drank. It was stupid, but it was fun to be part of something.

They purchased the lipstick from a street vendor, teased each other as they donned colours that did not compliment their skin tones, and found a tourist to take an adorable picture of them. As they moved away from the countdown, Maxine gasped and ran to a wall plastered in Apocastock posters. "Bonnie, look!" she said, a hand on either side of a nearly black and white poster of a dark-haired girl with her head thrown back, a melancholy expression on her face as she held herself in an embrace.

"Tomorrow we labour; today we play," Bonnie read

the words at the bottom of the poster aloud. "Did you know Pocket Rochelle was going to be there?" she asked.

"No," Maxine said, a distant longing in her voice. The festival was right in the middle of Bonnie's comedy tour, and in another country. She wasn't going to kid herself into thinking they could make that work.

Bonnie pulled out her phone. "Mirror her pose, babe," she prompted, and Maxine did, her blue lips almost matching Rochelle's blue nail polish—the only real colour on the poster.

"Now what about you in front of 30 Rock," Maxine said.

"It's not cool to be so eager," Bonnie protested.

"Bonnie! You're a homegrown New Yorker who gets to host one of the most iconic comedy shows of all time. Stop pretending to be humble."

Only one week earlier, Live Nation released her tour dates and opened ticket sales. It was a short run if you compared it to big-timers like Trevor Noah or Sarah Silverman—just eighteen shows—but her manager assured her that as long as they filled those seats and Netflix made back their investment, this was the beginning of something huge for her. "You'll be at the Garden before you know it."

"Yeah, right," Bonnie had said, but she would never admit that most nights she fell asleep to fantasies of a packed stadium, of the women who had carved the way for her lining the front row in a show of solidarity and sisterhood, proving a world wrong that thought women couldn't be as funny as men.

Together they spun towards Rockefeller Plaza, hand in hand. "I'm really proud of you," Maxine said as they navigated the summer crowds, and Bonnie, suddenly overcome with a wild emotion, chocked back a sob-laugh as she used a tissue to wipe the orange lipstick from her mouth.

23 days before Labour Day | California

A rocket scientist sat in one of the blue velvet armchairs that formed a small arc across the stage at Berkley University's Wheeler Hall. Beside her, a geologist leaned back in his seat, one eyebrow cocked skeptically. Next to him, a seismologist pushed his glasses up the bridge of his nose, his expression a mask of smug self-assurance.

Across the stage, an environmental engineer fidgeted in his chair, arms crossed defensively, while a priest in a stiff white collar sat ramrod straight, his gaze fixed on the mediator who consulted her notes from the chair on the far left, her brow creased in thought as she prepared to steer the conversation.

All seven hundred seats were full and a zoo of cameras and reporters crowded the open floor space in front of the stage, broadcasting the event out to countless networks and streaming platforms. The live YouTube stream alone had millions of real-time watchers. In the end, the event would challenge the Super Bowl for viewership.

On the screen behind the panel guests, a huge Rajiv Montgomery Noah was projected, a replay of his famous interview running to open the event.

"When a lion smells the smoke that will destroy his home, does he lie down and wait for the flames? Of course not! He gathers his pride and he sees them to safety. I am the King of the Beasts. I have smelled the smoke. I will watch you die."

The mediator stared straight ahead, reading from a teleprompter. "Strong words from a man who claims to know the hour of our doom. Mr. Noah professes to have been given a vision and has been using his vast wealth to build himself a place to ride out the storm." She turned to face the panel. "What do you make of this, Father Myers?"

The priest leaned forward, his intensity matching the deep lines of his brow. "We must remember that this is the same man who abandoned the feminine to gestate fetuses in a synthesized womb far outside God's plan, far outside natural conception."

"You're speaking of ethics," the mediator said, her tone measured.

"Yes. But also narcissism," said the priest. "This is a man who dares to take the place of God." He instinctively touched the cross that hung against his chest.

"One might argue that his discovery has brought a lot

of joy and hope," said the scientist, eyes alight with defiance. "That perhaps it is the opposite of what you're saying, Father Myers, that it actually elevates the autonomy of women."

Most of the panel rolled their eyes, save for the environmental engineer, who nodded in solidarity.

The priest adjusted his collar, his expression stern. "It's a fool's errand to predict the end of the world. Look at all who have tried before him. Fools. Always proven wrong."

"One time, it will be proven right," the environmental engineer said with a note of resignation. "It only takes one time."

"But what are the odds that an event of such magnitude could occur without warning from the scientific community?" the mediator interjected, shifting her gaze to the seismologist.

"Point zero zero one percent," the seismologist replied, his voice a projection of smugness as he pushed his glasses back up his nose.

"We are wise, but we are not omniscient," the geologist cut in. "We have only explored five percent of the ocean. We can only guess at the turmoil boiling up at its depths."

"Yet, Rajiv speaks of fire," the priest mused. "Can fire come from the sea?"

"As surely as the sky," the geologist replied, a hint of resignation in his voice.

The rocket scientist chewed her lip, her gaze flickering

between her colleagues before contributing. "We've explored even less of space," she said. "Though unlikely, something could have occurred millions of lightyears ago that set a course for the annihilation of earth within our time."

"And the chances of that?" the mediator asked.

"One in 10,000," the scientist replied, her shoulders tensing.

A sharp intake of collective breath spread across the room.

"Point zero zero zero one percent," she continued. "Look at the world population. Over eight billion. Approximately eight hundred thousand of those people are afflicted with Huntington's disease—a terminal illness. An asteroid could be a terminal illness for earth. Out of the billions of planets and stars, what makes ours any more protected than another? The odds of winning the lottery are 1 in 14 million and someone wins that every week. In a heartbeat, the odds become 100% to that lottery winner, or 100% to that person diagnosed with Huntington's."

"So we've never been safe?" the mediator asked.

"Safe? Of course not," she said. "Everything is in a delicate balance."

"Just look at our water levels," the environmental engineer said, cutting in. His jaw tightened as he spoke. "Every choice we make in our climate crisis fight, or lack thereof, draws us closer to our own potential destruction. Of our own doing. We are waking up too late."

"And yet, projections say human life can be sustained for multiple generations if we don't change at all," the priest argued.

"Sustain does not mean flourish," the environmentalist shot back. "At our current rate of destruction, if earth does not experience a massive reset, we will cross the point of no return. Nature responds to tension and disease through rebirth. If we allowed her to speak, she would ask for the extinction of humans."

The mediator allowed her gaze to sweep across each expert. "How much control do we have?" she asked.

"None," the panel members replied in almost perfect unison, their expressions grim.

"So why bother?" she asked pensively. "Why the ongoing research?"

"Knowledge is power," the rocket scientist said.

"Is Rajiv Montgomery Noah's knowledge power?" Father Myers asked.

"With no science to back it up, it is nothing but hearsay," said the seismologist. "But I will say this, we have been detecting some unusual activity. Some unsettled rumbles below Russia as well as the Atlantic seaboard that we haven't yet identified. As water levels rise, we are seeing increasing change in the shifting of tectonic plates. We have yet to identify the cause."

The environmental scientist scoffed and leaned back in his seat. "Of course you know the cause. There is no argument against the fact that climate change is wreaking havoc on our planet. It's cause and effect. For every ounce of carbon emission there is an answer from nature, and nature has been warning us for years."

"So you believe the claim of Mr. Noah?" the mediator asked.

"Not necessarily, but I will say that we have placed our planet in such a state of fragility that should some mass event target us, we have used up much of the resources that might naturally resist it."

"Meaning?"

"Meaning if you already understand how hard it is becoming to battle the California wildfires, imagine if something sparks those but multiplies it by a thousand," the environmental scientist said. "Even a hundred and we would be looking at a massive loss."

"Enough heat or impact at precise locations across the planet could ignite long-dead, even unregistered, volcanoes," the geologist said.

"Which in turn can trigger earthquakes," added the seismologist.

The rocket scientist arched an eyebrow, a wry smile playing on her lips. "Has no one considered aliens?" she asked, eliciting a nervous chuckle from the crowd.

"Don't be absurd," the priest scoffed, shaking his head in disapproval.

"So, are we doomed?" asked the mediator.

"Inevitably," said the environmental engineer. "Life is sacred and fragile and a perfect balance is required to sustain it. Earth *will* be destroyed. When is the only unknown."

"2nd Peter 3:10," said the priest. "But the day of the Lord will come as a thief in the night, in which the heavens will pass away with a great noise, and the elements will melt with fervent heat; both the earth and the works that are in it will be burned up."

"Charming," said the geologist with a huff.

"We all know earth has been threatened before," the rocket scientist said, smoothing her skirt. "65 million years ago an asteroid with a six-mile diameter hit what is now the Yucatàn Peninsula, wiping out most plant and animal species, including the dinosaurs."

"Long before space exploration or astrologists were in place to prevent such a thing," added the geologist.

"Yes," she agreed. "But we can only potentially prevent a disaster if we know it is there. Astronomers deem an object a threat if it comes within 4.6 million miles from us and is at least 460 feet in diameter. Earth has been surprised before. Do you remember the "City-killer" in 2019? The size of a football field! It passed less than 45,000 miles from us. An asteroid the size of a 747 came close in 2021. Both of these were only discovered a day before they passed earth. One day."

"Surely our space tech continues to expand to avoid

these surprises," said the seismologist, as uncomfortable with these facts as the rumbling audience.

The rocket scientist shifted in her chair so she could address the seismologist directly. "Of course, in 2018 Congress approved funding for a new mission to employ an infrared, space-based telescope specifically designed to search for potential threats, but it has yet to be launched. Research has shown us that the earth's rotation creates a blind spot, causing some asteroids to remain undetected. In 2008, astronomers discovered a small asteroid only nineteen hours before it crashed into rural Sudan. More than 30,000 near-earth asteroids have been located, 30% of those are larger than the earth can safely accept. But even smaller asteroids can cause significant damage. In 1908, a 164-foot rock exploded over Siberia, levelling millions of trees over eight hundred square miles. Another, in 2013, only sixty-five feet across, entered our atmosphere twenty miles above Russia, releasing the equivalent energy of thirty Hiroshima bombs. We are not safe. We are entirely vulnerable." She sat back in her seat, cheeks pink with the thrill of presenting hard facts.

"And what of the date?" the moderator asked. "Can anyone speak to Rajiv's prediction of this occurring on Labour Day?"

"It's a rather quaint bit of poetry, isn't it?" the priest said. "The history of Labour Day rests in the Toronto printers' strike of 1872 when the Typographical Union took up the fight of the 'Nine Hour Movement.' Before then, workers were expected to be at their post for twelve hours a day."

"And now, 150 years later, we have bestsellers touting a four-hour workweek," added the geologist sarcastically.

"Exactly," said the priest, exasperated. "This is merely a dramatic commentary on the sedentary work ethic of the modern workforce. And if a new world begins on Labour Day, so too will a new generation of workers, I suppose."

"Birthing pains," said the geologist. "There is always labour before birth."

"A little too Marc Forster for my liking," said the rocket scientist. "Contrived coincidence reduces the believability of what he's trying to say. Brad Pitt's character could never have been at ground zero for every inciting incident in that zombie movie—that just doesn't make sense. Suspended belief is broken."

"So even if a huge part of us trusts in the word of Rajiv Montgomery Noah, and even if there is actually science to prove its probability, this frivolous detail harms the quality of the whole?" the mediator concluded.

"That's the function of human trust," said the priest. "We can put faith in many things that seem beyond our understanding, but there is a line of ridiculousness that can't be crossed."

"Like a resurrection?" the seismologist interjected. "Do you know the size of earthquake required to move a two ton rock from in front of a grave? 9.5 magnitude. To only move a rock and not harm the people there, or even crush the tomb itself? Impossible."

"You don't believe in miracles?" Father Myers asked, his finger tracing his cross.

"Science is a miracle and I believe in science."

"And you think science backs up these Labour Day claims?" the priest pushed back.

"I think science backs up its probability," the rocket scientist offered. "Not the date, per se, but the inevitability that the earth will meet its end. It has never been a question of if."

The moderator turned back to face the cameras. "It's a questions of when," she said. "And as you've heard here today, we have conflicting opinions on the validity of Mr. Noah's prediction, and to borrow an old idiom, only time will tell. Join us back here on September 16 as we unpack the aftermath of the end of the world. If Rajiv Montgomery Noah is wrong, we will have much to discuss. If he is right, I suppose none of this will matter. If nothing else, let me leave you with this: live your days with purpose, do good, surround yourself with people you love and who love you. Whether the world ends in a few weeks or continues on for generations, do not become complacent. Live fully. Live brightly. Remember to recycle. Focus on what matters, and please take care."

The spotlights dimmed as the cameras cut the feed.

The crowd erupted in noise, people hurling questions at the platform, discomforted by the lack of sure information the presentation provided.

The experts were escorted off the stage, their expressions a mix of resignation and concern. Reporters began their own feeds, standing with their backs to the crowd to capture the unrest. No one was satisfied. Fear was palpable in the human stench of sweat as anxiety swept the hall.

"Is this the end?" one reporter asked a nervous man he had pulled from the crowd.

"I don't know," the man said. "But it doesn't bode well that not one expert can deny the possibility."

In the third row, a young woman with nearly white blonde hair held her phone in selfie mode, recording herself live to her followers as tears cut pale lines through her makeup. "I think it's real," she said, her voice quivering. "I think it's really real."

Chapter Fifteen
30 days before Labour Day | Rabbit Mountain

Jude parked the RV in the vast wasteland in front of the gates and approached the man standing just inside them with his arms spread wide, her camera lens trained on his grin and the strange world spread out behind him as he welcomed her.

"I can't drive inside?" she asked.

His teeth were as white as his hair and his smile seemed warm though his eyes observed her with the tilt of one who felt pity for another. "There are no vehicles in Eden," he said. "Did you ever notice that there are no vehicles used for good in the Bible? Certainly not in Eden."

"Are you a follower of the Christian faith, Mr. Noah?"

"Rajiv," he said, reaching out a hand. "Please call me Rajiv. Yes… and no, to your question. I hold to no one creed, but believe there is good to be gleaned from most traditions. I have yet to find one that reveres a vintage motor home."

Jude laughed and switched her camera to her left shoulder so she could shake his hand. "What if I called it my chariot?" she asked.

"Ah, yes. The chariots. Do you think it was a gift that Elijah was taken up in a chariot of fire?"

"I'm afraid my Sunday school lessons are a long way behind me," Jude said, though she vaguely remembered the story of the prophet.

"Ripped from the earth and carried off inside a flaming box of wood and iron—all this after standing witness to so many others being burned alive. His fate was the very same as those he cursed. So no, bright eyes. No chariots here. And no curses. I mean only to warn and save those I can—and though within these walls we will bear witness to horrors yet unseen by man since the days of Elijah, no flame will touch us." He still held her hand, now cupping it with both of his in earnest.

"You are a modern prophet then?"

"No," he said, eyes squinting in a playful manner. "All the prophets died."

"Everybody dies," she said.

"Yes, but the lucky ones die at the end of their life, not when it is taken from them. Come. Let me show you what lies beyond the veil."

"Why did you agree to this, Mr. Noah?" Jude asked as they crossed the gate's threshold. "You've said no to major news stations since the famous interview three years ago."

"You represent the good that is left," he said, pausing to push a button that would seal the gate behind them. "And please," he reminded her. "Call me Rajiv."

A soft meow cut through the air and they both looked out to see Edgar pawing at the RV window, calling after Jude.

Rajiv chuckled. "Perhaps you're not the only good thing."

"What do you mean by good?" she asked.

"You're not happy without seeking answers for yourself. Touching the evidence. Telling the truth about what you learn. A doubting Thomas who needs evidence. This makes you powerful and gives voice and answer to the questions of many who lack the wherewithal to ask for themselves. Your first film was very moving."

Jude was touched to know he had watched it. "But if you believe what you're preaching, this new film will never be made," she said. "Thirty days. That's what you've said we have left."

"You use tapes for that, yes?" he asked, pointing at the camera.

"Yes."

"And you have a fireproof safe in your motorhome where you store them for safekeeping?"

"Of course."

"That is why."

"Posterity?" she asked.

"This story will matter to those few who survive outside my walls. Now come and see what I have built for the future."

"So you believe people outside may survive?"

He shrugged, noncommittally. "If they've listened and done their due diligence, it is possible. Unlikely, but possible."

They stood against the edge of the dome. It stretched left and right as far as Jude could see, and to look up she couldn't tell how high it actually reached. The glass-like surface appeared incredibly thick and up to a height of two hundred and ninety feet.

"How big is it?" she asked.

"It covers thirty-five acres of surface land," Rajiv said, resting his hand against the dome and tapping his fingers as if he was greeting a pet.

"Surface?"

"Ah, bright eyes. There is much beneath the surface that you cannot see. Eden is an iceberg. More below than above."

"I read that you need at least an acre of farmable land per person to sustain human life," she said.

"You've done your homework. Even more if I expected to maintain the average North American diet. Which I do not."

He entered a series of numbers into a keypad that was all but invisible on the wall he told her was five feet thick, and an opening appeared in front of them.

The "wow" was past Jude's lips before she realized she had said it. Rajiv's Eden stretched before them, a sweet wonderland of delicious scents and verdant greens. They stood on a smooth stone path lined in fruit trees of various sizes, cradled in beds of clover, beyond which, Jude saw rows and rows of vegetable gardens. As they moved further inside, Jude could see paths that turned off the one they travelled, leading to new wonders. Every so often, Rajiv would point and say something with pride. "Sweet potatoes." "Soy beans." "Peanuts." "Kale." "The sunflower field."

Jude moved slowly and let the camera pan back and forth to take it all in.

Rajiv pointed down a path. "The hives are at the end there. There's an open meadow—almost all clover and some wildflowers. Dandelions too—for salads and teas. Maybe wine if we feel like it one season. Fresh honey will be such a joy."

"How did you do all this?" Jude asked.

Rajiv laughed. "I didn't. It's a skeleton crew today because I wanted to give you a pure view. Usually this place is bustling with gardeners and farmers and scientists and builders."

"And will they all be with you here when the world ends?"

Rajiv stopped walking and pressed his palm against the bark of a small apple tree. His shoulders drooped as if he'd suddenly remembered he bore the weight of eight billion lives. "No," he said softly. "One or two at most."

"How do you choose?"

"Did you give your consent?" he asked. "Did you drink what I sent?"

"I did," she admitted.

"You believe?"

"I don't know."

His smile was pained as he pulled a small black device from his breast pocket and he gestured her over. Jude stood before him, camera trained on his face as he held the black box in front of her stomach. It beeped and the small screen filled with text. There was a visible shift in his mood, drawing him even lower, and he raised his eyes to her, glassy with a shock of tears.

"What is it?" Jude asked.

"When were you diagnosed?" he asked gently.

Jude sucked in her breath and stumbled back against another tree. "What?"

"I'm sorry, Jude. You're so young."

Jude held her free hand over the space that once held her womb. She raised her eyes to where the sun was shining through the dome and through the leaves. "I had the hysterectomy when I was 27, but it had already metastasized. The treatment made me sick. I've got a year left, maybe less."

Rajiv seemed to age, his shoulders hunching forward to make him appear even shorter than he was. "I would take this cup from you if I could."

"I've made my peace with it," Jude said, but her voice shook. Her peace appeared fragile.

"That's a funny thing," he said. "Peace. We can accept the worst, but many of us stop striving for better. Not you."

"I have a purpose," she offered firmly.

"As do I." He tucked the scanner back in his pocket.

"I guess this means I don't get in?" Jude said, only half joking.

"I like you, Jude. Always remember that."

"Remember for thirty more days?" She was trying to be funny, but her question hung between them with the heavy intensity of a confessional screen.

Their path led between symmetrical rows of tiny homes. At a bench overlooking the centre square, Rajiv gestured for her to sit. From there, they had a clear view of both the fountain and the grand building beyond it. "In the Hindu faith, it is believed that life is eternal. Our essence goes on to be birthed anew in another form," he said.

"Even if the planet is destroyed?"

He sat in silence for a moment, pondering. Jude raised the camera to capture his answer as he spoke out to the view. "Eight billion souls. That doesn't just evaporate. We all go somewhere. I just know I don't get to find out yet."

"But I do?" she said, less of a question than a statement of acceptance.

Rajiv turned toward Jude and took her empty hand in his while she tipped the camera to capture the gesture. "You are the only human on the planet—besides my own family, of course—that knows if your ticket is getting punched. I wish it was a gift—knowing—and not a death sentence."

Jude pulled back her hand and touched her abdomen again. "Six of one, half a dozen of the other," she said with the shrug of one shoulder.

A smile flashed across Rajiv's face. "I remember my father teaching me that saying. Pure foolishness."

"Truth is not foolish," she said with confidence.

"No. Truth is never foolish," he agreed.

"Do you worry about being accused of nepotism? Having your family as chosen ones?"

"Ha!" The laugh erupted from him. "Who will be left to complain?"

"What proof do you have?" she asked.

"Proof?"

"Proof of this cataclysmic event?" she pushed. "How do you know?"

"To know something, to really know something, is to have it planted in your guts," he said with conviction. "It is instinct and faith. I have known this end for so long that it is part of me. I know it in the way I know the sad face of the moon or the colour of my daughter's eyes. I know it because it was shown to me and I was chosen to tell others."

"You were chosen," Jude echoed. "But you haven't *really* told, have you? Sure, you've warned of this impending doom, but you haven't explained how it will happen or what it will look like."

Rajiv nodded and lowered his head, staring at the ground. "Prophets are not also interpreters, Jude. I know only that the end comes and we must prepare. I know there will be fire because that is what was shown to me. I do not know why it will come to pass, only that it will."

Jude mulled over this confession and found no comfort in it, recognizing how he had both denied and accepted his role as prophet since they started talking. "I remember learning about a vision in the Bible," she said. "About angels with many eyes. I have been more afraid of heaven than dying since then."

Rajiv chuckled sadly. "You see? Interpretation breeds fear. Prophesy stands as a warning, a perpetuation of free will. It either sparks curiosity and action, or curiosity and mockery."

"Will you show me more?" Jude asked. "What about the underground?"

"I will," he said, pressing his hands to his knees and rising.

"Do you have animals in here, Mr. Noah?"

"Two of every kind," he said and laughed. Then, "We have some. Those that will provide what we need for a pleasant survival: eggs, milk."

"Meat?" she asked.

"Not like you think," he said. "Raising meat costs far too much in resources and ozone."

"But an animal will inevitably die."

"Yes," he agreed. "And so might people. We are equipped with a self-contained crematorium that will reduce the waste. We have 'small pods that can be placed within the mountain like a mausoleum."

Rajiv led them to the left of the grand house—a building as large as Jude's old high school.

"How do you choose the animals?" she asked.

"With great care and precision," he explained. "I've been working in partnership with a lab, breeding the cleanest specimens of chicken and goat we can attain."

"And what of comfort animals? Dogs? Cats?"

He shook his head. "We've not the resources for that. People must learn to gain their comfort from the gardens and the trees."

The path they followed stretched to where the dome butted up against the mountain at the entrance to the old Rabbit Mountain mine.

Jude had accepted her mortality, but it was the first time she'd considered Edgar's. Were they fated to pass from the earth at the same time? He was still just a kitten.

"And what of the species that aren't represented here?" she asked. "What becomes of them in the new age?"

"I'm not exactly sure," Rajiv said. "I like to believe that even though what comes will be fully devastating, if we can survive here, perhaps some creatures and humans can survive elsewhere. Of course it is possible. The truth of the flood is written in geological evidence all across the globe, though I believe the Biblical story of the ark was full of hyperbole. Two of every living thing? Unless that ark was a portal to a much larger dimension, to represent all creatures of the land, the sky, and the sea, is impossible." He laughed lightly then carried on. "Consider this: two termites are on the ark. In order to ensure survival, one of those must be the queen. A queen can lay as many as 3000 eggs in one day. Scholars say that though it only rained for forty days and forty nights, the ark remained closed until the waters dissipated. That took more than one year. On a boat made of wood, how sea-worthy would it remain, and for how long, if termites were appearing at a rate of 3000 a day?"

"So the myth is sunk?" Jude asked wryly.

"Sunk indeed!" Rajiv said with enthusiasm. "I do not believe two of every kind were on that boat. I believe there was survival beyond the ark."

"Even though God said there wouldn't be?" she pushed.

"In all my study of the Old Testament, I only have one conclusion," he said.

"And what is that?"

"God was fear. There is a lovely redemptive arc through the New Testament Gospels before it returns to how it started. The Bible is bookended by fear."

"And *your* gospel?" Jude asked.

"Hope," he said.

They had arrived at the face of the mountain where a large opening was honed into the rock, leading to silver doors.

"Come along," Rajiv said, pushing a button that opened the elevator. "I will show you where we will weather the storm."

Chapter Sixteen

3 days before Labour Day | New York City

Bonnie entered Maxine Blooms quietly. She had learned she could silence the old-fashioned bell if she pushed the door open just four inches, reached up, and held it while she shouldered herself through the opening. She liked to sneak in and watch Max work. Something about that woman in an apron made her heart race. She sat on the little stool by the counter and watched Maxine as she built a tall arrangement on the worktable in the back corner beside the glass-walled refrigerated room. When she concentrated, Max talked to herself, and Bonnie found this adorable. She couldn't hear what she was saying, but by the gentle bob of Maxine's curls, she soon realized it was lyrics. She was singing. Bonnie pulled out her phone, made sure the sound was off, and snapped a photo. When she posted it, her caption read: *A rose among thorns.* The small ding of Maxine's phone pulled her concentration away and she saw that Bonnie had just tagged her. She spun around.

"Why do you do that?" she asked, poking her head into the shop, her tone annoyed but playful. "You can't be sneaky like that. That's not fair."

She wiped her hands on her apron and met Bonnie in the middle of the space between them. She smelled of the petals she'd just been handling and Bonnie loved the way her tiny body fit into her arms.

"What if we went to Eden?" Bonnie asked.

"Why? What do you mean?" Max said, pulling back from their embrace.

"I don't know. I just think you're feeling nervous and weird about everything, and maybe seeing it in real life will help you accept how silly it is."

"You want to be like those weirdos who go to Roswell for an alien encounter?" Max asked.

"And all they find is a weird diner and zero aliens," Bonnie countered. "It will show you there's nothing to worry about. Come on. It could be fun."

"Bonnie, it's like a three day drive."

"Or thirty minutes from Mission Island."

"What are you talking about?" Maxine's voice started to rise. "What did you do?" Her eyes grew wide.

"Apocastock, babe! We're going to Thunder Bay! Pocket Rochelle is playing Sunday night and then we can hop one of her shuttle buses to Eden to watch the countdown! We're VIP, baby!" Bonnie pulled out her phone and brought up the flight passes. "Can you think of a better way to celebrate our seventh year together?"

Maxine grabbed the phone out of her hand, not believing her. She scrolled through the information, her hands shaking. "You're serious?"

"It's the end of the world! I've already talked to your assistant and she's going to run the shop. We leave tomorrow. Happy anniversary!"

Maxine protested. "We can't afford this."

"Oh, come on! We can live on ramen all next month. It'll be worth it. Plus, I've got that sweet tour money coming in now. This is just the beginning. Sushi every week some day soon!"

"But don't you have shows?"

"Nope," Bonnie said. "Tour contract. They didn't book anything over the Labour Day weekend because of all the hullabaloo, and I'm not allowed to book anything else myself while I'm under contract with them. We'll go to Thunder Bay for the long weekend, then you can come back here, and I'll go on to Toronto for the next weekend show. It's perfect, really."

"Janice really said she'd cover the shop?"

"She really did. Call her yourself. Work out a quick plan."

Maxine grinned, excitement beginning to replace trepidation. "Both or neither," she said.

"Both!" Bonnie replied. "Go finish that order, call Janice, and then we need to pack. I have a car coming at 8 a.m. tomorrow to take us to the airport."

30 days before Labour Day | Eden

The elevator was surprisingly bright, not the dank and dim box Jude had expected from the mining documentaries she'd watched.

"What kind of mine was this?" she asked.

"Silver," Rajiv said. "It's been through many hands and evolutions with its last regulated dewatering in 1967. Needless to say, we had our work cut out for us. Shall we go to the depths and make our way up?"

Nerves prickled along Jude's neck and she felt the weight of the earth around her. "Just how deep is 'the depths?'"

He chuckled. "The power station is about 290 feet down. Twenty storeys." He caught her wide eyes and smiled. "Peanuts," he said. "The CN Tower is 1817 feet and people use the stairs on it!"

"Still," she said, her hand grasping the brass bar that wrapped around the elevator. "What is the power station?" she asked.

He explained as they began their descent. "Lithium batteries. Hundreds of them. They will power everything from our filtration system to our medicinal grow-op."

"Medicinal?" Jude said, cocking an eyebrow.

He winked as the elevator dinged and the door slid open into another world.

To her right, Jude stared down a long shaft awash in the blinking lights of countless digital control panels. To her left she could see a shorter hall, but just as wide, where pumps gurgled and tanks bubbled with churning water.

"This way," Rajiv said, leading her into the power station, pushing aside the heavy transparent curtaining that blocked the entrance. "To control the humidity," he told her, answering the unspoken question.

Batteries were piled into stacks of eight on either side of the shaft, stretching all the way to the end of the wide hall.

"Thirty-five feet," he said. "All batteries. More than five hundred of them."

"You need all this?"

"One ten kilowatt hour battery, when used modestly, can power a home for eight hours."

"So how many homes do you need to power?" Jude asked. In the viewfinder of her camera, the setting looked like something from a science fiction movie.

"We are sustaining two hundred human lives. Electric necessity and consumption will be far less than required in a typical modern home, but it's still a tall order, and I'm not even convinced this will be enough. But, as you can see, we've used every inch. Caused quite a rift in the market. Those off-grid hippies aren't too thrilled. Lithium has been on back order for over a year now." He barked out a laugh.

The hair on Jude's arms stood on end as if she could feel the electricity in the air. "So how does this actually run your system here?" she asked.

He tapped on a box that appeared every ten power banks. "This inverter transforms the power the batteries capture from the sun into what we need to run our filtration and lighting system. And, of course, every possible household need above ground." He laughed again. "Except internet, of course. The world will be better off without that demon, don't you think?" He traced a finger along the edge of a battery. "A person is not their carefully curated online presence. Not their follower count or their digital footprint. Here, we'll be free to be truly human. To feel dirt under our fingernails again, like it was always meant to be. Removing the internet invites space for freedom."

Jude considered the analog equipment she held in her hand and wasn't sure she disagreed. "Okay, but… the sun? We're twenty storeys underground."

He pointed to the thick blue conduit that appeared everywhere: along the floor and up the walls, disappearing right into the rock. "This carries the solar that is captured by the dome and feeds it into the batteries."

"But doesn't a lot of it get lost during transport?" she asked.

"Some, but it's minimal. This system is so insulated, it's a wonder you can't feel the sun's heat through the conduits."

"Yeah," Jude interjected. "Why isn't it colder down here?"

"Each battery generates a little bit of heat. A little bit times five hundred results in a balmy basement."

"Okay… so what about when everything blows up and the sun is gone? That's what you think is going to happen, right?"

"The sun isn't disappearing, Jude. It will merely be covered. For how long, we don't know. But we do have a plan. In the initial days, power will be conserved. Against the mountain outside we have four capsules we can open from inside. In these capsules are spider robots designed by our partners at NASA and modelled after the Mars Rover. Powered by radio signals, they are designed to clean the panels, giving us open access to whatever sun power there is."

"Have you named them?"

"The robots?"

"Yes. Have you named them?"

"No, but we've been calling them the Roombas."

"Lame," Jude said and he laughed.

"Would you like to name them?" he asked.

Jude tilted her head and didn't protest when Rajiv took the camera from her hand and turned it on her.

"Jude Abbott, I grant you the honour of naming our dome cleaning robots," he said. "What will it be?"

Jude thought for a moment and then knew. "Elenor, Rita, Prudence, and Martha," she said, staring coyly at the camera.

A smile beamed across Rajiv's face. "Yes," he said. "Nearly perfect."

"Nearly?"

"If you're going to name the robots after songs by The Beatles, you should certainly include your own. Hey Jude?"

Jude shook her head. "No. No. I don't want to be remembered through a robot."

"Fair enough," he said. "You shine brighter than a robot."

"We all shine on," she said, feeling a rich kinship with the man she interviewed.

"Ah… there… *he* seemed to know something was coming, didn't he?" Rajiv said.

"I visited the apartment where he was killed," Jude told him. "In New York City. I stood on the pavement where he bled. There were candles melted against the sidewalk and people were laughing as they walked by, and I just stood there and cried."

"I met him," Rajiv said, plopping that down between them like a bomb as he handed back the camera. "During his peace movement. I gave him a flower. I had a small brass lion my mother had given me that I carried with me everywhere. He saw it and he told me I was that lion. I was 13 years old and my parents were dead. 'We have to be loud, son,' he said. 'We have to roar to be heard. Roar for me.' I had been too afraid, too intimidated, too small to make a sound. But I never forgot." His voice held the weighty quality of grief, with cracks at the seams of each sentence.

"Wait," Jude said. "That can't be true."

"What do you mean?"

"Rajiv, if your Wikipedia page is correct, you weren't even alive yet during the peace movement."

He paused and then bent over, laughing heartily with his hands on his knees.

"Rajiv…?"

He righted himself, his cheeks flushed with the effort of his laughter. "Jude, I do believe that is something I dreamed. I've carried it so long and replayed it so often that I guess it's become part of my true story."

Jude matched his smile, nodding. "I get it. I'm totally convinced I definitely had a coffee date with Andrew Garfield at the Moondance Diner."

They shared a laugh, wiping tears from their eyes.

"When I wandered into Central Park and saw cropped-top Instagram girls taking selfies on the Imagine mosaic, I wanted to roar more than anything," Jude said. "But I had been too afraid."

"Yet here we both are now. Being loud when it matters. Me with my message. You with your stories." He nodded at the camera. "When a soul impresses on us, that's a hard thing to shake. And why you'd ever want to, I don't understand. Whether in dream or reality, he accepted your tears, sweet Jude. He accepted them into his memory and he said, 'You are a lion. Roar.'"

Jude choked back a sob, overwhelmed with a feeling she couldn't articulate, feeling truly seen inside that deep hole in the ground.

"Elenor, Rita, Prudence, and Martha," Rajiv said, placing a gentle hand on her arm. "Four ladies to save us."

Jude didn't respond, just followed him quietly back through the plastic curtains and into the water centre.

At the very back of the space, a tank as large as a YMCA pool swarmed with dark bodies, separated by size into lengthy channels. Jude recoiled at the sight of their long whiskers. "Catfish?" she asked.

"They will provide some much needed protein, healthy fats, and B12. Good oils. They're much easier to maintain and breed than some of the more popular fish."

"I thought you were going to keep the dome population vegetarian?" she said.

"Well, yes, mostly," he agreed. "But health has to take precedence over principals. Of course, I won't force-feed any resident if their own scruples won't allow them to partake, but ensuring access to good protein is essential."

"And this water?" she asked. "Where does it come from?"

"We've tapped into a deep, underground river. It's why this shaft has been dewatered so many times since the mine was first channelled."

They walked the full length of the tank so Jude could capture its magnitude. The closer to the back they went, the more prominent a strange scent became. Once at the rear wall, Jude saw a large pit in the rock floor. The smell emanating from it wasn't totally unpleasant, but she couldn't quite place it. Earthy. Wet. A little like the ground after a good rain when the worms came out.

"Fish manure," Rajiv said.

"Seriously?" She'd never considered the fact that fish produced waste that would have to be addressed, but of course it made sense.

He pointed out an automated machine that was moving along the base of the tank. "The waste lands on the bottom and that vacuum pumps it into the pit. Much of the moisture leeches back into the ground and then from there it is harvested for fertilizer and transported all over the dome, from the potato crop to the fruit trees."

Jude jumped then laughed when a fish arched out of

the water and splashed her.

"They think we're here to feed them," Rajiv explained.

"Are you worried about flooding? What if your pumps can't maintain once you lose full sun access?"

Rajiv sighed. "Yes. I'm worried. But what can I do? I am putting my faith in the system, come what may. My hope is that we have access to the new world beyond the dome by the time the system fails. Because it will fail. There is no doubt. We don't know how long we have. But we have longer than those on the outside, and every additional day is a gift. Best case scenario: the atmosphere cleans itself enough for human habitation much sooner than our projections."

"Worse case?"

"I have built the most beautiful coffin for two hundred of the world's most deserving people."

"And you can live with that?"

He smiled sadly and his eyes shone with a faraway look. "No," he said. "I will die with that."

"How will it feel to be the oldest man in the world?" Jude asked.

Rajiv handed her the same scanner he'd used to check her chip when she first arrived. "I won't have to carry that burden too long," he said. He nodded at the scanner and then dropped his eyes to his own belly. "Go ahead."

Jude set the camera on a ledge and then held the scanner out as she'd seen him do, letting it go to work. Within seconds the screen showed a red X with the words "Renal Failure," beneath. Rajiv Montgomery Noah was rejected from his own experiment.

"I do recognize the narcissism required to lay claim to a spot that should go to a healthy soul," he admitted. "Aside from my family and my doctor, you, Jude, are the only one who knows. I am trusting you with this."

Jude chewed her lip and then nodded to the camera that was propped opposite them, capturing the moment.

"Right," he said. "But by then it won't matter, will it?"

"How long?" Jude asked.

"How long do I have, or how long have I had it?"

"Both, I guess."

"I am a long-term statistic from the Bhopal explosion of 1984. Do you know of it?"

Jude shook her head.

"Thousands of us who were close enough to the blast to breathe particles of the poisoned air are paying the price all these years later. Just part of the collateral damage. Do you suppose Arnold Schwarzenegger will play me in the movie version?" And then his face fell. "I suppose not."

Realization dawned on Jude, not because she understood the reference to such an old film, but because she suddenly understood the potential loss. "Because he'll be gone?"

"They all will. Or most of them. Hollywood will be obliterated."

"Channing Tatem?"

"Gone."

"Taylor Swift?"

"Gone."

"Ryan Reynolds?"

"Gone."

"But he's perfect."

"We think that about so many, don't we?"

Jude sighed. "The tragedy of it all."

"Indeed."

"And you?" she said. "You would take the seat of someone more...?"

"Deserving? Yes. I would. Every new world needs a leader to map the new way. I am that leader. I am their Moses. But like Moses, I may not live to see the Promised Land."

"So, you're their Jesus. Sent to die that others might live?"

Rajiv laughed then, a hearty laugh that turned into a dry cough.

"How sick are you?" Jude asked.

"Sick enough to know my time is coming. Not sick enough to stop doing everything I can to ensure humanity endures. We are the ugliest animal, evolving over millennia to become the worst version of ourselves. Here I separate the wheat from the chaff; here I weed hate from grace; here I direct a dance and remove the devil."

"What if you're the devil?" Jude asked softly.

"Is that what you believe?"

"No," she admitted.

"Jude, I promised to save two hundred souls."

"Yes."

"And I *will* save two hundred souls. I am not counted in that number."

"Ahh. So Eden begins with two hundred and one?"

"Something like that," he said, with a wink and a smile.

"Are you afraid?"

"I am."

"Are you sure?"

"I am."

Chapter Seventeen

2 days before Labour Day | New Mexico

Penny felt giddy and nervous as she let Jessie lead her out to the bunker. It seemed to her like it had been "nearly" finished for a lifetime, but today, Jessie said it was officially done. He had one final surprise for her.

"No peeking," he said as he let go of her elbow. She heard the click of the lock and the painful groan as he pulled the heavy door open. Through the blindfold she could only see bulbous shadows and strange flashes of light, all painted the burnt orange of the scarf he'd used to block her vision.

As they stepped inside, she was pleased to find it smelled quite fresh. She'd spent the last week of evenings helping Jessie put down a subfloor of treated plywood and layers of Dollar Tree woven floor mats that had made a pleasant, rather bohemian final touch. After a thorough dusting and the vigorous effort of a lint-free rag and Mr. Clean, the space sparkled. As much as an underground hole could sparkle.

Moving deeper into the bunker, she could sense when they passed the pantry and the toilet and then when they entered the tight sleeping quarters.

"I know you've been worried about privacy and stuff, and so I made you something," Jessie said.

He undid the blindfold gently, careful not to pull her hair as he loosened the knot. She felt her heart bloom in a burst of warmth as she took in the space.

He had strung lines of twinkle lights, dim and battery-powered, to add a little whimsy. "They take double A's and we won't use them all the time, but I thought it'd be nice," he said. And it was. Between each army cot, he'd hung a colourful scarf—also Dollar Tree—to create a sense of walls. In the final berth, he'd pushed two cots together, topped them with a thin camping mat, and the extra duvet from the farmhouse. A decorative pillow lay against the plain shams.

Penny laughed and hugged him. "It's beautiful!" she said. "Thank you."

"At least we can pretend we are alone," Jessie said.

"I wish this was here when that film lady visited."

Jessie wanted to tell her that she brought all the light and colour that any space needed, but all he said was, "Yeah."

Days before, they had listed out every neighbour in a two concession span—there were forty-seven of them—and they built a chart of pros and cons for who to invite into their space. They had to rule out the large families for obvious reasons—they didn't know how to provide for the mental, emotional, and educational needs of small children. Meredith was an alcoholic, Brendon smoked like a chimney, and Pete was a known philanderer with a very public herpes infection. It was actually easy to narrow it down to ten: three couples and four singles, ranging in age from 23 to 58.

Armed with a little stack of white envelopes and handmade invitations Penny had built with scrapbooking leftovers, they went door to door, delivering hope.

You are cordially invited to spend the end of the world within the bunker of Mr. And Mrs. Peters. Should you choose to accept, please bring with you only two changes of clothes and any non-perishable food items you are currently in possession of. Please arrive on Labour Day no later than 9 a.m. Once the door is locked we cannot guarantee entry. This invitation is non-transferable and offered in good faith. Godspeed.

Because they had chosen well, the neighbours were kind, but they were also dismissive. "I don't know if any of them will show up," Jessie admitted.

"We've done what we can," Penny said, more to assure herself than her husband. "There's nothing else left."

30 days before Labour Day | Rabbit Mountain

Jude could smell the "medicinal hall" before they pushed through the plastic sheeting on the second level. In her visits to interview other preppers, pot plants were not uncommon. "Servin' ourselves so we can care a little less and a whole lot more at the end," one steely-eyed brute had told her at an old World War Two bunker in Kansas.

"Wow," Jude said as her camera lens filled with plants taller than her. "These are healthy."

Rajiv chuckled and plucked a leaf from one of the nearer plants. He rubbed it between his thumb and forefinger before lifting it to his nose. "Six different strains," he said. "Both sativa and indica to serve all our needs. I had my team do extensive research so we only have the best of the best. Plus, a strong collection of seeds in our seed library."

"Seed library?" Jude wandered down one of the rows where the leaves were more purple than green.

"Of course," Rajiv said. He let the crumpled leaf fall to the ground and licked his fingers. "We have a sealed catalogue of whatever seeds we thought needed saving for the new generation."

"Smart."

"What would you save?" he asked her.

"Black-eyed Susan's," she said. "And daisies." Both grew along roadsides all over North America and had started to feel like home to her.

Rajiv laughed. "Okay, but what about food?"

"Easy," she said. "Potatoes. Is there anything more versatile?" She vaguely remembered a story about a man who survived in space on potatoes.

A grin spread across Rajiv's face. "Come," he said, leading her back to a cross-cut where they entered a wide cave of low and bushy plants.

"Squash and pumpkin," he said, indicating two distinct beds separated by a highway lane of stone. Then he pointed into the corner. "And watermelon. The level below us is all corn. All our berries and smaller vegetables—peas, beans, peppers—will grow above ground. Tomatoes too. Potatoes are one level up opposite the holding camp."

It smelled of pure earth away from the medicinal plants and Jude bent to touch the soil. "And you used fish manure in here?" she asked.

"Yes, along with the topsoil, of course."

"And all these greens. What will you do when you

harvest? Do you have some massive composting system hidden under here too?"

"Of course we do," Rajiv said, ducking around a curve in the rock that revealed a large holding area full of big, black bins. "Worm farms. We feed the compostables into the top. The worms digest it amazingly fast, and it falls through the bottom as nutrient-rich compost that we recycle back into our growing system." He pulled a long drawer from the bottom of one of the bins to show Jude the near black soil being produced.

"Impressive."

"And this feeds the mushrooms." One cave deeper and she was standing in a wonderland of fungi.

"Amazing!"

5 years before Labour Day | Toronto

Geraldine cradled the sealed jar in front of her with the reverence of one who held the cremated remains of a dear loved one. And, in many ways, that was exactly what she was doing. She entered Rajiv's office with the kind of gentle movements she was known for and it was several moments before Rajiv even noticed her quiet presence as she stood just inside the door, not wanting to interrupt, but desperately needing to speak with him.

"Gerry," he said, finally looking up from the papers strewn before him. "Is everything okay?"

She hesitated a moment, allowing a deep wave of grief to pass through her body before she approached his desk.

"It's time for me to go," she said.

Rajiv dropped his pen and leaned back in his chair. "What do you mean?" he asked.

"The children are grown and can take care of themselves. I want to see the world. While there's still time."

Rajiv knew by her tone and the shadow across her face that she meant it, and the reality of a life without her hit him with a severity that made him unable to speak for a few moments.

"I have loved this life here with you and your family," Geraldine said. "I have loved watching them grow into the amazing people they are. It's my turn to grow now."

"We still need you," Rajiv managed.

She shook her head.

"I need you."

"Rajiv, you think that, but it's not true. You have had almost twenty years to show me that you need me and you haven't done that. Your work needs you. You do not need me."

The truth of her words cut deeply and he felt tears spark to his eyes as he pushed off from the desk and came around it to stand before her. "You know I love you," he said.

"Yes," she agreed. "In your way."

"And you love me."

She didn't deny it and instead, pushed the jar into his hands. "I am leaving this for you. Care for it like it is a third child. This starter has been in my family for generations. It's how I can stay in your life. I can't properly store and care for it if I'm travelling. You can think of me with every new loaf of fresh bread."

Rajiv looked down at the jar and traced the top with one finger. "Eat this in remembrance of me," he said.

Geraldine laughed, but it lacked any mirth. "Yes," she said. "Eat this in remembrance of me."

They gazed at each other silently until both had tears on their cheeks. Rajiv placed the jar on his desk and then cupped her face, tipping his forehead down until it rested against hers. "JarJar," he said, and then he let his lips meet hers. She did not resist, seeming to melt into him as she received his affection, reciprocating with her own kisses, sealing their goodbye with the kind of aching passion that is only ignited by a love that is never quite right.

Though it was certainly their last, this was not their first kiss. They had, in fact, experienced many moments of physical connection over the years, always with the exquisite kind of longing that answered needs of the body but never fully responded to the needs of the heart. In the heat of it, it was always perfect and satiating, but in the moments and days that would follow it brought a heavy kind of emptiness that could only be described as sorrow. And so, they'd come together. Again and again in an attempt to feed that monster of attraction and loneliness. An unhealthy cycle of lackadaisical lust and affection built on convenience and misaligned passions that did nothing but build a wall until it was too high to allow true happiness or connection.

Shaken, grieving, broken, and warmed by two decades of tender memories of precious moments, they separated. As he watched her leave he knew a piece of his heart was leaving with her and his mourning period would last until the remainder of that selfish organ finally stopped beating.

He would never love again.

Chapter Eighteen

"Has there ever been a community built without a church?" Jude asked.

They were sitting in the square, Jude having returned for the second part of her tour, the sound of the fountain their background music as workers tended the fields around the perimeter.

Rajiv smiled and leaned back, gazing up into the sky which could be seen clearly through the protective bubble far above them. The air was fresh. Jude wondered how long that would last once the world exploded and the filtration system was fighting to find anything amidst the ash and smoke.

"An appropriate comment, coming from an Abbott. Do you feel misrepresented here, Jude?" he asked.

"What do you mean?"

He turned to face her. "Surely you know the etymology of your surname."

Jude shook her head.

"An Abbott is the head of a monastery. There is spiritual longing written right into your DNA."

"Ha." Jude rolled her eyes without humour. "Why do you even know that?"

"There is much to be said of a name, don't you think?" he asked.

"I guess I haven't really thought about it," she said.

"I looked it up as soon as I knew we were going to meet, Jude. You are named for the patron saint of lost causes who incites believers to save the world from the fire —a heroic saint and the leader of a church."

"Perhaps we should trade names, Mr. Noah."

"No, no," he said. "With your camera you bring about a new kind of salvation. Knowledge is the saviour of the new world. You are going to be the seed of its future."

Jude didn't understand what he meant, but didn't push him to explain. "And *your* name?"

"Ah yes. Rajiv. In ancient Sanskrit it means 'striped.'"

"Like a tiger?" Jude asked.

Rajiv laughed. "Perhaps. Perhaps something different."

"By his stripes we are saved," Jude said softly,

remembering the scripture from an interview she did with a nun for her first feature-length documentary. The sister had claimed the stain of her menses was the woman's experience of Jesus's wounds. "These are my stripes," she had said. The clip didn't make it into the final cut.

"By his stripes we are *healed*," Rajiv corrected her. "Fascinating, isn't it? The Christian obsession with the suffering of Christ. Frankly, I would like to be saved through an act of joy rather than an act of pain."

"And Noah?" Jude pushed.

"I took that name for myself. My mother helped me receive it while she was on her deathbed. The disease that is taking more than four decades to consume me took two days to take her from me. She was much closer to the epicentre. I caught it on the wind, carried across many kilometres. Her death was sealed within minutes of the explosion, she just didn't know it until she couldn't get out of bed and my father lay dead beside her." There was no grief in his voice, just facts stated plainly.

Jude thought of her parents back in New Mexico, a fact heavy with grief. "Without a church, where will people go to find solace? Isn't that the point of the church? A place to feel at peace?" She herself had wandered into sanctuaries along her journey, seeking quiet, seeking answers to questions she didn't know how to ask. She loved the architecture and the smell and the way everyone whispered in respect.

"All of Eden is a church, dear girl," Rajiv said. "Here you sit on one of its pews. Each of these homes will be a confessional and a place for communion. Church is not an institution, church is a community."

"And what god will you serve?" she asked.

"When I was a child, I sat in a staunch sanctuary with women who brought jellied salad to the potlucks and men who wanted to talk about business and children who wanted to rip off their shiny shoes and their ties to climb the trees outside. And we all stared forward at a man who spoke for another man about another tree that no one should ever want to climb, and yet we were to celebrate that and nibble the flesh and drink the blood of that ultimate tree climber. That was 'going to church' and I always knew it was missing the heart of the matter."

"Which is…?"

"Which is that we are on this world to make it better. To create as a creator has created us. Who we worship is not important as long as it is not ourselves. We are here to serve one another, and in that act of humility, we serve our god. But we will not do it in stiff ritual once a week. We will not. We will do it all day and all night. Our survival will be our worship. Our survival is sacred."

"Will there be prayer?"

"All of life is one long prayer, Jude. When we wake, we whisper thanks. When the ground is dry, we whisper please. When our hearts are heavy, we whisper why. When we make love, we cry out in exultation. For every good and perfect gift we say Amen. Let it be."

"And in times of trouble?"

"In times of trouble, this population will rally around one another. Because we will not be a Sunday morning foxhole. This will be a daily congregation, serving its god by securing the future within these holy walls."

"You've been accused of being a communist."

"And?"

"That doesn't bother you?"

"Why should it? Do you know the roots of communism? At its core it paints the most beautiful vision of humanity."

"*Utopia?*"

"Indeed."

"I studied it in school," Jude said. "But things always look different in the real world. Better on paper than in the flesh. Even though it was perfect, people are still people. And people need a leader."

"I will be their leader," Rajiv said with confidence.

"But you don't believe in government," Jude pushed back.

"I believe in a unifying creed to bind us to one another. An agreement for the good of the many. Even now, my daughter is finalizing the draft of our constitution. There will be rules and expectations, of course, but no one man will be above another."

"The farmer is as valuable as the surgeon?" Jude asked.

"Exactly. We are one body. Together we form many parts. As a whole we will be perfect. Each part of the body will perform its role because it is the role it is blessed with. Through every good and perfect gift, we form the ideal human society."

"Scientist?"

"Yes."

"Midwife?"

"Yes."

"Chef?"

"Yes."

"Economist?"

"There is no money in Eden."

That gave Jude pause. "Right. Communist."

Rajiv took her hand. "In the early days, we will be consumed by our grief. There will be anger and denial and a darkness that bores deep into our cores. But then we will rise—"

"On the third day?" Jude interrupted.

Rajiv chuckled. "Wouldn't that be something. I mean rise out of the darkness of our hearts. We will be born again into the new world where one's self doesn't matter, only our gifts. And when we allow those gifts to serve the whole, we turn Eden into Nirvana."

"But people are still people."

"I think you underestimate the power of the algorithm that determines who resides within these walls."

Jude studied him quietly for a moment before finding the courage to ask her final question. "Except you and your children."

He let go of her hand and rose to his feet, moving toward the fountain where he stood with his back to her. "Nepotism," he finally said.

"Yes. I know we've already touched on that, but what if you or your children are the reasons it doesn't work in the end? What if one or all of you lack the thing that the algorithm seeks out in order to guarantee order?"

"You don't have enough faith, Jude."

"I don't need faith, Mr. Noah. You do."

He turned back to face her. "I guess the best and worst part of that is that there would only be two hundred witnesses should one soul turn wrong. But I *do* have faith. I do. *This* is the new world."

Jude sat in silence, allowing his conviction to sink into her and find its meaning against her own views of the world. It was a beautiful thing to know ones place in the universe and she knew she was lucky to have found hers in film-making. But faith? Sure, she had faith. She had faith in her family. She had faith in Edgar. She had faith in her RV. She had faith in her cancer. All things that continued to do what they had promised to do.

"I am afraid," she finally said.

"I hope it is gentle," he said.

"I hope it is quick," she replied.

From the centre of the square, Jude could turn and see tiny wooden houses in concentric semi-circles that spanned back toward the fields, only made imperfect by the placement of the grand house which stood as a massive watchman over the community of two hundred homes. The precision of the design was concise and impressive.

"It's perfect, isn't it?" Rajiv said proudly.

"Indeed." Jude approached the fountain, capturing its precise sculptural shape with her camera. It was a man, but not. It was a woman, but not. There was something decidedly Greek about it, yet it lacked sexuality. It was beautiful, but it was also unsettling. Robes billowed in stone around the figure, masking its body, and yet a feminine clavicle stood out between masculine shoulders. An outstretched hand held an open book upon the cover of which was inscribed the lion insignia of Rajiv and his Eden. Water poured from between the stone fingers. The other hand pointed due east, though Jude only knew that because Rajiv told her. "It will always point to where the sun used to rise and it will be a reminder to pray that it will rise again," he said. One leg was raised up on a marble boulder, bare feet and long toes white against the black stone, the robes formed in such a way that it seemed a seat or throne appeared in them. On closer inspection, Jude saw loops in the sculpture, places where substantial metal rings were hidden among the folds of the garments. "What's that?" she asked, pointing.

Rajiv's face grew solemn. "Even the most perfect people are unpredictable," he said. "When Adam sinned, he was excommunicated. We can't do that here. There will be nowhere to go. And so, when someone breaks the laws of Eden, they will atone for that sin by being chained to our cornerstone. This fountain marks our foundation, our law, and our future. If anyone jeopardizes that, they will pay the price at the foot of our new civilization."

"Isn't that a little antiquated?" Jude asked, ignoring the fact that a cornerstone should rest in a corner, not the centre, but she liked the imagery. "It's basically like your version of stocks."

"Precisely," Rajiv agreed. "Most antiquated ideals have more wisdom than the shininess of modernism. Don't you think we would have been much further ahead in our climate war if we hadn't torn out all the railway infrastructure and instead invested in energy-efficient trains, rather than dump billions into a brand new electric infrastructure that the average working adult cannot afford? Do you know the carbon cost of producing one electric vehicle? It's roughly double the production footprint of a typical internal-combustion engine. Tell me how that makes sense. This," he said, pointing to the fountain, "is a symbol of humanity. To be respectful of your fellow man means to never be tied down. To show disrespect, ones spirit is repressed, chained to that which sparked your poor behaviour. Public humiliation might seem barbaric, yes, but in a society of emotionally evolved humans as we are building here, the threat of it should be enough. I pray that it is."

"Why not a simple jail cell? Remove the wrongdoer from the public eye and therefore remove the celebrity of their action. Like in professional sports when they stopped airing the people who ran onto the field naked. By removing the audience, they removed incentive to do the thing."

"Streaking is different than crime, Jude."

"I suppose."

"And there is a place. A place I hope we never have to use. Where we can put someone who is putting others at risk, or, god-forbid, hurts someone."

"Do you ever wonder if by putting systems in place for the thing you want to avoid, you are, in turn, inviting that very thing?" she asked.

"Manifesting?"

"Well, yes."

Rajiv ran his hand over the side of the statue. "We all fall short," he said.

"But we don't have to fall down."

He took her elbow and led her to sit on the edge of the

fountain. "When God created the world, do you think he wanted the people to fail?"

"If God is perfect and claimed to make man in his image, why then did he make man worthy of failure?" she asked. "It seems to me that God is maybe not as perfect as he wants us to think he is."

Rajiv smiled. "So we *are* made in his image."

"I suppose we are. Can I see your home now?" Jude asked.

"Of course." Rajiv stood and began leading the way to the imposing brick structure before surprising her by veering to the right of it, approaching the first tiny home.

"But I thought…" Jude began and Rajiv laughed.

"That's how the media spun it. Crazy Rajiv with his mansion in a bubble. No. We are all equal here. I am above no one. I will serve my kitchen duties just like everyone else. Come." He pushed open the door with a raised number one—much like a motel door—and gestured for her to follow him inside. There was no lock.

Whitewashed walls made the small space appear bigger. A small black sink was embedded in a butcher block counter. An electric kettle and a bowl of fruit sat beside it. One long shelf held two plates, two bowls, two mugs, and two glasses. A small round table with two chairs stood beneath the large front window. A small love seat pressed against one wall with a little coffee table in front. Shelves were built into the lower undercarriage of the narrow staircase and a door where the stairs were their highest opened to reveal a composting toilet.

The loft held a double bed, a side table, a narrow dresser, and an armchair. Four wooden pegs protruded from one wall where three outfits hung. Linen pants and tops, identical except in colour. White, sand, and brown. Jude touched the first outfit and it was deliciously soft. The fourth was pyjamas, linen again, but included long pants, shorts, a tank top, and a long-sleeved t-shirt. Drawers under the bed were where Jude expected to find undergarments and the like. "It's all so plain," she said.

"Not plain," Rajiv corrected. "Simple. If I provide every resident with what they need, and if every resident is given the same thing, there is no need for jealousy. Sameness is a tool for harmony."

Jude cocked her head. "I went to an all girl's high school, Mr. Noah. Our uniforms were horrific. And I have never seen more 'otherness' than in that space."

"Yes, but each girl came from a different home where different luxuries were provided or denied. Here, we are truly equals."

"Which is why you will have a home like all the others?"

"Precisely."

"And they're all the same?"

"Yes. Except for the bookshelf."

They wandered back down the stairs and Jude paused

at the bookshelf beneath them.

"We took great care to curate a shelf for each resident that best represents their likes and favourites," Rajiv told her.

Jude pulled a book off the shelf. "*The God of Small Things,*" she said. And then, "A little on the nose?"

"Not at all," Rajiv said with a chuckle. "Roy is a delicious novelist. This one, perhaps, is a little more on the nose." He pulled a beautifully bound copy of *Utopia* off the shelf.

Jude laughed. "Indeed. But each resident having their own small stack of books is hardly a way to preserve literature. Do you have a digital database so the world library is preserved in the event you are right?"

"A database," Rajiv said, smiling. "Yes. Of a sort."

They left his humble dwelling and Jude followed him up the impressive steps of what the world assumed was his home. He pushed both doors wide and allowed Jude to step inside where she stood speechless as her eyes grew hot and a fat tear spilled down her cheek.

"Our database," Rajiv said.

A massive room lay spread before them, the centre of which appeared like a ballroom, gorgeous parquet floor, polished to reflect the artificial light. Tall windows alternated with the tall bookshelves and rolling ladders that wrapped the space. A loft circled the room in its entirety, accessed by circular wrought iron staircases in each corner.

The ceiling was a mini dome of intricate stained glass that stretched to fifty feet at its apex. Directly across from where they entered, an archway offered a portal to whatever lay beyond; carved into the rich wooden frame was what Jude assumed to be the official creed of Eden: Wisdom over comfort; community over self; love over fear.

Jude walked the space slowly, touching spines, occasionally wiping a tear away. This was a library of dreams. She'd visited some impressive collections before—it was all part of her digital rebellion—but never had she seen something so vast and inclusive. Classics, biographies, politics, poetry, even a full shelf dedicated to banned books. She laughed when she saw this. "Texas will roll over in its grave." But then she fell sober. Texas was so close to home. In a locked glass cabinet she could see fragile first editions by F. Scott Fitzgerald, Virginia Woolf, Ernest Hemingway, CS Lewis, JR Tolkien, Stephen King. An ornate door at the back pushed into a room wrapped in vinyl records with various listening stations situated throughout the space.

When they came back into the main library, Jude indicated the loft where thousands of books lined up in identical brown leather with gold font on the spine. "And what is that collection?" she asked.

"Wikipedia," Rajiv said with a shrug.

"You're serious?"

"It's not one hundred percent current, obviously, but it's close."

"But why would you—?"

"Because it captures the state of the world at its ending. What better tool of history do we have than the Britannica of the people?"

"That's insane."

"Yes," Rajiv agreed. "I had fifty-seven full-time employees of library science on this project. It's taken five years."

"In-sane," Jude repeated. "And residents can just come in and use this space?"

"Of course."

"And borrow books?"

"Yes."

"You know you could have created a digital library and saved all this space." Though even as she said it, she knew what a loss it would have been to dedicate this beautiful room to something less grand than story.

"We have done both, but to put all faith in new technology is the work of fools. History has proven paper stands the test of time. It is more valuable than any microchip. It stands at the heart of humanity."

Jude laughed. "But everything you've achieved is because of technology. The synthetic womb? Of course that couldn't have happened without wild advances in science and tech."

Rajiv smiled. "Yes. Man's capacity to replicate the creative powers of a god are vast, and the possibilities, if we hadn't destroyed the planet in all the ways we have, are beyond anything any of us could imagine. And yet…" He wandered to a low shelf filled with heavy books and pulled a substantial tome from among other spiritual texts. "…the written word has survived thousands of years," he said. "*The Rigveda* dates back to 1500 BC and yet here I hold a copy in my hands. When is the last time you saw an iPod?"

"Touché."

He showed her through the rest of the building that included a beautiful washroom with fifteen flushing toilets and sinks, fifteen pristine shower stalls, and an attached gym with state-of-the-art equipment for both cardio and strength training. The opposite side of the building housed an industrial kitchen and dining hall for two hundred. "Family style dinner every night," Rajiv explained. "Each resident will serve in the kitchen on a rotation, supporting the chef."

"And what will the food be like?" Jude asked.

"High in fibre and grain and almost exclusively vege-tarian, as we've already discussed. On Fridays we will eat fish."

"Isn't that a religious thing?"

"In some cultures. I just like the alliteration of Fish Fridays."

Jude laughed. "Fair enough. I've only had catfish once in Chicago and it was deep fried. You won't grow sick of it?"

"No. And we certainly won't be deep frying it. It can

be prepared in a variety of ways. Ever had jalapeño aioli with a goat's milk base?"

Jude shook her head and Rajiv presented a chef's kiss. "Divine," he said. "It elevates fish tacos to a new level."

"You'll have tacos here?"

"Sure. Sometimes. And fillets and cakes. The chefs have developed a one month meal plan. No repeats."

He led her up a wide staircase that took them out onto a rooftop patio that covered the entire surface of the non-library part of the grand house. "We will have shows and ceremonies here," he told her. "Once people are settled and have found their place."

"Shows?"

"Sure. Live music. Small plays. Many talented people are going to be living here, Jude, and a showcase of true talent is always good for the soul."

They approached the edge of the rooftop which was wrapped in a glass railing with black trim. The view of the dome was breathtaking and Jude moved from one side to the other to try and absorb it all before they returned inside.

The tour ended in a lovely, modest office where a photo of Rajiv's son and daughter sat on the desk.

"Thank you for this, Rajiv. I feel good knowing this will be a safe place, that maybe when everything settles, the world will have a chance."

"If we don't have hope, we have nothing," he said.

"Hope is the star that guides," Jude quoted.

"What is that?" Rajiv asked.

Jude pulled a copy of Edgar Albert Guest from her bag and handed it to him. "If it's already in your library, please put it in your home," she said.

He accepted the book and opened it to where she had inscribed the following: *No matter the trouble of this world, always make space for the hope of tomorrow. Jude Abbott.*

His eyes glistened as he closed the cover. "You are only the second person I've met for whom I've wanted to break the rules," he said softly.

Jude stood silently as he struggled to still his trembling chin.

"I have a friend in the city who I desperately want to bring with me," he told her.

"What's stopping you?" she asked.

"He is old and he would take the place of someone young. And you…" Rajiv wiped a hand over his face and shook his head slightly, eyes raised to the ceiling as he blinked quickly. "You, Jude, are a great treasure and I have so loved getting to know you. I will feel your absence." He sat in the large leather chair behind the desk and pulled a skinny drawer open. He removed a small orange bottle and set in on the desk between them, right on top of the book of poetry. "I don't want you to suffer," he said, tapping the white lid. "These will knock you out. You'll drift away. You don't have to feel it."

Jude hesitated only a moment before she picked up the bottle.

"Don't take more than four," he warned. "If I am wrong, you will wake up hours later with a headache. If I am right, you will dream your way through."

"I thought it would mean something to witness the end of the world," Jude said.

"For what?" Rajiv asked. "For whom?"

Jude shook the bottle like a sad maraca then tucked it in her bag.

"You'll know if it's right when the time comes," Rajiv said.

Jude worried her lip and then nodded. "Thank you."

"Do you have a CB in the RV?" he asked.

"I do."

"I'll check on you," he promised. "Channel 29."

"Thank you," she said again.

Sweet beloved,

For every day we are alive, our chance of death increases. I know you know this. The longer we live, the closer to death we become. It is why, as children, Christmas seems so far away, and as adults we say, "Haven't we just done this?"

As sand moves through our hourglasses we get heavy with mortality, days are shorter, sleep feels wasted, and when we have the choice between laughter and hustle, we choose hustle because we think legacy means leaving concrete behind. It doesn't. I assure you. Legacy is the spark you've left in someone's eye. I understand that now. And just as they say you can't teach an old dog new tricks, I think, maybe, I am beyond the legacy that matters. No, instead, I will leave a kingdom in my wake, a kingdom womb for the new generation. You won't laugh at this. It isn't funny. It is, in many ways, the most tragic thing of all.

When I was 8 years old I went with my mother on a fourteen hour train ride to see the holy guru at the Jagannath Temple in Puri. As we sat lotus in the inner sanctum, he stood over her, his hand on her head, and said, "You are a single drop in the ocean. Time is meaningless. It does not exist. You are guaranteed nothing but right now. If you dive deep, you will be sustained. If you remain on the surface, the sun will resorb you. We are all of the sun and the sun desires her children. Be a drop that feeds the earth and you will have found a purpose."

My dad was with us. He couldn't sit lotus, but that didn't matter. He didn't believe. I knew because he chewed gum while the guru spoke and his feet stunk. That was the biggest horror of all. Popping gum and a smell like rotten pear that even the most divine incense could not cover.

I knew my mother thought it disgraceful, but she never said a word. She was grace incarnate. "I am a single drop in the ocean," she breathed into the enlightened space.

My father believed in two things: baseball

and Jesus. In that order. Though he
wouldn't want you to think it. He laughed
when we left the temple and I saw the
guru's legacy in his eyes.

For my mother's birthday, only a week
later, he presented her with a tiny corked
bottle on a chain. In it, a single drop of
water. As he put it around her neck, he
said, "You are more than this. You are the
whole ocean." Waves gathered in her eyes
and I saw my father's legacy there.

Three years later, when he lay dying, the
chemical burns so deep, all his
handsomeness stolen, my mother had taken
that vial from around her neck and put it
in his hands and said, "If I were the
whole ocean, I could wash away your pain,"
not even thinking about her own pain that
was boiling her from the inside out.

He hadn't been able to speak by then and with
tear ducks sealed shut by the burns, he
couldn't even open his eyes because of the
pain. When they took his body away, it left a
yellow-pink stain on the sheets and I thought,

this is his new legacy, and I wondered if it would be Jesus or Babe Ruth that would meet him at the final home run of his final season.

Child of Earth, I write this from the foundation of the guru, the foundation he planted in my heart on that day he anointed me with words to my mother. I have dived deep. I will sustain my own single drop for as long as the earth will have me. I pray you do the same, and if you cannot, I pray the sun is kind and that your rejoining her will be a divine moment of homecoming, that it will be quick, that it will be like a prayer, that somehow, a legacy will remain.

Everyone dies twice. Once when we rejoin the sun, and then again after the last time anyone thinks of us. Know this. I will think of you always. I will carry you with me as long as I'm able.

Chin up, bright eyes. Our future is guaranteed as long as I prevail.

Rajiv Montgomery Noah

Chapter Nineteen

7 days before Labour Day | Rabbit Mountain

With her solar panels set up on the roof of the RV, Jude had ample power for editing on her laptop, which was good, because she had hours of tape to go through. Conversion alone took a painful amount of time as the tapes required an almost real time play-through for her digital editing software to accept the content of the analog mini-tapes. Piecing a documentary together was arduous, the slow process requiring many breaks where she would go and wander around the slowly growing tent city. She had interviewed some of the people, but most were just there to party. Warm beers were already cracked while she was just pouring water over her French press. Coffee in hand and raising it to fellow "watchers" was how she met Brett. He had pulled into the spot beside her RV during the night ten days before the pronounced end of the world.

The first time she interviewed him, her heart had split in two and she felt so instantly in love with this strange man that she didn't know where to put her feelings.

He drove a 2004 Dodge Caravan, "the only thing my mom had left in her name when she passed," and he'd pulled out both rear bench seats to outfit it with a narrow bed—raised up just enough that thin storage totes could fit beneath—a cooler sat between the front seats with a Coleman stove on top. A five gallon water jug, half full, was fastened into the passenger seat with the seatbelt, and two more sat on the floor in front, wedged in the foot well.

He had a kind, round face, a little thick in the middle with broad shoulders and long dark hair dusty with the terrain. His eyes were so sad they felt like a poem. When he said yes to an interview, Jude had arranged him sitting on the lip of his Dodge, the sliding door open so his un-made bed was visible.

"Why did you come to Eden?" she asked him when all was settled.

He looked directly into the camera lens, his face stoic, though as the silence stretched to fifteen seconds, his eyes grew shiny. "I came here to die," he finally said.

"So you're a believer?"

"Maybe," he said. "Or maybe I'm a wishful thinker." He scratched at his wrist and Jude noticed the scar for the first time. He watched her notice. "I've never been brave enough," he said. "These were just deep enough to put me under psych watch. I was never really in any danger. They said it was a call for help. I told them I'm just too chicken-shit to follow through. I'm a coward. I thought maybe if I came to the party at the end of the world, I wouldn't have to be afraid any more."

"And if the world doesn't end?"

Another long stare before he pushed off the edge of the van and walked to the back where he showed her the tube he had attached to the tail pipe. It curled up and into a hole drilled through the van body, sealed with white caulking.

"If the world doesn't end, I will start my van," he said.

Jude raised the camera from the pipe to his face and saw that he meant it.

"Why?" she asked.

"Because the world is too big and I am too small and I have never done anything to make it better."

"I'm sure that's not true," Jude said.

"Why? Because you know what it's like to be adored? Look at you. You're beautiful, driven, independent. I bet there's never been a moment in your life when you haven't been and felt loved. You don't know loneliness, do you? Even driving in that old RV, you're never truly alone.

You've got love following you wherever you go."

"I'm sure you do too," Jude insisted.

"No. That's the thing. Everyone who has it, takes it for granted. Everyone who doesn't, just wants to die."

Jude put down the camera and backed into her own folding chair beside the RV. "I'm sorry," she said.

"Why?" he asked sharply. "This has nothing to do with you."

"I don't know."

He accepted that and they settled into an easy silence while Jude's heart shattered.

She studied his big hands and groomed nails, the sneakers with worn laces and the flannel shirt with a torn pocket. She liked his heavy brows and the intense, wet brown of his eyes. His lips were large, feminine, lovely. He wore exhaustion like an extra layer, it hovered around him, a shadow that was invisible but easy to see if you paid attention. *Maybe that was the thing,* she thought. *Maybe no one had ever paid attention.*

The next morning she emerged from the RV with two coffees. They watched the sun rise over the tree line in the two folding lawn chairs she kept under the RV bed, their silence comfortable, his loneliness a little less heavy. Every morning, the same routine. Their chairs got a little bit closer and his shadow got a little bit lighter.

4 days before Labour Day | Stanford University

Five male mice roamed a plexiglass enclosure. Across a clear divide, five female mice scurried. On the opposite side of the room, an identical prison stood as a twin of the first. For eighty-six days, the scientists observed them. On one side, the male mice had been force-fed Rajiv's Kool-Aid. On the other, it was the females. Every twenty days, the divider rose and the mice had done what mice do. During the first cycle, seventy-nine pups had resulted from little rodent unions. On the second cycle, there were only eighteen pups. By the third cycle, reproduction dropped to one litter of six stillborn fetuses. Not wanting to jump to a conclusion too quickly before the inevitable request for funding and human trials, the Kool-Aid mice were brought together in one tank and the non-Kool-Aid mice in another. Now, nineteen days after that final switch, the small team of scientists watched all five, untainted female mice, begin the process of live birth, pushing healthy, fully formed pups into the world. In the Kool-Aid tank, the mice behaved normally, but not one had even conceived—and careful observation had proven that it wasn't for lack of trying.

"You know what this means," one of the undergrads said, her voice tinged with a hint of fear.

"We've known for a while," the principle investigator said, adjusting his lab coat.

"How are we supposed to break this?"

"We can't. Not yet." He pushed his glasses up on his head and rubbed his eyes. "We have to make sure the issue translates to humans." Already, he was drafting the opening paragraphs in his head. *Scientific American* wasn't going to know what hit them.

"But the gestation period is so long."

"We can test through extraction," he explained, ignoring the obvious ignorance of the question. "We can observe conception and see how it takes. That won't take too long. I think we'll quickly see if an embryo is viable. We just need the volunteers. That's going to cost more than the department usually allots for medical testing."

"And the hypothesis is…?"

"This 'micro-bot' is creating enough of an electromagnetic force through its transmission that radiation is killing the host's fertility. We've observed it happening as quickly as forty days from ingestion in the mice; therefore, we can postulate that within two years, any human who drank the Kool-Aid may find themselves infertile, or, at the very least, less fertile than before they took it."

"Okay, but that means we can't really start human testing until two years from the first ingestion."

The professor sat heavily and rolled his chair back against the whiteboard that tracked the mouse activity.

"Shit," he said.

"Yeah. Shit," the undergrad echoed.

"Well, we have to tell someone," another student said. "Didn't estimates put the Kool-Aid delivery at over one hundred thousand?"

"At least," he agreed.

"What if we can figure out how to kill the signal? If it's the transmission that's causing the radiation, can't we develop some kind of kill-switch? Like an antidote?" the student asked.

"So, what? Aluminum foil helmets?" the undergrad mocked.

The sarcasm was ignored. "That's to stop signals getting into the body. How do we stop a signal from coming out?"

"Dear God," said the professor.

"What else is there?" she pushed. "Surgery? The bot is so small, if we could actually locate it in the body, maybe it could just be extracted with a hypodermic needle. We could set up clinics, spread the fear. Invite people to pop in for a free procedure."

"And who will pay for that?" someone shot out.

"The government," she said. "Once we tell them what we're up against they'll be all over it. Birthrates are already going down. They're going to want to fight it."

"Remember the last time the government set up free clinics in order to 'save' its residents?" the professor said.

"Sure, it covered maybe seventy percent of the population, but what have we heard since then? Nothing but blame and regrets. If we try to offer another 'mass solution' the country will revolt. Trust was lost. This isn't how to regain it."

"So then…?"

"I don't know, but that's not our department. We report the findings, someone else has to figure out what to do with it."

No one in the room was satisfied, but this was the nature of the hierarchy. Research could only report. Delivering this thesis was going to dump a burden on a government that already had too many irons in the fire. He suspected it would go nowhere. He suspected nothing would change, at least not until the birthrate plummeted even further than the projected levels. It seemed that, whether he was right or wrong, Rajiv Montgomery Noah had set an extinction event into motion. Whether fire or infertility, humanity was about to take a hit.

Chapter Twenty

2 days before Labour Day | Eden

There were two dozen of them. Nineteen men and five women. They stood in a straight row inside the library of Rajiv Montgomery Noah's impressive kingdom, beneath a high dome they did not fully understand. Save for Daniel and Moriah, who stood on the end, this was their first time in the presence of the man who had captivated the world with his claims, though all had been fully briefed and signed on the dotted line.

They were dressed identically, all in black: a black long-sleeved cotton shirt, snug black pants fitted with a black leather belt through the loops, black combat boots.

They were all of darker complexions, with stern jawlines and steady hands, save for the woman with the blonde curls that tumbled over her shoulders like water.

Each had signed an extensive NDA and pocketed a whopping deposit for their services, the other half of which would be deposited with their beneficiary immediately following the reaping. Not that it mattered in the end. They were military-trained warriors employed to execute a mission. The fee included their discretion.

Rajiv paced their ranks like a drill sergeant, but there was a warmth to his eyes. "You are my pride," he said. "Your service and attention will be forever remembered and documented as a sacrifice that saved the world."

No one moved or spoke.

A large bulletin board on a metal frame with wheels stood behind Rajiv, outfitted with a detailed map of the world. 199 pushpins decorated the map. 177 red pins to represent himself, his children, and the targets across North and South America. Twenty-two green pins to represent the home of each other person in the room. Ideally, the pull of the reaping would have spanned the entire world, but with personnel limits and time constraints, he'd been forced to condense the lottery to one side of the globe, fully satisfied that the list his algorithm had created was a powerful mix of professional expertise, pristine DNA, and exquisite beauty: the three main requirements for the start of a new humanity. He had, of course, never disclosed this to the greater public. Anyone outside the Americas was sent a placebo drink mix. They would assume their information would be entered into the algorithm, but they were sorely mistaken and falsely allowed to believe in this lottery ticket. The twenty-four before him came from all the places that bred genius and would add enough worldly culture and personal history to the final numbers that he was satisfied his vision hadn't been compromised. They had each ingested the Kool-Aid upon arrival as insurance of their identity and worthiness, and the algorithm affirmed that Rajiv had made informed and wise choices.

"You know why you are here," Rajiv said. "It was all explained in your invitation. I trust the payment was adequate and the goodbyes you shared with your families were sweet. Know that their final days will be spent enjoying the luxuries that payment afforded them. It was a gift. Treasure the memories of their smiles." He continued to pace. "Among you we have scientists, mathematicians, medical professionals… all—save for my own children— with military training. You are the best of the best and it is you who will execute the reaping. Daniel is your team leader. Daniel," he motioned for Daniel to step forward and he did, moving up to stand beside his father. "Daniel will be your team leader. You will answer to him and follow his direction. Through the com-packs in your masks, you will be in constant communication as you collect our population from across the Americas. Your process will be tracked from here through the embedded cameras. Are there questions?"

The men remain stoic but the blonde woman raised her hand. It shook slightly in the air.

"Yes," Rajiv said.

"Why?" she asked. "Why not invite them of their own free will as you did us?"

"There is no time," Rajiv said. "Forty-eight hours from now the world will end. We need to strike quickly and we need to do it now. People must not be given the time to think or they will wait too long and it will be too late. We need every one of the people on those lists to ensure our future existence here. You have twenty-four hours to gather them and return them to me. The jets are fuelled and waiting. Armoured trucks are standing by on the other end for your collections. Use aggression if you must but do not harm any of them. If their family tries to stop you, gas them. It will incapacitate them but they will not be hurt. This must be executed without casualty and without mistakes. If you do not return, I will close the gates. There is no maybe anymore. We've lost that luxury.

"It's kidnapping," the woman said.

"Yes," he agreed. "In a way."

"It's illegal."

"Chin up, bright eyes. You forget that each adult has given their consent. Besides, two days from now, every law will be beneath the ashes." He wandered to a table, his movements casual yet calculated. He lifted one of the beautiful masks that rested there. "They will follow the Lord," he said as he ran his fingers along the lush mane. "He will roar like a lion. When he roars, his children will come trembling from the west." He looked up and saw confusion. "From the book of Hosea," he explained. "In the Old Testament. Everything I've done is because a vision was planted in my heart. I take on the visage of a lion because my own mother pressed that identity into my palm when I was just a boy at her deathbed. I built an Eden so the lion might lie with the lamb. Do you see? But first, the lion must become the shepherd."

After collecting their labelled masks from the table, the crew filed from the building and marched from the dome where an armoured truck blocked the entrance. One by one they climbed inside, blocked from the view of the gathering crowd by strategically placed blackout screens.

Crushed inside, the lions sat quietly as the truck pulled away, taking them to a small private airfield where they would split up and take little jets to their designated destinations.

2 days before Labour Day | Rabbit Mountain

Jude watched as an armoured vehicle left the gate before she grabbed her backpack and approached. Guards blocked her path, but she pleaded with them, asking them to reach out to Rajiv that he might meet her at the gate. After a quick consultation over a walkie-talkie, the guards moved aside to allow her beyond the screens blocking the view into Eden. It didn't take long for Rajiv to appear, floating down the main road from the centre on an electric scooter, a sight that in any other situation might have been comical.

"Jude," he said. "Everything is in motion."

"I can see that," she said. "You didn't show me the scooter before."

He laughed. "We have a half dozen of them stored in a garage on the side of the big house. A dozen skateboards, twenty bicycles, two Segways, one golf cart. They may or may not get a lot of use. We will have rare occasion to come all the way to the gate after today, I'm afraid, but perhaps someone might like to get to the goat pen or the pear tree a little quicker." He leaned the scooter against the wall and approached so they were mere inches apart.

Jude slipped her backpack off and handed it through the gate. "This is for you," she said. "Just in case."

Rajiv pulled the zipper open to reveal stacks of mini-tapes and an old camcorder with a charging pack.

"I copied them all," she told him. "It's the raw footage from the doc project. Nothing is edited. I want you to keep these. Just in case it's as bad as you say and a fireproof safe isn't good enough. And that's one of my older cameras. It's not great, but you can at least watch the tapes with it. If anyone ever wants to."

Rajiv placed his open palm on the top of the tapes like he was a priest blessing them. "This is important work," he said. "I will keep it safe."

"I'll be here," Jude said. "Until the end. Or until whatever happens happens. I'm still working on pulling this thing together, but there are hundreds of hours of footage I've had to go through. I don't know how far I'll get, but at least the story will be preserved if my efforts don't pan out."

"Take a sad song and make it better," Rajiv said.

"That's all I can do. If you're wrong, I will leave. I imagine you won't open the gates right away. What you would be facing, I expect, is some kind of major legal accusations. I promised my family I would come back to New Mexico. Spend my last months with them. I still feel healthy, but we both know that one day soon I won't. One day soon it will catch up with me. The desert air is good. It might buy me a little more time. So that's what I'll do. If you're wrong. If you're not..." she stepped forward and patted the backpack. "Remember me."

Rajiv put his hand over hers. "I let you into my heart," he said, sealing their goodbye.

She watched as he turned around with the backpack, following the path like Dorothy to the Emerald City, weaving the scooter back and forth playfully. Though the idea of death (and angels with a thousand eyes) still scared her, she hoped he was right. Everything she'd learned on the road showed her that the world could do with a hard reset, and she was almost done with it anyway.

Crowds were jovial as she made her way back to the RV. The party was ramping up. She didn't expect to sleep much that night.

2 days before Labour Day | Thunder Bay

The Holiday Inn Express and Suites was packed with people planning to attend the festival the next day; people who, like Bonnie and Max, chose a day pass rather than the full weekend pass. They had discussed camping out with the hippies for the full experience, but with Bonnie wanting to keep her energy up for the rest of the tour, Maxine worried about leaving her shop for so long, and the fact that they didn't really care about the Friday and Saturday headliners, the decision hadn't been difficult. The hotel had a shuttle to take concert-goers to the main parking lot on the island where the Mission Marsh Boardwalk could take them to any of three stages. It would start transporting Sunday ticket-holders as early as 8 a.m. the next day. The excitement was palpable as they navigated the hallways to their room. Maxine flopped on the bed while Bonnie dumped their bags in a corner. "I still can't believe you did this."

"Believe it!" Bonnie said, pulling a bottle from the

front of her bag that she'd snagged in the airport. "You see any cups?"

Maxine popped off the bed and ducked into the bathroom, returning with two water glasses. "We're classy ladies tonight," she said.

Bonnie grinned as she opened the bottle with the little corkscrew on her jackknife. "Every night," she said, pouring two equal portions into the cups Maxine held.

They clinked their glasses in a hearty cheers and drank. "There's a hot tub downstairs," Bonnie said.

"No," Maxine responded, taking Bonnie's drink from her hand. She set the glass on the side table then put a knee on either side of Bonnie's lap, straddling her while she started to unbutton her top. "We're not leaving this room tonight."

2 days before Labour Day | Mission Island

Rochelle de Lioncourt sat in front of the little makeup mirror in her van applying star stickers in a half moon along her temple. The vintage Chevy had seen her band all the way from Old Quebec and now they were settled in the field beside the abandoned factory on Mission Island: the designated "green room" for all the Apocastock musical guests.

The band members were setting their tents up outside.

She had claim to the back bench that, with the push of a worn button, folded down into a semi-comfortable bed as long as you didn't think about what it was used for in the early 80s. There hadn't been a fight over the bed. The van belonged to her, bequeathed by the uncle who encouraged her musical pursuits since her first piano lesson when she was 6 years old. That van saw eleven Burning Man's and seventeen summers of northern tree planting before the tumour stole her uncle and the keys passed into her hand.

Portable solar panels were set up so they would have some power at their site, but she didn't expect to spend a lot of time there. In the spirit of her uncle she planned to embrace this experience for what it was, lean into the excitement, and bask in their fourth headline show. The electricity in the air told her that something was coming. She didn't believe in the end of the world, but she sensed a change and her brain was already working to pull new lyrics from the ether to capture that feeling of anticipation.

Tonight, VIP ticket holders would be inside the factory for the "Hard Launch Rave" and she was definitely going. She had her 90s themed outfit already laid out before she began lining her eyes with a sparkly blue pencil. It wasn't like she couldn't be "of the people." She had gained increasing popularity across Canada but wasn't yet a household name aside from the feminists and the LGBTQ2S+ crowd—for some reason, her work resonated loudly with them though she had never publicly claimed a spot atop any of the letters. She didn't think it was anyone's business, and their manager encouraged her to stay mum because the speculation added more intrigue. Her lyrics on love, beauty, climate change, and feminist modernism—while also avoiding the immature angst of many pop stars—made her current and catching.

With one arm covered in a full tattoo sleeve and the other loaded with witchy bracelets, she was the quintessential lead singer. At first glance, one might mistake her for an emo chick, her dark hair and eyes giving her an introspective and hard edge, but on close inspection, her French/Asian heritage gave her a softness that leaked around her style. And her music? Well. That was something altogether unexpected and charming. She'd been called the dark Joni Mitchell of her generation—writing songs about the state of the world with a haunting undertone and a political theme that pushed against convention and promoted critical thinking and social change. Her style wasn't heavy. It was more theatrical and musical—though one reporter did refer to her music as "orchestral thunder"—years of piano lessons pouring into her wicked attacking of the keys in every show she put on. If music was her heart, dance was her pulse. She scrunched her teased hair and pulled the heavy combat boots over her long socks, the florescent bands at the top sure to catch the black light when DJ Young Yaper dropped the bass and the rave crowd ignited into a pulsing band of collective ecstasy. She was going to church.

Chapter Twenty-One

1 day before Labour Day | Thunder Bay

When hotelier Samuel Parker went to bed on the night of the reaping it was with the full intention to rise the next morning, kiss his wife, and guide she and his son to the prepared tunnel dwelling beneath their hotel.

When Samuel fell asleep, it was with the peaceful assurance that he had done everything he could to ensure a future for his family. He had spoken to his friend, Rajiv, to say goodbye.

"But it is not goodbye, my friend," Rajiv had said. "It is until the sun breaks through the ash—for then we shall see each other again." Rajiv was confident the tunnel re-model beneath the Prince Arthur would sustain them and so Samuel adopted his optimism, accepting it as truth.

When Samuel started to dream, it was of a canola field and a woman in a white dress and a little boy with golden hair and how their hands felt in his as they walked through a heaven of yellow.

When Samuel's heart stopped it was because of an undiagnosed condition that would have been caught had he listened to his wife and gone for his annual check up, which he had neglected for three years.

When Samuel died, it was the kind of enviable, pain-less death that everyone hopes for, even though the pain they avoid is immediately passed on to their loved ones.

When Imogen found him cold beside her the next morning, she wept and wailed and called for her son. To-gether they washed his face and hands and laid him out straight and stoic on the bed. He did not look dead. He looked like he was sleeping. His face pale, his features serene.

"You know what he would say," she said to her son as they both looked down on his still form. "He'd say, 'well, my love, I *did* want to be cremated.'" She laughed, but then she fell to the ground, her body curled in on itself in sorrow.

"We have to go," her son prodded. "We have to get to the tunnel."

"The tunnel. Yes," she said, her shoulders shaking.

"I would like to keep his ring," her son said.

"Yes," she agreed. "You should keep it."

He lifted his father's freshly washed hand and slid the insignia ring off his cold finger. "Would you like his wedding ring, Mother?"

"No," she said. "He should take it with him." But then she changed her mind. "Gold melts in fire," she said as she removed it and slipped it onto her thumb.

1 day before Labour Day | Thunder Bay

The sun burned white and hot through the triple-paned glass of the Holiday Inn Express. Maxine groaned and pulled a pillow over her head. Her phone buzzed and she slapped blindly at the bedside table, knocking an empty wine bottle to the floor. Her head pounded. If she remembered correctly, they'd almost emptied a second bottle before blissfully passing out in a tangle of hotel bed sheets.

She smiled despite the migraine thumping behind her closed eyes, remembering the Spotify dance party and love making this room has been witness to the night before. "Bonnie. Babe. We didn't close the blackouts last night."

Nothing.

She flopped her arm across the bed, feeling for her

partner. She raised herself up on her elbows and surveyed the room. "Babe? You in the bathroom?"

She could see the bathroom door was open, the light off. She also noticed the lamp was missing from Bonnie's side.

"Bonnie?" She crawled to the edge of the bed and peered over to see the lamp on its side, bulb shattered into the carpet. Panic swelled into her throat. How crazy did that dance party get?

"Lesbian landing strip!" She remembered Bonnie yelling her signature, not-funny-but-made-her-laugh-anyway, catch-phrase during a Tegan and Sara deep cut as she belly-flopped onto the bed.

"Bonnie?!"

Still nothing.

Maxine pulled the duvet with her as she got out of bed, wrapping it around her naked form as she checked beside the desk and in the closet and out on the tiny balcony. As she approached the bathroom a shine caught her eye and she bent to pick up a gold wedding band. It had belonged to Bonnie's grandfather before he passed and Bonnie hadn't taken it off since the day the funeral director asked if it should be buried with his body. Yet here it was. A bread crumb.

Maxine rushed to the door, hardly registering that it was ajar, peering out in the hall to find nothing but ugly carpeting and a couple picked-over breakfast trays.

Bonnie was gone.

All the news stations were hyper with stories of abductions. There was something about a satellite malfunction caused by "an unanticipated but not abnormal solar flare." Contact had been lost, regained, and then lost again with the International Space Station, but this was "nothing to panic about." The station-nauts appeared to be in good spirits on last contact and nothing seemed out of the ordinary. "It's rather routine to lose brief contact with the station," a representative from NASA told a CNN reporter. "There can be many causes and it is always resolved in short order."

Maxine flipped from channel to channel, looking for answers. "Both or neither," she kept repeating to the television as if that promise made between two people would change what had been taken from her. She played with Bonnie's grandfather's wedding band and wiped at her tears violently—so violently she was nearly slapping herself. Her face grew red with her efforts.

Unable to sit still any longer, she threw what she could see into her duffle bag and raced from the room and down to the front desk. "My partner's been taken," she cried, slamming her bag to the floor and her palms down onto the counter. Three staff members were gathered around a monitor behind the desk.

A little woman with fuzzy hair came and took Maxine's elbow, guiding her back around the desk to stand with them. Security footage was on the monitor. Maxine watched in black and white as three people in lion masks raced through the lobby with a struggling form between them, the infinity tattoo visible on a flailing arm.

"That's her," she breathed. "That's Bonnie."

"Sorry, love," the little woman said.

"What should I do?" Maxine asked, her shoulders folding forward as hope left her.

"I don't know. We could call the cops? Report her missing?"

Maxine slid down the counter until she was sitting on the cold tile floor. "She's not missing," she said. "We all know exactly what happened to her." She watched with a helpless curiosity as jovial kids in hippie beads and torn jeans congregated in the foyer. Concert-goers. She dug in her bag for her ticket and threw the lanyard around her neck, forcing herself to join them. *Bonnie wanted me to go to this concert*, she thought. *Maybe I'll find some answers there.*

"Dude!" a young man in a straw hat said, pointing to her badge. "You got the Pocket Rochelle VIP. That's wicked! You get to go to Eden, man!"

And he was right. Maxine felt a rush of warmth spread through her. *This ticket gets me to Eden. Bonnie will be in Eden.* She took a deep breath, shouldered her bag, and followed the excited crowd onto the bus.

Bonnie didn't cry out when she found herself in the back of the van even though, all around her, she could heard the sobs of others in the darkness.

She knew what had happened. Her head pounded with a wine hangover. She had a foggy memory of being removed from her room. She'd caught the shape of beautiful Maxine asleep in their bed—the lump of her body rising and falling with the soft snores she always denied every time she drank. Hands covered Bonnie's mouth as they took her, so she couldn't call out a warning. She couldn't say goodbye. She stretched toward her lover, her heart pounding and breaking. "Maxine!" her soul cried. With her thumb, she pushed her grandfather's wedding band up her finger and let it fall. The man who had grabbed her made such little noise during the kidnapping that she could hear the ring bounce on the carpet.

Regret had never been so sharp. Bonnie felt it pulsing through her body, felt it spin around the chip that was embedded somewhere in her stomach. She had asked for this. She could almost taste the ghost of the Kool-Aid on her tongue.

Maxine's voice echoed in her head. "Both or neither. Both or neither."

Bonnie sat up and leaned against the cold wall of the

van. Why her? Sure, she drank Rajiv Montgomery Noah's stupid concoction. But it was a joke. It was just a thing everyone was doing because it was funny. Sure, she gave her consent, inasmuch as the fine print she didn't believe had told her, but this was too much. This was taking it too far, wasn't it? As an expert in jokes, she knew this one wasn't landing.

The van pulled to a stop and the people on board were herded directly into a bus where a medication was administered to keep them docile. Bonnie didn't fight it. What was the point? She leaned her forehead against the cool window and allowed it to bounce there as the bus resumed their trip.

She didn't know how much time had passed, but it felt like a lot. She knew she wasn't far from the famous Rabbit Mountain site of Eden. The sun was high in the sky when the bus joined a line of other buses all headed the same direction. She looked at the people around her. Most were quiet now. They all understood.

The masked people who had gathered them were not cruel—gentle even. "You are the future," they'd said to her as they dropped a pill into her palm and waited for her to swallow it.

It didn't make her feel high or dizzy. It just made her care a little less.

The bus pulled into a huge hangar and everyone was allowed off to use the washrooms. They were escorted to a far wall where rows of cots were arranged like corpses after a massive disaster. "Rest," they were told. "More will join us and tomorrow we enter Eden together."

Food and water was distributed but Bonnie wasn't hungry. She curled into a bunk and finally cried.

Chapter Twenty-Two
1 day before Labour Day | Mission Island

Maxine stumbled off the shuttle bus into the chaos of Mission Island. The palpable excitement of the crowd crushed her, a fist clenching her heart. She felt sick. Her roiling stomach begged for food, but she hadn't been able to finish the toast she'd grabbed from the hotel breakfast bar. It had turned to cardboard in her mouth. Even the coffee had been tasteless. She could still smell Bonnie on her skin. Her nerves pulsed through her body and she spun Bonnie's ring nervously on her thumb.

What am I doing here?

No one had helped her at the hotel, not really. They

pretended to care that Bonnie was missing, but Max was more of an inconvenience than anything—an extra body in the throng of excited music fans. When the shuttle bus arrived she had allowed herself to be shuffled on with the noisy crowd, sitting down beside a large woman in a back seat, tears dripping off her chin.

"Oh, honey," the woman had said.

"My partner is gone." Maxine told her about the messy hotel room and her suspicion of the reaping. "Both or neither. That's what we promised each other. When we took that stupid drink, we thought it was a joke."

And why Bonnie? How did a stand-up comedian earn a spot in the two hundred? How was that worth more than a flower artist? She immediately hated herself for the thought. Kings had jesters. Of course crazy Rajiv Montgomery Noah wanted a comedian. What good was a little woman who knew you shouldn't mix irises with chrysanthemums when you had someone who could bring light into the darkness?

She moved with the crowd along the closely shorn grass path. If Bonnie had been beside her she would have noticed how beautiful it was. Old growth trees formed a natural canopy over the path, strung with lights so that thousands of bulbs glowed into the morning dimness cast by the shadows of the branches. Long hours from that moment, the night would be full of magic as darkness fell and the lights bloomed.

The path emerged at the main hub of the event where

vendor tents surrounded the central pavilion. Generators filled the air with a steady hum and steam pumped from the top of a long line of food trucks. Already, a wavy row of people stood at the coffee truck, bleary-eyed extended-VIP ticket holders, on the island since Thursday night, the stink of two days and a factory rave clinging to them like a scar. She'd seen the tent city before the bus dropped them at the main gate—a rainbow field of canvas that would continue to grow as more people arrived for the final night. Before too long, the other food vendors would be doing a steady business too. Large signs marked the way to each featured location of the festival. Maxine followed the arrow to the main water stage.

Fifty metres from the shoreline, a large platform stood in Lake Superior, built on pressure-treated stilts and created specifically for the event. Gentle waves lapped the edge and the Sleeping Giant, one of Lake Superior's most famous natural landmarks, rested in the background, framed between the heavy scaffolding that held the lighting rigs.

Maxine lowered herself into the grass, facing the stage where Pocket Rochelle would stand in mere hours. When they'd looked at the location on Google Maps after Bonnie bought the tickets, the waterfront was lined with pretty landscaped gardens, but now there was nothing but the historical plaque on a cement monument right in the middle. The event planners had obviously decided the crowds would ruin the gardens. The lines of new sod were evident where they had uprooted the flowers and levelled the area.

She watched as a boat loaded with gear approached the stage and a small crew unloaded and began setting up for the first act of the day: a Thunder Bay local who had won a songwriting contest.

Two acoustic stages were scattered throughout the park where smaller bands would present stripped down versions of their songs in the company of trees and wannabe hippies. The water stage was for The Big Event. Saturday night presented the raging talent of Alias Grace (so named for the famous Margaret Atwood novel) a leather-wearing, punky gang of hipsters who had been called a cross-breed of Rage Against the Machine and Aerosmith. They weren't Maxine's favourite, though she and Bonnie did love singing along to "The Noise is Why We're Aching"—an anthem for anyone who felt marginalized and unseen in the era of social media.

Tonight, Pocket Rochelle would push her voice into the sky. Tonight, Maxine would die a little more as her body absorbed that sound without Bonnie keeping her warm at her side. Tonight, Maxine would watch her girl crush crush it as her own heart became pulp within her chest.

She knew nothing of Rochelle except that her haunting eyes and gravelly voice moved her. Even that song about grocery stores. She was stirred by the slight French accent. The year before, Bonnie had dressed as Rochelle for Halloween, covering her shaggy haircut with a long dark wig and donning a loose men's dress shirt over skinny jeans and boots. It was hot.

Hit with another wave of sorrow, Maxine pulled herself up from the grass and followed a sign that said "Forest Bathing." It was stupid of her to come. This was supposed to be *their* thing—their little getaway together in the midst of Bonnie's tour. Apocastock was meant to be the levity within the storm; the joke they could share together.

No one was laughing now.

The path she followed opened into a clearing in a circle of trees where people were sitting crosslegged throughout the space. A woman in a white dress played a strange little harp, and a man beside her played a recorder. Not a flute. A recorder like she remembered learning in fourth grade music class. The two together created a haunting melody that wrapped itself around her throat.

Someone handed her a small square of carpet and leaned in very close to whisper in her ear. "Choose a spot for your bath. Embrace the silence of the people so you can absorb the conversation of the trees. This is the most intimate moment you're going to experience on these grounds. Let it take you where you need to go. Let yourself be loved."

Maxine found a spot near a small cusp of delicate white flowers and assumed the lotus position on her carpet. It was just large enough to protect her bottom from the damp ground. Her knees stuck over the edge. She looked around at all the people and saw joy. Faces were turned upwards to catch rays of morning sun that were beginning to peek through the canopy of trees like heaven holes. She watched the strange musicians and felt their unfamiliar melody move from her throat to her chest. She closed her eyes, spilling tears as she did so, finding the rustle of leaves and the call of a distant bird like a balm to her spirit. She heard water too but wasn't sure if it was an estuary passing by or the rush of her own sorrow bubbling over her edges. She wept silently, but it rocked her whole body. Time passed and she found herself in a cave of warmth as bodies surrounded her, embracing her in a platonic humanity that created a womb of refuge. No words were spoken. Just bodies together, binding a healing in tune with Mother Nature. She sat. She accepted. She cried. She absorbed. She bathed.

Music that didn't match the clearing began to spill over, bruising the magic. Maxine felt the bodies leaving the space, but still she sat. The sun was warmer now and the harp had stopped. A hand landed on her shoulder. "Stay as long as you need to," a voice whispered.

Maxine opened her eyes to see the harp player.

"Stay until all that heaviness has seeped into the dirt."

"I'm not heavy," Maxine said. "I am so vey, very light."

The woman smiled and stood. "That is very, very good."

But it wasn't good. Being 146 pounds lighter meant that she was 146 pounds lacking and that meant that 146 pounds of Bonnie was out of reach, somewhere beyond her control or touch. Somewhere scary.

She didn't feel better, but she did feel capable. Today was going to be the longest day of her life.

When the news about the meteorite broke, people shrugged it off as a practical joke. The announcement came too soon after the expert debate that went viral; too ironic that the very thing they warned of from that stage was happening so quickly. It was shockingly easy to disregard a thing that only belonged in a Michael Bay movie.

More than a full kilometre wide and heading directly toward Moscow with an expected point of impact within less than twenty-four hours, the wider world went from casual amusement to terrorized panic. "As it enters our atmosphere, we anticipate seeing some pieces break off and head toward other locations in the east, but that can't be determined until we track the entry. For anyone on that side of the Atlantic, our best advice is to seek shelter immediately."

And, like most North Americans who choose ignorance over acknowledgement, the majority of the

United States and Canada continued with their #blessed lives, ignoring the panic overseas, ignoring the fact that an intense collision between the earth and a space rock could have rippling effects that reached them before the long weekend was over.

Hiding in a blindspot, just as the rocket scientist had warned, the rock was first discovered by an astronomer's apprentice named Lisimba in Abuja, Nigeria as he did his nightly tracking of the space station and his hero, Victor Korsakov. A call to his mentor at NASRDA began frantic connections and confirmations with other space research facilities around the globe. There was no mistaking what was coming their way. And there was no escaping it.

The supreme commander-in-chief of the Russian Armed Forces went silent, as did his entourage, and rumours spurred that they had locked themselves away in the unconfirmed secret bunker within Mount Yamantau.

Google released a special report saying the most searched item was something along the lines of "what happens when a meteor hits a nuclear warhead?"

Moscow saw a mad exodus of panicked people without leadership. Highways backed up and people started out on foot, carrying valuables and babies and birdcages with cheeping budgies in a futile attempt to escape even though projections set the potential destruction at reaching a spread of over 100,000 kilometres if the rock hit at its current size—though, of course, expectations were that atmospheric entry would cause as much as half to break off into smaller pieces with various trajectories. This made space for some hope for the people of Moscow, but even more space for fear for anyone else in the northern hemisphere.

On Mission Island, where the signal was spotty at best, the few people who had Google alerts set up and actually managed to see the breaking news shrugged it off. Moscow was far away. The party was right now. Though there were some scattered conversations, no one seemed overly concerned. Apocastock would not be silenced.

1 day before Labour Day | Eden

Rajiv closed his laptop slowly, a sad smile across his face, the weariness of his burden almost too much to bear in the weight of this new ironic poetry. He held the brass lion in his hand, worrying its side with the pad of his thumb, the carved texture of the fur and mane almost worn down to a dull, smooth gold after many years of tension.

"Lisimba," he said to the quiet room and his daughter grunted from the desk on the other side where she diligently worked on the final paragraphs of Eden's constitution, her typing more urgent now that they knew their timeline was sure.

"What's that?" she asked, not looking up from her screen, the frayed threads of her bracelet catching on the edge of the desk as if to remind her she had as much to lose as everyone else.

"Lisimba," he said again. "The name of the asteroid." He set the brass beast on his desk and patted its head with the tip of his finger. "It means lion."

1 day before Labour Day | Mission Island

As the opening chords of Pocket Rochelle's first song floated across the water, Maxine sank onto the grass at the edge of the lake. She'd claimed her spot hours before, unable to bring herself to partake in any of the other stage activities, nor had she needed to eat or visit the long string of porta-potties because she had no appetite for food or drink. The lapping of the water had lulled her and she knew she'd slipped into a weird nature nap several times through the day, visions of Bonnie in various states of pain or fear jerking her awake each time. But now the crowd thronged and she had stood with them as PR took the stage and now, while the opening stanza built into a slow crescendo she had no strength left to stand. "Today we sing, tomorrow we fly," Rochelle said into the microphone as the crowd roared its approval. "Tomorrow we labour; today we play."

Maxine knew from Rochelle's social media that she was taking The End of the World as seriously as the rest of them: a good reason to celebrate, but nothing to really worry about. Of course, Rochelle's partner hadn't been snatched from their bed in the middle of the night. Maxine had tuned in to Rochelle's live Kool-Aid party three months earlier and felt some sort of strange kinship when she saw they had received the same colour. *Sisters*, she had thought foolishly. *Soeurs bleues.*

This was her first time seeing them live and Rochelle was more haunting and beautiful than any filtered Instagram photo. Being this close to the real person caused a warmth to bloom in Maxine's chest that confused her in the light of her Bonnie Baby feelings.

She knew she was crying, but she made no move to stop it, allowing it to become part of the whole experience. Rochelle found her there on the edge of the water and held her gaze, singing directly to her, filling her soul with something that felt a little like hope, touching her on a spiritual level that even the forest bath hadn't reached. "We will not fold to ignorance," Rochelle sang out as she launched into the pre-chorus of one of their most well-known songs.

"We'll hold the line!" the crowd sang back.

"Hold the line," Maxine echoed in broken sobs.

When the last note had faded in the distance and the Sleeping Giant snored with the lapping of gentle waves and the crowd had begun to make their way to the old fac-tory for Rave Trois: Night Three with DJ Young Yaper, one of Pocket Rochelle's roadies approached her and asked if she would come with him.

"Why?" she asked, wiping her eyes.

"Rochelle wants to chat."

The bottom of the world fell out and Maxine gaped at him. "Why?" she echoed her first question.

"Beats me," he said, offering a hand to help her from the now damp grass. She swayed slightly, not eating all day finally catching up to her.

"I'm a little dizzy," she said.

"We got cookies," he told her, and led her along the waterfront to a basecamp around the corner of the island where Rochelle was sitting on a folding chair, holding a steaming mug.

She was breathtaking, her dark hair stuck against her warm cheek, flushed from an incredible performance and a wild response from an excited audience. She stood to greet Maxine, putting a hand on either arm before pulling her in for a tight hug. "I watched you," she whispered as she held her. She smelled like sandalwood and vanilla. "I saw all your tears. You are like a song."

Maxine felt herself melt, softening against Rochelle, two small women clinging to one another in a strange and unexpected moment of communion.

Rochelle stroked her back. Maxine sobbed.

"Come, *mon amour*," Rochelle said, leading her into the tent and opening a folding chair for her. "Everybody out," she called to the crew and bandmates that were milling around a snack table.

Maxine sat and Rochelle placed her own chair to face her so that their knees touched when she sat. A confusing thrill shot through Maxine's body. "Now," Rochelle said, taking Maxine's hands. "Tell me everything."

Maxine spilled her heart until 4:00 in the morning, eating three paper plates full of cheese and crackers and apple slices and chocolate dipped granola bars. After her second cup of coffee, Rochelle gently took the cup from her, turning her hand so her palm faced upwards. Slowly, she traced the infinity symbol on Maxine's wrist, making her whole body go hot with confusion.

Rochelle's nails were short and unpainted but as she rounded the bottom of the symbol, her finger tipped up and her nail grazed the delicate skin, sending a wild shiver through Maxine. She thought of how that finger danced across piano keys, striking them with such a confident burst that it was a wonder the whole instrument didn't crumble under her performance, and then this, here, this gentleness from that same finger. She wanted to be a major chord under those hands. She wanted to be played. She wanted to be a song on Rochelle's lips and a poem in her belly. A sob hitched up from her gut and she raised her other hand to try and catch it, but it tumbled out and Rochelle leaned forward in her folding chair and wrapped her arms around her.

"I am an F-sharp-minor," Maxine said because one of Bonnie's musician friends had once told her it was the ugliest chord to play on a guitar.

Rochelle held both sides of her face and touched her forehead with her own. "Oh no, *mom amore*, you are a Major 9th, you just can't see it yet."

Chapter Twenty-Three

Labour Day | Rabbit Mountain

As the horizon began to grey with the hint of a coming morning, Jude poured hot water into the French press and sighed at the smell of it. Edgar weaved around her feet as she waited the six minutes for the grinds to finish wetting. She picked him up and nuzzled his face with her nose. "What do you think, buddy?" she asked him. "Is this our last cup of coffee ever?" She wasn't sure how she felt. She wasn't exactly sad; she was hanging in a place between grief and acceptance that was uncomfortable but survivable. *Survivable.* Ha! "That's a joke if I ever heard one," she said as Edgar squirmed to get free. She dropped him onto the bed and he curled up against the needlepoint pillow, yawning.

Two coffees in hand, she stepped outside to greet Brett who waited for her in one of the old lawn chairs.

"Good morning," he said. He was wearing a button-down flannel over a t-shirt and worn blue jeans, and Jude smiled to realize her own flannel was almost matching his.

"Good morning," she said, handing him his coffee and sitting beside him.

The steam rose thick and white and their breath shot out in front of them as they sipped, the air chilly with the tease of autumn.

Together they watched the sunrise, an explosive display of colour that usually didn't show up this deep in the mountains. It was like the sky knew something was coming and it wanted one last chance to show off.

"Thank you," Brett said as the full sun finally broke through. "I didn't expect a friend for the end of the world."

Jude took his hand and led him into her camper without a word, both their coffee mugs left on the dirt beside their chairs, the last few swallows destined to grow cold before whatever was going to happen evaporated them from existence.

Labour Day | Thunder Bay

When Imogen Parker and her son, Rasmus, entered the Prince Arthur Hotel, they brought nothing with them but the rings on their fingers and the clothes on their backs. The tunnel had already been outfitted with everything they were going to need to make it through the foreseeable future.

"Good morning, Mrs. Parker," the concierge greeted them. "Will Mr. Parker be in today?"

"Not today, Daryl," she said, keeping her voice even. "He's attending to some personal matters." It would do no good to spread her sorrow, though she felt shocked that he couldn't see the tattoo of her husband's still body sealed on her eyes, because it was all she could see.

"Very good," Daryl said. "Is there anything I can help you with?"

"No, thank you. Just picking up a few things for him from his office."

"Be sure to call on me if you do need anything." Daryl tipped his head.

"Of course. Thank you."

Imogen and her son headed toward her husband's office, but veered down a secondary hallway as soon as they knew they were out of Daryl's view. They went through a swinging door and down a service elevator where they took a private staircase (a far improvement from the dangerous ladder stairs Rajiv had first encountered there) to the area between the coded basement door and the vault door.

As if they were breaking into a bank safe, Imogen slowly turned the combination lock first one way then the other until there was a click. The numbers were their wedding anniversary and she felt her loss anew as she turned the crank and the seal released with a dramatic hiss. Lights came on as the door opened, revealing their new reality. A smile laced with sadness spread across her face as she saw one of the last additions Samuel had made.

"I have a surprise for you," he had told her. "You'll see it as soon as we enter the tunnel."

Hanging from the ceiling in what would now be known as the "foyer" was one of the original Prince Arthur Hotel chandeliers. One of the intricate beauties that hung throughout the lobby and the suite hallways. How he had removed it without raising suspicion was a mystery. An image of the Grinch filled her mind. "…there's a light on this floor that won't light on one side…"

The low tunnel ceiling meant that she could touch the fixture by raising her hand. The lowest crystals were just shy of brushing the top of her son's head.

Beyond the foyer, a comfortable living room was set up with expensive leather furniture. Oil lamps sat on each of the three side tables. A bookshelf held a small library of favourites and the family list of I-really-should-read-this-classic-someday titles. Apparently, someday had arrived. There was a battery-operated turntable and a stack of sealed vinyl records beside a small upright piano. She ran her fingers along the keys. "You didn't have to bring this here," she said. It was the piano from her mother's apartment she'd neglected cleaning out since her passing seven months before. She trilled a few notes.

"The music books are in the bench," her son said. "She would have wanted you to have it here."

In the kitchen, long, steel pantry shelves were loaded with non-perishables, and a sink provided fresh water that pulled from the harbour—just two hundred metres away—into a sophisticated filtration system that also dispelled their grey water right back out to Lake Superior. A shower (cold water only) stood as a frosted plexiglass box at the end of the pantry, with a washing machine beside it.

A tiny closet held a composting toilet that captured methane and converted it into the energy needed to power the lamp over a small raised garden with leafy greens and herbs. A monthly emptying of the composting barrel would provide powerful (odourless) nutrients for the planter soil. It was a project piloted by one of Rajiv's chief scientists and a system he was employing on a larger scale within his Eden.

Five "stalls"—open-ended and separated by thin

plywood walls—were outfitted with beautiful beds and bedding, oil lamps, and a minimal supply of clothing: one pair of jeans, one par of jogging pants, three t-shirts (one long-sleeve, two short sleeved), two sweaters, one flannel shirt, five pairs of cotton sports socks, two pairs of wool socks, seven pairs of cotton underwear. A trunk in the last bedroom held a couple goose down parkas, ski pants, heavy winter boots, and five oxygen helmets. A supply of tanks lined the back of the last plywood wall.

At the end of the tunnel, a huge bank of batteries flashed their little lights into the darkness—a mini version of what Rajiv had in the mines. Power lines ran along the same conduit as the water lines, out to a solar bank three hundred metres off the harbour point. There was no guarantee the lake would survive what was coming, but they certainly trusted that anything mounted on the roof of the hotel would not stand. They were to conserve energy whenever possible, only tapping into the batteries when necessary. A digital monitor was mounted to the wall by the batteries. It read 97.8%, 49.8hrs. Everything was currently running off the hotel's electricity.

Imogen's son stood at the bedrooms. "There are five beds," he said.

"Yes."

"Who are the other three for?"

Imogen sighed. "I don't know. Your father was waiting until the last minute to bring them in so as not to create any kind of panic. He didn't tell me. I trusted him."

"We can save three," her son said.

"But who?"

A small screen was mounted in the living room. Though it currently ran the live stream of the scene outside Eden, it would soon be rendered useless. There was an old VCR and some tapes on the bottom of the bookshelf, but those would only be indulged in should the sun return and allow their battery bank to remain charged.

Imogen sat and watched the crowds in front of the gates of Eden, her son's hand on her shoulder as he studied the faces that flashed past the camera. Joyful, fearful, entertained, terrified, anticipatory. They were all waiting for something, and it became clear that it was either death (fear), or the hilarity of a billionaire who got something wrong (entertained).

He kissed his mother on the forehead. "I'll be back," he promised.

"Where are you going?"

"Do you trust me?"

"Don't leave me here alone. I'll die here alone."

"Do you trust me, Mother?"

She nodded, fresh tears in her eyes.

"I'll be back before it happens. Don't open the door for anyone except me."

Labour Day | Rabbit Mountain

We all seemed to wake at the same time. The plane banked and I felt my stomach drop. We were going to land.

A dull pain pulsed in the crook of my arm and I looked down to see where a tiny bruise formed around a little pinprick. I felt a tightness at my ankle and saw a tension bandage around where I'd slammed it against the door frame as I was removed from my home. I didn't think it was sprained, but the bandage would protect the bruise from further bumps and I was grateful. I gazed out the window at a barren landscape, desertlike and destitute, almost colourless as the pre-dawn doused everything in foggy grey-scale, split through with the black line of the tarmac; though off in the distance I could see a lush, green stretch of nature—old trees heavy with leaves. If I craned against the edge of my window frame I could just see the wall I knew from so many news programs and tabloid stories.

"Noah's Ark," someone said from the other side where they had a more direct view.

Early sun beamed off the massive dome as it crested the horizon and I had to look away. My shoulder was sore and slightly itchy. When I rubbed it, I found a small Bandaid. A woman across the aisle from me was wearing a tank top. She too had a Bandaid on her shoulder. Strange.

When we landed, the lions directed us to follow them from the plane and onto a bus which would take us to the gate. The air was cool and fresh. I'd read about mountain air before but never experienced it firsthand. There were companies who started selling it in canisters, but I always thought that was foolish. Now I understood. It was lovely.

Tents were pitched all around the exterior, story chasers wanting to catch a glimpse of Rajiv Montgomery Noah's "End of the World," hoping to go viral and find their own moment of fame. Security wearing lion masks held them back as the bus slowly moved toward those famous Eden gates. People waved flags over their heads, some held homemade signs: *Take me with you!* "Heaven is a Place on Earth" pumped from speakers mounted on top of an old Volkswagen, Belinda Carlisle singing the anthem the world had adopted from the 1980s to identify the insanity of Rajiv's vision.

None of us spoke and we did our best to avoid eye contact with the mob of fans who pushed to get close to us. It was as if we all knew we needed to treat this moment with an air of reverence—though no one knew why exactly—and those camped-out nut-cases had no place in this picture of our deliverance. It was our duty to ignore them, despite the fear that coiled in our guts.

Dear Ryan, it's almost time. I'm going to be locked away now. You thought you'd be the one to do it, but you were wrong. How does that feel? Bitter? Are you relieved? Are you scared? Of course not. You don't have enough empathy to feel fear. If I survive this, you will too. Because though I don't want to think of you, I know I will. That is the power of a scar. You are my scar. I hope you're thinking of me when the fire comes. I hope I am your scar. I hope you remember what summer tastes like before your tongue melts.

Labour Day | Mission Island

"Let's go find her," Rochelle said, filling two matching Yeti cups with fresh steaming coffee.

"What do you mean?" Maxine asked, accepting the mug and inhaling a scent that would usually remind her of slow mornings with Bonnie in their small apartment in East Harlem.

Rochelle flicked the tag on the lanyard around Maxine's neck. "VIP," she said. "We're going to Eden and you're coming with us." She leaned back to yell beyond the tent. "Yo! You guys ready to go?"

Affirmations from beyond the canvas brought both women to their feet and, together with the full Pocket Rochelle band and other VIP ticket holders, they piled into a bus and joined a caravan of vehicles full of people hoping to catch a glimpse of the end of the world.

Labour Day | Rabbit Mountain

When Jude unbuttoned Brett's flannel shirt, she could smell the baby wipes he'd been using to clean himself. His own musk cut through, but it was mild and intoxicating. He caught her hand before she got to the last button. "Slow," he said, gripping the back of her neck and planting the whisper of a kiss against her ear.

Every part of her ached for him and electricity shot through her when their skin touched, but she obeyed, she let him lead, she surrendered to his slow investigation even though her body screamed for more. His lips and tongue sent shivers through her as he explored. Slowly. So slowly.

"Brett?" she pleaded, but he would not rush, savouring each agonizing and explosive second until they were both finally free of their clothes and lying in her bed. Even then, he rose above her slowly, every movement intentional and exquisite in its timing until they both knew they couldn't go on. He held back as she found her plateau, not caring that the thin RV walls would barely dampen her cries, and as she pulsed with the pleasure of the moment, he allowed his own ecstasy to break through. As they arched together in those final seconds, Jude opened her eyes to find him watching her too. They fell back to the mattress in a sweaty, beautiful mess, and as she stroked his face she saw the truth. "It's gone," she said.

"What?" he asked, kissing her with the kind of deepness that made it seem like he was ready to let it all happen again.

"Your shadow," she said. "It's gone."

He held her against his chest. "No, it's not," he said.

"What do you mean?"

"I mean it's part of me. But you are like a prism. And sometimes a prism can push light where it hasn't been accepted before. I can hold a shadow, but I can also hold light, if you'll let me."

Jude lay against his shoulder, tucking her head into the cave between his chin and collarbone as she ran a finger around the fine hair on his chest.

"Yes," she said. "I think I will let you."

And in that moment, she knew she loved him. Loved him in a way not ever captured by her own lived-experience or anything she'd ever caught on her camera. It was as if every definition of living had been stripped back to only this moment and she finally understood what it meant to be alive. And what it would mean to die. Her heart broke and sang in a tumultuous harmony. His presence dug into the tumoured shadow of her body and replaced it with colour. She was whole.

He tipped her chin up and pressed his lips against hers with a softness that reminded her of a woman. "If this is our last day," he said, "I am so lucky it gets to end here."

They lay tangled together until the heat in the closed RV became too much and the commotion beyond swelled to such a crescendo that they needed to see what was going on. As Jude tugged her tank top over her head, Brett pulled her in for one last kiss. This one was not slow. It was deep, intense, bruising, sending shocks to her toes and new heat to bloom between her thighs. When they came apart, even the colour of his eyes seemed to have changed. Lightened.

"I need to use the washroom," he said, and Jude laughed at the way it stopped the romance. "Thank you," he said, his body turned toward her as he stood at the door, pulling his t-shirt on, suddenly shy.

Jude pushed her hair out of her eyes, feeling the sweat of their lovemaking on her forehead. "You're welcome," she said, and it was the Amen at the end of a beautiful moment.

The RV door sprung shut and Jude smiled after him as she saw him jog off through the windshield. The porta-potties were set up almost two acres away on the far side of the field. Buses were filing in off the Rabbit Mountain Road. *This is it,* she thought. *Here are the chosen.* She grabbed two beers from her little fridge and went outside to watch.

The crowd pulsed with excitement. Jude sat in a lawn chair and sipped a cold beer with lime. The desert-like state of the damaged land in front of Eden meant there was nothing to block the sun from getting to her solar panels so her power supply had been more than adequate to last through the long month of anticipation. Her food stores were running low though. No fresh meat or vegetables for over a week now. No milk either. It kept her morning oatmeal thick, but she didn't mind so much.

Edgar walked in and out of her legs, his tail tickling her thigh as they watched the buses pull up in front of the gate. "There they are," she murmured to him, setting down her drink and picking him up, nuzzling her nose into his fur. She hadn't had a proper shower for more than a month, but he always smelled fresh and clean and didn't care what state she was in. He licked her chin where a small drop of beer glistened. She decided that if today ended and she was still alive, she would use the solar shower—though she didn't like the idea of washing Brett off her body. It felt good to have a whisper of his scent on her skin. She liked it.

Where she had been one lonely vehicle sitting in a desolate wasteland, she was now surrounded on all sides by others. Cars, trucks, tents, tractors, ATVs. It was as if the whole population of Ontario and beyond had shown up to watch the great fall of Rajiv Montgomery Noah. Or so they hoped.

Jude found herself wishing for more time with him. She wanted to know more of his story. She wanted to dig beneath the eccentricities to unlock his genesis. It was the missing piece of her doc. It would have been incredible. Exclusive access to the one man everyone was talking about. She would have definitely won another prize. Maybe even a Pulitzer. Not that it was exactly journalism, but it was spectacular, what she'd been allowed to witness. Once the tour had ended though, she had no more right to him or his kingdom. He hadn't been cruel about it, just matter-of-fact. "I must focus on the final touches so I can welcome the survivors," he had said.

She had fought against a desire to blast her tapes to the living world. If it was all going to end, why did it even matter? But she cared about the man for some reason she couldn't quite put her finger on. His passion inspired her. His drive reminded her of herself and so she felt a bit of a kinship. And now, in the end, she thought that she believed him, and she wished him the best.

As if he'd known he was on her mind, she heard the CB in the RV crackle to life and she rushed inside with Edgar in tow to answer.

Labour Day | Thunder Bay

Imogen toggled the radio and pleaded into the receiver. "Rajiv. Rajiv. This is Imogen Parker. Are you there, Rajiv? Samuel is dead. Rasmus is gone. I don't know what to do. Rajiv. Rajiv are you there?"

She was left with nothing but static air and a low hum

like the line was busy. She kissed her husband's ring, curled into a tight ball on the couch, and prayed that her son would return before it was too late.

"—you there? This is Rajiv. Respond back."

Jude grabbed the mouthpiece and held the receiver button. "Mr. Noah. Yes, I'm here. Go for Jude."

"You see the buses?"

"I see them."

"It won't be long now."

Jude bit her lip and stared out to where the chosen from the first bus were being slowly herded together in a tight group, while soldiers—lions—held back the pressing crowd. "I'll be watching until the end."

"You are a bright spark, Jude. I'm sorry your body betrayed you. I would have liked to get to know you better."

"Thank you." She chocked back a sob.

"You will find the next thing. I will not forget you. Your tapes will one day tell the story. Are they in the fireproof safe? Have you protected them?"

"I have."

"Very good."

"Have you protected your copies?" she asked.

"Your legacy lives on, Jude. Take care, bright eyes. Over."

"Good luck," Jude said. "Over."

The signal went dead and she let the receiver fall.

Chapter Twenty-Four

Labour Day | Rabbit Mountain

Bonnie saw the crowds long before she saw the gates of Eden. It looked like the scene from a music festival. Tents and people everywhere. It even seemed festive. She could hear music pumping across the space, so loud it cut through the cheers of the crowd as the buses appeared.

They're here to see us, Bonnie thought absently, running her fingertip around the space where her grandfather's ring should have been.

She knew a large amount of them came from where she was supposed to have been: Apocastock. Had Maxine gone? How was she navigating this new, terrifying reality? Bonnie tried to imagine how she would have reacted in Maxine's position, and she knew she would have torn the hotel down, fighting to find her love in the rubble of a promise they had both made.

What if all of this was true? What if the world really was ending and she was being handed a future? A future without Maxine. She didn't want it, but the pill she'd taken and whatever they'd put into her arm when she fell asleep pulled the fight out of her and she could do nothing but follow the other sheep off the bus.

Labour Day | Rabbit Mountain

We were about to meet Rajiv and I didn't know what to expect, I only knew I'd never planned for such a meeting. I wanted to shower. I wanted to hide. The media had painted him as such a maniac and I was in no way prepared to face a maniac. What if we were just pawns in his psychotic game? What if we were being led to our death rather than to our salvation? With just a small distraction I could slip from the line and disappear into the crowd of watchers. I felt a hand on my arm and saw a lion fall in step with me, his fingers around my bicep as if he read my thoughts. I swallowed a fearful sob. *Ryan or death?* I remembered the crunch of my rib that time he'd shoved me into the kitchen island. All I'd asked for was one evening that he'd stay home and keep me company. When I hadn't stopped crying, as I stood bent over in the kitchen, clutching my side and begging him to love me, he'd slapped me hard across the face and told me to "Grow up!" and "I like you better bent over like that." *For better or for worse?* We didn't know better. It had always been for worse—even in the early days when I thought it was exciting and good. I felt a tear slip down my cheek. *Dear Ryan, I hope you enjoy hell. You've earned a room with a view.* It occurred to me that even if my "for better" was death within these dome walls, I would welcome it because it meant a different kind of freedom, which I'd been praying for since I lost my own willpower.

Labour Day | Rabbit Mountain

Like docile cattle, the captives stood in a row nearly two hundred strong as the buses pulled away, giving the crowd a fair look at the chosen. Heavy security kept the crowd back by twenty-five metres.

A frantic scream rose above the din. Bonnie felt the vibration of her own name and she swung around, scanning the crowd. "Maxine?" she called out, but her voice was lost in the noise. A flash of black hair. "Maxine?"

A hand landed on her shoulder. Gentle. "It is time," a lion said.

Bonnie turned back to face the mountain and then moved obediently with the line and the lion as they walked single file toward the gates.

Something soft brushed past her ankles. She looked down but there was nothing there. She thought she heard her name again, screamed in a tone that dripped with pain. She blinked slowly, not quite understanding why she was walking, but walking anyway. She didn't turn around again.

Labour Day | Rabbit Mountain

Jude watched as the final buses were unloaded. Weary travellers stumbled out, fear clearly sketched across faces that were grey, no matter their ethnicity. She heard a devastating scream as more and more transports expelled their loads.

"Bonnie!"

She watched as a small Black woman rushed forward only to be pressed back by the guards. She fell to her knees, arms forward on the ground in a supplicating prayer. Jude felt her heartbreak and was drawn to her.

She wrapped an arm around the weeping woman and directed her back toward the RV, noticing, too late, that Edgar had followed her.

"Edgar!" she cried as he darted through the legs of the guard line. "Edgar!" But he had disappeared among the legs of the prisoners. *Perhaps he will have a tomorrow after all,* she thought as she sat the distraught woman in a lawn chair and put the cold beer meant for Brett in her hand.

"Someone you love?" Jude asked, nodding toward the gate where the people were being filed through under heavy guard.

The woman hiccuped and raised the beer to her lips. She lowered it without taking a drink.

A man approached them, two people following him like a funeral procession, their faces traced in tears. "Who have you lost?" he asked her.

"My Bonnie," she said.

"Do you want to see her again?"

"Fuck you." The words fell out of her like a sob, like she'd never said them aloud before.

He knelt down in front of her and placed a hand on her knee.

"Hey—" Jude said, but he raised his other hand to calm her.

"I have a place. It might keep us safe. You might be able to see her again. It's not far. But you must come now."

The woman set her bottle on the ground without saying a word and followed after the man as if in a trance.

Jude wiped her eyes and tried to find Edgar in the mass of people, but he was gone.

She looked for the woman. She was gone too, her beer tipped over beside the chair and dripping onto the ground. Jude rescued it and raised it to her lips. No need to hold back. She took a long pull from the bottle then allowed her eyes to scan the mountain for a sign of the pods Rajiv had said were hidden there. She thought she saw a small crack that might have been a seam for one of them. "Fair thee well, Lovely Rita. Keep the sun captive." She held out the beer in a solo cheers as Belinda Carlisle began her song again. And again. And again. And she waited for Brett to return.

Labour Day | Eden

The gates swung open as we approached. Despite their heaviness and size they didn't make a sound, instead opening like the arms of a lover, inviting us into a warm embrace.

The beauty within was shocking and the path we walked was long. Simple but pretty tiny houses lined narrow cobblestone streets that led to a large centre square with a spouting fountain sporting a graceful humanoid creature I couldn't identify. We filtered in silently, the only sound the water in the fountain and our shoes against the ground. I remembered my slippers and felt foolish, but I also knew it didn't matter.

He's not bringing us here to die. He's bringing us here to live. He's built this place for us. He wants our happiness. He is not a troll. He is not a maniac. He is misunderstood… I tried to talk myself into a state of calm, but my body trembled. The baby kicked.

We were a mass of two hundred souls. That's what the news stations and newsletters had said. That's how many Rajiv Montgomery Noah had committed to save. Every colour of skin, every shape and size, yet every face had a beauty that was near breathtaking, and no one could have been older than 35. I thought of my swollen body and the extra weight I was carrying in my own face—how I felt less attractive than I'd ever felt before—and I knew they'd grabbed me by mistake. Ryan was who they wanted: smart, accomplished, cool, cruel Ryan. They were going to send me back.

A new knot of fear formed in my stomach and slowly began to twist.

The massive double doors of a large white brick building opened and two people emerged.

Rajiv Montgomery Noah and Moriah, his daughter, navigated the stone steps, passing between the heavy pillars and a pair of white iron lions as they came to stand before us.

"Welcome," he said, his voice projected with a lapel mic that pumped out from speakers mounted all over the dome. I was shocked to see how small he was, his daughter towering over him, his shoulders slightly turned forward as if he suffered from scoliosis. He lacked the powerful stance I'd witnessed on television, but his presence was captivating nonetheless, and his voice reached inside me to a place that harboured hope, the soft curve of his accent making him sound gentle and trustworthy.

"I trust your journey was comfortable," he said. A rumble of discontent rippled through the crowd. "You must accept my sincere apologies for the way in which you were removed from your homes and places of work. We had no choice but to strike swiftly. We had twenty-four-hours to secure each one of you before authorities inter-vened. I understand if you're wrestling with confusion or anger, but you must trust me when I say this is for your survival. With me, your future is guaranteed. Look around you. This is the new world."

Doubt plagued me, yet I liked the sound of his voice, it had a singsong quality that put me at ease and loosened the set of my shoulders.

What will he do when he realizes they brought the wrong person?

"Perhaps you're wondering why you were chosen," he said, somehow having gotten inside my head. "Perhaps you think you're here by mistake. Let me assure you, we have made no mistakes. Using a sophisticated algorithm we determined, from the entire human population, the very best; taking into consideration all things, from DNA to skill-sets to anything else you might think of. There are no mistakes here, I promise you that. Your identity was confirmed against our computers while you slept on the planes and trucks that delivered you. You are here because I required you to be here. You are here because you are the future. In three hours, the world as you know it will be no more."

A rumble of conversation carried through the crowd, recurring themes of doubt and wonderment as I rubbed the small pin-prick bruise on my arm.

What was to become of us?

Labour Day | Eden

Edgar navigated the throng of legs like a snake. He knew the smells beyond the strange wall were far more exciting than this barren dirt patch. He had smelled the freshness—the *aliveness*—on Jude both times she returned from her long trips inside as he yowled and cried at her to ensure she knew her disappearances were of the utmost inconvenience. He craved the green of nature and he knew nature hid in the place she kept vanishing into. In fleeting thoughts, images of Jude's face flashed across his memory, but the idea of grass and bugs and goats pulled him with a natural force far beyond the love of his mistress. Of course, he didn't have a memory to tell him what goats were, but a musky scent lingered on Jude's skin that smelled of beast and of friend and he needed to roll in it.

He was a shadow, darting in and out and around. Hands shot down to grab him, but he was too set on reaching his goal to allow a mere human animal to feel more than the briefest touch of his fur.

He camouflaged himself with great speed and distraction as he became part of the procession that led through the gate. He could smell the ugly sweat of the people around him and his instincts swelled with the sound of crying as a memory of Jude's tears shocked his brain. The salt on his tongue as he'd lick them, the way she would soften and fold herself around him, how her body felt a little like a mother when he kneaded her with the pads of his feet, how she would pet him and he purred. He almost turned around, wanting her familiar scent over the animal scent of these beasts he wove amongst, but then he saw a flash of green and he forgot all about Jude.

He dashed ahead, zipping up the first tree trunk, jumping to the next like a squirrel. Were there squirrels here? Jump. Jump. Climb. Jump. Until he came to the grass near the beehives where the buzzing made him think he was losing his mind with joy. He flopped in front of them, rolling onto his back, purring into the earth, biting at the green spikes that wiggled around his body, so absorbed in his own bliss that he could no longer hear the wailing of the crowd.

Labour Day | Eden

We were led down a new path through abundant fields and lined up at the entrance to the old mine. How long ago had we disembarked the buses? It felt like hours. The mountain loomed over us, its shadow teasing with thoughts of cool air, but unable to touch us beneath the protection of the dome. It seemed fully climate controlled and though it felt like we were outdoors, I knew we were trapped within this massive building made of glass… or whatever material it was made of—he'd told us in one of his newsletters, but I couldn't remember. If Rajiv was right, if the world really was ending today, and if we actually survived within this structure, did that mean we were destined to live out the rest of our lives within it? The realization that my brief moment being carried from my house to that armoured van was potentially my last real moment outdoors struck me deeply and awfully. I reached into my pocket and pulled out the crushed chrysanthemum I'd grabbed when they carried me off. It still possessed its peppery scent and I fingered the paper-like petals as a last-ditch attempt to hang onto what I may never have again.

Dear Ryan, if the world doesn't end, please take care of the chrysanthemums. Give all my possessions to the Goodwill, hell, burn them in the courtyard, but please, save the flowers.

A profound wave of grief passed over me as I thought of my mother and my sister. I said a little prayer, hoping that Rajiv was wrong.

Slowly, people disappeared into the mine in groups of nine. The major news network was broadcast on the side of the dome for us to watch as we waited our turn… "More reports of missing persons are coming in. Though there is no evidence of bodily harm, property damage has been extensive. Speculation says that billionaire Rajiv Montgomery Noah is finally executing the plan he's spoken of for years… Authorities have been dispatched to the Eden site to investigate… We are still tracking the meteor that is on a trajectory toward Moscow. We're receiving reports of mass panic and blocked highways as people try to leave the city. Russian government has been unresponsive from where they are hiding…"

A few minutes later, deployed drones captured images through the exterior of the dome, showing a group of people being slowly disappeared into the mountainside.

Another ten minutes and police vehicles were pulled up to the gates, top lights spinning wildly, megaphone held to the lips of the point man. "Rajiv Montgomery Noah, please come forward."

Rajiv drove a golf cart to the entrance and then wandered forward as if on a Sunday afternoon stroll, showing no concern for the assault rifles aimed at him. He walked right to the gate, so close they could have grabbed his collar had they thought to reach through, not that it would have accomplished anything but the bruising of an old man's ribs. Their interaction took over the broadcast screens. "I am the only person who knows the code to unlock this place," Rajiv said. He wiped at the sniper dots on his chest as if he were brushing crumbs from his shirt. "You can kill me, but that won't release these people. They have all asked to be here, and no one has asked to leave. This is a closed community. And this—" he gestured to the surrounding land full of vehicles, tents, and excited people "—is private property upon which you are trespassing."

"What are your demands?"

"Demands?" He smiled, amused at the ignorance that tried to stare him down. "Demands? These people are my only demands. You've spent years mocking me, now you will reap the fruits of your foolery. I would love to save you all, but sadly, even my funds have reached their limits. I wish you well. I hope, for your sake, I am wrong. You have only a few hours left. You should be home with the ones you love." Rajiv reached a hand to the wall beside the gate, pressing his palm against a sensor pad. A loud click shot an ominous definition across the row of police, and from above, the dome shifted as a piece lowered on the inside of the gate, sealing Eden from the world beyond, shoring up the five foot thick and ten foot high wall of concrete and iron that would forever protect the dome.

Rajiv still wore his smile, a little smug now, knowing he'd won, knowing what was in motion could never be stopped as he returned to the mine, the drones following him from outside until he too disappeared into the mountain.

Chapter Twenty-Five
Labour Day | Mount Yamantau, Russia

A violent argument was happening between the supreme commander and his military advisors. Spittle flew from the mouth of the general as he emphasized for the fifth time: "Force cannot detonate a nuclear warhead!" But the supreme commander couldn't hear him—*wouldn't* hear him.

"I have a duty to my people," he insisted. Leading the country with the largest nuclear arsenal was only a benefit if those weapons were aimed elsewhere. "If the power of a meteorite hit could force the detonation protocol, it is our duty to eject those weapons out of our country."

"Even if a space rock could cause an explosion, it would simply scatter the radioactive material," the general said. "It would not result in a nuclear bomb."

"So we choose to pepper Russia with radiation?" the commander said, his voice rising by several increments.

"If the rock doesn't break into smaller pieces as it enters the atmosphere, we will lose Moscow," the general explained. "If our weapons are also destroyed in that hit, we will lose a vast number of our wider population as radiation poisoning takes them."

"And if we deploy those weapons to bury themselves in the ocean?"

"There is no time for that."

"So we all die. From impact or from radiation. Or, we eject our weapons and maybe save some."

"We cut ourselves off at the knees if we give up our weapons."

The supreme commander sat at his desk and formed his hands into a pyramid under his chin. "We are gravely wounded either way," he said. "This would help to level the playing field. We need to act and we need to act now."

"I will play no part in this," the general said. "It's a call to war."

"No one is thinking of war right now. Sinking unarmed weapons into the Atlantic is not an act of war, it is an act of mercy. It is the only chance we have to preserve our people, to give any that escape Moscow a fighting chance."

"I will not allow it," the general said.

It took little more than a cocking of the commander's head before a pistol appeared in the hand of one of the security guards and the general fell into a crumpled heap, a neat hole in his temple.

"Initiate Perimetr," he said. "Ask them to alter trajectories to preserve life if they can. This is not an act of war, this is an act of protection for my people."

A phone was pulled off the wall and orders barked into the receiver.

Labour Day | Rabbit Mountain

Maxine allowed the man to lead her. He held her hand gently. She liked his face. "I am Rasmus," he said, putting his mouth close to her ear so she could hear over the din of the crowd. He reached back and pulled the two who followed them closer. "This is Jasmine and this is Damien. Jasmine has lost her sister, and Damien, like you, has lost his partner."

"And you?" Maxine asked.

"I have lost my father."

"Maxine!" a voice called through the throng.

"Bonnie?" she swung around.

Rochelle ran up to her and Maxine shook her head

slowly. "I watched her go in," she said. "I didn't get to speak with her or touch her." The steadiness of her voice shocked her. It was as if she'd resigned herself to this new Bonnie-less fate. Sadness was her future. She turned to Rasmus. "Is there room for one more?" she asked.

Rasmus's eyes rolled off to the right and they all stood watch as he ran calculations. He pursed his lips, studied Rochelle, then brought his gaze back to Maxine. "Yes," he said, though he knew the bunker had only been properly outfitted for a total of five.

"Come with us," Maxine begged, taking Rochelle's hand as if she'd earned the right for such familiarity. "He has a place."

Rochelle looked back out to the crowd. "I thought it would be romantic to watch it all happen with a crowd. I should find my bandmates…"

"There's no time," Rasmus said. "In or out?"

"Both or neither," Maxine said and immediately hated herself.

They all piled into an SUV and Rasmus took them away from the throng. The radio repeated all the craziness that was happening, but Maxine reached forward and turned it off.

"Thank you," said Jasmine, a hitch in her voice.

Concert traffic was thick as they approached the city. "That festival was supposed to be our anniversary celebration," Maxine said with sadness.

"This is the kind of anniversary no one wants to cele-brate," Rochelle said. "I might write a song about that."

After a short drive through heavy traffic they pulled into a small parking lot behind a hotel. Maxine looked at Rasmus with doubt. "Trust me," he said, holding out his hand, and she took it.

He led their tiny group through staff hallways and then through a coded door until they stood before a vault. He spoke into an intercom box on the wall beside the door. "Mother, it's me." Then he spun the combination and broke the seal with a loud hiss.

The door opened and all four guests gasped at what lay before them.

A woman rushed forward and attacked Rasmus with a desperate embrace.

"My mother," Rasmus said. "Imogen." He untangled himself from her grip and held her at arms length. "You see?" he said. "I am fine. I am back."

Maxine could see the thin line the women tread, tears hanging in her eyes, hands trembling. She reached out to her. "I'm Maxine. Max."

Imogen touched her face. "So pretty," she said. "Welcome."

She gestured for them to follow her into the space. Rasmus sealed the door and spun the dial with a finality that caught Maxine in the gut.

They were only half-way through the tour when the

ground began to shake. Gathered around the little screen in the living room, they all watched the chaos at Eden.

Labour Day | Eden

The goats did not want to be Edgar's friend. Nor did the chickens. But Edgar was not a quitter; he was a hunter. A friend hunter.

The chickens were fun, but they were mean. One hit him with the tip of its wing and hurt his eye. The goats were different. They were more annoyed than mean. The smallest seemed most amenable to Edgar's presence. Edgar liked the sound it made—it rattled between his ears and Edgar yowled back, rubbing up against Goat's hind legs. Goat kicked, but only the first time. Edgar knew he would win her over.

Another goat, the bigger one with horns on its head, had a smell that made Edgar giddy, but he didn't like Edgar to get too close. Edgar had to settle for rolling in the straw after the big goat left.

When a human approached with a bucket, Edgar watched from behind a yellow bale as white liquid shot into the metal pail with a *sckwishk sckwishk* sound. He tasted the air with his tongue and thought he was in heaven. When the human left, he snuck up behind Goat and caught a drop of the white stuff on his tongue and he almost died with pleasure. This wasn't like the white stuff Jude would give him—Jude… where was Jude? He hadn't seen her for a while now—this was richer and warmer with a little of that musky perfume the big goat wore like a coat.

The next time a human approached, he didn't carry a bucket. Edgar was disappointed. The human made clicking sounds and spoke in gentle tones and Edgar knew he was kind. The human put ropes around the goats' necks and led them down a path to a hole in the mountain. Edgar stalked them from behind, keeping himself shadowed as he marched down a line of sweet potato plants.

Where was Goat going? And where was Jude? And *where* was Goat *going*?

The human came back and did the same with the twenty chickens. He didn't put ropes around their necks. Instead, he coaxed them into white boxes. These too disappeared into the mountain.

Everything became very quiet. Even the bees had stopped their humming. Their hives were wrapped in thick blankets. Why, Edgar could not imagine.

He did not like the silence. Jude always had music playing. Where was Jude?

He sniffed at the mountain where his friends had disappeared. He could still smell them. Them and the stinky humans who he'd followed before. He could not smell Jude.

Edgar padded back to the goat pen and dug a nest in the hay where the big goat usually lay. He placed his chin on his paws and he waited.

Labour Day | Eden, the mine

I and the eight people I stood in line with were directed onto a small elevator. With the door closed we couldn't help but be touching one another. I squirmed in the cramped quarters but knew complaining would accomplish nothing.

One man prayed aloud in Aramaic. A woman, slightly older than me, stood straight, the set of her shoulders firm, yet tears coursed down her cheeks as she clasped a crumpled photograph of three children to her chest.

One masked man rode with us. He operated the buttons, sending us into a slow descent that caused my belly to drop. The whole contraption rattled and groaned as we descended deeper and deeper into the earth.

One by one he put a bag into each of our hands. "We will be down in the mine for three days," he said. "In these bags you will find a blanket, some toiletry items, a flashlight, four bottles of water, and enough protein packs to sustain you until we return to the surface. You must ration your supplies. It is most important that you remain calm. Collect your strength and try to use the time to rest and resign yourself to this new way of life. When we do come back up, everything will be different."

His hand brushed mine as he passed a bag to me. "Yours has three days worth of prenatal medications. Be sure to take them. The health of your child is of the utmost importance."

"Thank you," I whispered. I recognized his voice as that of the kind man in the hangar.

He pushed his mask back so it rested on his forehead. I felt a rush of heat move through me as I gazed on his face for the first time. His skin was dark and smooth, his eyes large and reflective, blue like water, softened by a warmth I knew I didn't deserve.

"I'm Daniel," he said. "If you need anything, you come and find me." He tucked his hand into my empty one in a gesture of welcome that took me by surprise. His hand was large and the way it fit against my palm felt natural and good.

"Aiya," I said. I didn't want to let go.

"We will see each other again, Aiya," he said, his smile rising to his eyes, taking back his hand and leaving mine inexplicably cold.

The light flickered overhead as the elevator cart came to rest. Daniel opened the door and gestured for us to leave. The air was cool and damp. I felt his hand on my arm and I looked back to lock eyes with him once again before he shut the door for the journey back to the surface.

"It will be fine," he said and I nodded dumbly, needing to trust something—anything.

A woman led us this time. She too had worn a lion mask but now pulled it down so it hung around her neck like a dramatic scarf. Eden had been shut off from the world, they had no access here, so deep in the ground, which meant the crew no longer had need of anonymity. We were all in this together.

She led us down a long hall at the end of which stood a wide opening draped in thick plastic. She pushed it aside and took us into a massive chamber in which a huge white tent stood. Within the tent, cots sat row upon row. It looked like a hospital triage centre' from an old war movie.

"Won't we run out of air?" I asked.

"We have a system in place for that. As long as our batteries maintain, we will all have plenty to breathe. Select a bed," the woman said. "Men on that side, women on this side. There is to be no sexual activity. You must respect this rule. At the back of the tent you will see an exit. Through those flaps you will find a row of portable washrooms. When this goes down you can expect all power to be lost. We could be in darkness for up to twenty-four hours before the grid can be restored with our backup solar battery packs and generators. Sleep as much as you can through this time. It will speed things up for you. This will not be easy, but it will be survivable if we all remain calm and cooperative."

Clutching my little survival pack, I wandered past a large bird cage containing four canaries and then along the rows of women's beds until I found one as close to the washroom exits as I could. With a baby pressing against my bladder, I knew I needed to plan my stay well.

The cot was dressed in white sheets and had one white pillow. There was a folded up tracksuit—grey—and a pair of heavy socks piled neatly at the foot of the bed.

"It's like the Four Seasons," a girl said from across the aisle. A bathing suit hung off the frame of her cot. "How'd your seizure go?" she asked. "They got me at the public pool. I didn't even have any clothes until I got down here." She pulled at the waist of the jogging pants. "Not sure this is any better, but at least it's dry."

I told her my story.

"What do you think your husband's doing right now?" she asked, noticing my ring.

"His assistant," I said.

Chapter Twenty-Six
Labour Day | Leslieville

Ryan knocked the bitch up so she wouldn't leave him. Not that she ever would, she was a timid mouse with conservative morals and a nice rack, but this would seal the deal. Planting a baby in her would lock her down for sure. Problem was, he didn't even want a baby. He wanted a hot wife who looked good on his arm at professional events, who didn't stick her nose into his business, and who put out whenever *he* wanted it. The irony was that the putting out (or the "putting in" harr harr) turned her from hot to cold. Not that he even wanted to touch her now. Her slender frame was bulbous with his offspring and he found himself repulsed when he looked at her, even if her breasts were even perkier than before.

He used to call her Babe. Now he didn't call her anything, just spoke to her like he might a barista. "Get me a 19-year-old with a shot of juicy ass, would ya."

In the beginning there had been tenderness. She had been sweet, he had been charming, her laugh alone had made his pants a little tighter. Oh, he used to love to make her laugh alright. But then he discovered how it felt to make her cry, how by knocking her down he unlocked some primal desire within himself so that he could hardly wait to get to the office, lock the door, and roughly guide Gwen down until she was on her knees in front of him. She'd have kicked off her shoes by then and the sight of her bare feet would almost take him over the edge before she'd even unbuckled his belt. Fat wife at home, slut assistant at work. Ain't life grand? Yes, there had been tenderness, but now he knew passion—red, burning, angry passion—and it was better than love.

Labour Day | Russia

Seventeen 800-kiloton nuclear warheads were housed in the blast range vicinity of Moscow, Russia. For sixteen of those, codes were manipulated to send them plummeting into the ocean without detonation, rendering them useless, strange discoveries for an underwater explorer centuries down the line should humanity indeed rebuild after what was about to transpire. In the chaos of the closing time clock, while the whole planet tracked the meteorite as it sped towards the huge city, one warhead launched fully armed, a careless mistake by a rushed decision that would surely change the world forever should there ever come a time that the world remembered this moment.

Labour Day | Eden, the mine

Screens mounted around the mine tent showed three different feeds. One was the major news network, one an internet satire show, and the third, a countdown clock. Twenty minutes until the end of the world. The numbers disappeared and Rajiv Montgomery Noah's face filled the screen.

"Residents of Eden," he began. "Once again, I welcome you. Your fear is understandable, but I implore you to be strong in this, Earth's final moments. You will have much time over the next few days and weeks to mourn what you have lost, but you face a lifetime of celebrating what you have gained and what you can do for the future of the human race. In your weeping, I pray you find a small dash of gratitude with which to cultivate your new life here." He paused there, his eyes shifting away from the monitor then drifting back, glistening. "My heart is broken for the nonbelievers. I did everything in my human power to spread the word I was given and yet not one world leader would heed my warning. There could have been many of these safe-havens erected around the globe, yet they all called me a fool. Well, today the jester inherits the kingdom." A tear slipped down his face and his daughter appeared behind him, her hand resting on his shoulder. "My daughter and I have only one dream and that dream is you. Bear with us through this trial and we trust you will grow to love us. It won't be long now." The monitor switched back to the countdown.

Eleven minutes.

One of the feeds panned over the crowds gathering outside the gates. They had their own countdown clock and the jubilee they seemed to exude reminded me of old videos I'd seen of New Years Eve in New York City. No one out there seemed to be harbouring the same fear I was feeling so deep in the earth. It didn't seem the news of the meteorite had dampened any spirits. Russia was so far away, I supposed. And we were all experts at ignoring the atrocities across the ocean, naively believing they didn't affect us.

Still, we were not in a good state, even here in the sophisticated west. Everyone knew that, though no one (besides Rajiv) truly thought it meant the end was nigh. The oceans were swelling. The melting ice caps had seen to that. Soon every shore-bound city would be a haunt for mermaids and scuba divers. You would be able to pay a handsome sum to take a glass-bottom boat out to see the Statue of Liberty. They'd create some sort of encasing bubble that protected the flame somehow. I'd watched a documentary about that once, showing how preserving the flame meant things would turn out okay in the end. The logic never made sense but I liked the imagery of it though it meant little to me. Projectionists said it would take another two centuries for the waters to reach the centre of every major landmass. My children and I would be safe from a global flood.

Eight minutes.

In the final days, Rajiv Montgomery Noah claimed a new planet, spinning on its own elliptical orbit, would come in line with the moon in such a way that it would cause a gravitational push that would confuse our tides. The crossing of orbits would ignite an influx of meteors, causing the biggest shower ever seen—pieces of space rock, too big to be disintegrated by our atmosphere. If we were lucky, they wouldn't hit anywhere near our five major nuclear epicentres; but at the very least, they would strike the earth, destroying anything in their path, causing enough disruption of the earth's crust that plates would shift, earthquakes would begin, spreading across the globe like dominos, volcanos would erupt, spurred to boil in all the commotion. Rajiv called it a Trifecta of Destruction. NASA had called it ridiculous and could find no solid proof to back up the claim until Lisimba was discovered mere hours ago, barrelling straight for us—straight for the nuclear epicentre of Russia, of all places. Though the mood outside the gates of Eden remained celebratory, the shift to solemnity in the news rooms was obvious.

Four minutes.

"…the strangest thing," a voice was saying from one of the news broadcasters. "Reports are coming in of millions of dead fish lining the shores of beaches across the world." The screen flipped through a collection of photos and short videos grabbed from various social media outlets. The sand was black with the bodies of sea creatures. Fish, dolphins, sharks. I looked away and squeezed my eyes shut.

Two minutes.

"Oh god," the girl across the aisle said. She grabbed her pillow and hugged it against her.

"We've got eyes on the meteorite!" an excited newscaster announced, the screen showing a wide shot of Moscow's impending doom. "It's breaking up!" We could see pieces big as houses calving off from the mother-rock that remained impossibly big.

"Maybe it will all fall apart before it hits," someone offered. "Maybe it's just a show, just a shock to scare us straight."

"We're stuck here either way, aren't we?" someone else reminded them.

The television exploded with an alarm. "Russia launches nuclear attack on Canada. Claims it is an accident. Residents of the GTA should seek shelter immediately."

Confusion ensued as the newscasters tried to make sense of the information being fed into their earpieces. "It sounds like in a rushed attempt to unload warheads from the Moscow area, one was accidentally employed for attack rather than destruction. Russia claims this is not an act of war."

The screens switched to an old interview with Rajiv. "My mother told me it would be a trinity of destruction: sky, earth, and man."

"It seems the prophesy of Mr. Noah is coming to pass. Early inquiries reveal no connection between Moscow and Rajiv. Kiss your loved ones," the newscaster said. "We don't know what's next."

Labour Day | Leslieville

Ryan's head was a little cooler as he navigated the Jeep through traffic on his way back home. He'd spent the night on the couch in his office after a day of ravenous "love making." He'd had Gwen twice that day: once in the handicapped stall of the seventh floor bathroom and once against the photocopier after the last professor left. He'd hit the big green start button as he'd reached his climax and a bright light had assaulted them while she screamed her pleasure (because she knew he liked it when she did that) and the machine had spit out an image of her face pressed against the glass, looking pained, like someone awaiting the guillotine. Nothing had ever excited him more. He could feel the folded paper in his pocket now and he couldn't wait to look at it again. He was going to hide it behind the framed painting of a misty tree that hung in the bathroom—half bare, half lush—one of Aiya's prints from her "Seasons" series which had seen some small success in little galleries across Canada (and two in the US).

The radio was spewing nonsense about Rajiv Montgomery Noah's "reaping" and something about a space rock heading to Moscow and how everyone was scared of bombs. Pure nonsense. He changed the channel, but it was the same thing everywhere.

"As promised, Rajiv Montgomery Noah of the Rabbit Mountain Eden, is following through on his promise. All across North and South America, people have disappeared from their homes and their places of employment, one account even states a woman was pulled from a grocery store, her cart and screaming toddler left abandoned in the produce aisle. Like the rapture, this unprecedented event is wreaking chaos on families and businesses alike."

Ryan laughed. "Bullshit!" He one-handed a Tic-Tac bottle and shook a few into his mouth. He could smell Gwen on his fingers and he laughed again. Aiya would never know. Not that he wanted to protect her, but because it was hotter to have a secret; it made him that much more powerful over her, even if she didn't understand why.

There were moments, brief though they were, when he wondered what had become of them—though he knew the answer. His father. He had become his father. He wouldn't go out like that man though, no sir. The bottle didn't have a grip on him. Sure, he loved a bourbon on the rocks, but he wasn't led by it. His liver was right as rain, fuck you very much. He adjusted his pants. He was led by something else.

When he first saw Aiya, it was her light that attracted him. He didn't believe in auras or any of that crap, but she was... *glowing*. And so young. He'd gone to the art show because it was his duty to placate these students—most of whom would never amount to anything; most of whom would go on to work retail, or get their teaching degree. And there she was, a first year art student allowed to show with the graduate students because she was just that good. She'd worn a mini dress and tall boots that drove him crazy and the way she put her lips against the champagne glass she was only just old enough to drink, the way they always looked wet, and how her eyes flashed around the room with nervous excitement. Later that night, when he took her small hand and raised it to his lips like an archaic prince, he told her she tasted like summer. "You should taste the rest of me," she'd teased, tricking him into thinking she had the experience of a 40-year-old in the body of a teenager. He offered $3,000 for her oil on wood of a woman by the sea, and she'd been his.

"I own you," he'd whispered into her ear much later that night.

"Yes," she'd breathed, exhausted after the education he'd freely offered.

And he owned her still.

He tried to imagine bending her over a photocopier, but he couldn't do it. She didn't bend that way. She liked him to be slow and gentle. Slow and gentle is how you grow tired of someone. Slow and gentle is why you find the opposite in a Gwen: a slouch at the desk, but a wizard beneath it, if you get the drift.

He noticed the open door before he saw the broken glass, the two together caused rage and terror to collide in his brain. He went blind for a second before racing into the loft.

"Aiya?" he called as he entered the living room. A spilled mug of tea had stained the expensive wool rug and he swore. "Aiya!"

Nothing.

He ran down the hall, checking the bedroom, the bathroom, the studio. "Aiya!"

Had she done it? Had she left him?

His eyes landed on an envelope, propped against a glass on the kitchen island. "Mr. Efron," it said in skilled calligraphy. He tore into it.

From the desk of Rajiv Montgomery Noah,
Rabbit Mountain, Eden

Mr. Ryan Efron,

On Sunday, September 6, your wife, one Aiya Elaine Efron, who gave her consent through the opt-in option laid out in my digital newsletter (with which she engaged on May 30), to ingest a chip that would give us access to her full medical history, projected health expectation, educational transcripts, professional curriculum vitae, and immediate location. A sophisticated algorithm developed by the top minds in current tech selected her from a pool of more than eight million potentials as a positive and needed addition to our surviving force. On her consent, she has been collected and detained for transportation to Eden where she and your unborn child will assume an integral role in the perpetuation of the human race. She is safe. She was not harmed. We will support her in her grief and ensure that your child is raised in a home that is full of love that he might also attain his fullest potential.

This loss is deep. Please accept my sincere condolences and eternal thanks for the sacrifice you have made. May your final moments be warmed by the memories of your wife and the light she brought into your life. For though this world descends into darkness, it is the promise of a new day that brings us hope. Chin up. Your loss makes you a hero.

Yours, Rajiv Montgomery Noah

Labour Day | Eden, the mine

People continued to filter in from the elevators in groups of nine. We all wore the same shell-shocked expression, terri-fied, curious, unsure who to trust. I didn't know how to behave around so many beautiful people. I grabbed the sweatshirt from my cot and pulled it over my head as if it would hide my plainness. I became a whale. I thought of all those dead sea creatures plastered across the shores and the screens and I hated myself and my ugliness. Three days down here and it might begin to smell like those shorelines. I wasn't sure I could take it. I hated tuna.

One minute.

There were still a few empty beds. They were bringing one last group down on the elevator. It felt like all the air had been sucked out of the chamber and we'd been left, frozen, suspended in a perpetual moment of waiting. I thought I might lose my mind.

0:03

0:02

0:01

0:00

A hush fell over the room. The tension was palpable. On the television screens the crowds outside wore cruel expressions of mockery as the timer ticked past zero. A large sign bobbed in the background, painted with the words *We Told You So!* Ripples of laughter bubbled up to pulsing screams, finally turning into a chant: *Let them go! Let them go! Let them go!* To the wider world we were now victims. Hostages. I felt no fear of my captor, truly I didn't. I coveted his kindness. What I feared was the unknown. What would happen now?

We watched the rock hit Moscow. Though reduced to half its entry size, it still took out almost 2000 square kilometres of the city. The violence of the hit caused tectonic plates to shift, beginning the slow work of worldwide chaos as earthquakes started, blooming out from ground zero, stirring monsters from the depths that hadn't been disturbed in millennia—Ecuador, Hawaii, Italy, Mexico, the Philippines, Washington. Even in the chaos of the immediate aftermath, new meteors were being discovered, coming out of the blindspot and barrelling toward the earth. We watched as a reporter pulled out their earpiece and ran from the broadcast stage.

Rajiv spoke to us again through the screen, his voice gravelly with emotion. "Here we witness the beginning of the end. The destruction caused by Lisimba and its various pieces has started a chain reaction that we will soon feel. The irony and tragedy of it all is that the launching of the warhead saved no one in Moscow, and though it will bring about a swifter end to those it meets mere minutes from now, they would not be saved had it not been launched. There is a time to be born and a time to die. It is all as it must be."

Chapter Twenty-Seven
Labour Day | New Mexico

Extension cords ran down from the farmhouse into the bunker, firing up the television that broadcast the happenings at Eden. The Peters knew it was coming. They knew everything. It wasn't like RMN had kept secrets. He had revealed it all. He didn't even want money—he had enough of that—he just wanted ears to hear what he had to share. He wanted to save the world. But the world wouldn't let him. His final email had nearly broken their hearts. They'd read it together, hunched around the laptop, weeping freely as they realized this really was the beginning of the true end.

"It will be the worst day," Jessie told his wife.

"We'll make it," Penny had said.

"Do you think we'll ever get to see that documentary we were interviewed for?" Jessie asked.

"No. But I wish we could."

They had entered the earth as Rajiv Montgomery Noah gave his final speech from within his fortress: *Demands? These people are my only demands…*

They held each other as they watched the camera pan the group assembled within his walls, the two hundred he had saved through the hunting of his lions.

"Look at them," Penny said. "They're all so beautiful."

"Of course they are, Penny," Jessie responded. "Why wouldn't they be? If you had the means to restart humanity, wouldn't you want to pull from the very best genes? He was honest about that too. He told us that his program found the best of the best of the best. I'm pretty sure gorgeous matters… even at the end of the world the beautiful people have a leg up on everyone else."

"Humph."

"Are your feelings hurt, love? You know I think you're perfect."

Tears streamed down her face. "I want to be there, with those people."

"I know," he said. "But we're not and so we have to move on. We have to survive. We have to do just as he told us to do."

"I'll miss the sun."

"I'll miss McDonalds."

She'd slapped him then. Lightly. Playfully. "Idiot!"

And he kissed her. The kind of hard kiss that squished her nose and would have looked ugly on a movie screen but that held more words than anything he could have said out loud. She loved him desperately. End of the world or not, she was content. He was her world.

A rumble shook through the ground, vibrating up into their chests, like the uncomfortable, invigorating invasion of a rock concert.

"It's starting," Jessie whispered.

"Oh god," Penny cried, tucking her face against his shoulder.

Labour Day | Leslieville

Ryan couldn't contain the emotions that plagued his body when he read the letter. Rage, fear, abandonment, hate, horror. He carried Rajiv's note to the sink and let it fall against the bottom. He pulled a drawer open and grabbed a barbecue lighter which he used to light the paper. He grabbed a bourbon bottle and a glass from a shelf, opened the bottle and ignored the glass, pulling a swig straight from the tapered lip. He spit a little in the sink and the flame barrelled upwards, singeing his eyebrows before settling back down and eating through the rest of the note.

On her consent, she has been collected and detained for transportation to Eden where she and your unborn child will assume an integral role in the perpetuation of the human race.

"Bullshit," he said to the sink when nothing remained but a tiny pile of ash. "Aiya!" he called out.

He wandered back to the living room, stepping onto the tea-stained carpet and sitting in the exact spot his wife sat when he left the morning before. The seat was cold, like she'd already been gone for years. Like she'd never been there in the first place. He pulled the photocopy of Gwen's face from his pocket, but it didn't give him the dopamine hit he needed. He took another long drink of bourbon. "Aiya!" There were tears on his cheek. *What was this?* He wiped at his face and tossed the photocopy onto the coffee table. Gwen's twisted face was ugly. He dribbled some of the alcohol onto his hands to sterilize away her scent. It added to the carpet stain. *How could she?*

The thing was, he'd done it too. He'd signed up for the newsletter—ironically, of course, so he could be part of the conversation at work and at the club. Aiya had mentioned it. He'd said, "You better not fall for that shit," even though he himself had fallen for it. He drank the orange Kool-Aid and it reminded him of his mother.

"You taste like summer." That's the first real thing he'd ever said to Aiya. Summer. He never even knew a season could have a taste until he'd met her. What a woman. What a gift. "Aiya!" He was sobbing now, regret pouring out even though, in the deepest part of him, he knew that if she walked through the door right now he'd hit her—or worse—for making him worry.

Their wedding photo was on the side table. He lifted it and pulled it out of the frame, letting the thin glass fall back against the table where it broke into three pieces. He wondered how it would feel to run one of those edges along Aiya's white thigh. He wondered how it would feel to hold her in his arms one more time. Startled, he suddenly realized he believed this whole insanity. He believed in Noah's Ark. He believed he was going to die. And he thought that maybe, just maybe, he actually did love his wife in his own strange and broken way. He wanted her there with him.

The wedding photo showed them standing on the front steps of the First Presbyterian Church. They looked happy. Young. Alive. He tore the picture down the centre, separating them. He tossed himself to the floor. He held Aiya up before his face, taking another swig from the bottle without closing his eyes, and then he let his head fall back.

Labour Day | Toronto

Two kilometres above Pearson International Airport, an 800 kiloton nuclear warhead exploded. The leader responsible for launching it was already dead, killed when the shockwaves from the meteorite that hit his city crumbled the mountain he hid within.

A massive fireball instantly vaporized the airport, airplanes, and all structures surrounding it, producing an immense blast wave which crushed even the heavily built concrete structures. Within half a second, all metal construction within the Congress Centre and Grandstand Casino was melted, as was the asphalt in the streets even before the blast wave hit, tossing burning cars into the air and flattening buildings. As the fire moved into Brampton and Mississauga, all combustible materials illuminated by the fireball spewed fire and black smoke. The Guardian Lions outside the Royal Ontario Museum, markers of the Qing Dynasty of 1650-1750, exploded into violet projectiles, and all the glass and metal that made up the angular architecture of the gallery melted into a bubbling stew. The CN Tower tried to topple but was almost fully consumed by flame and melted away before it could touch the ground. Toronto Island disappeared entirely. Moving into

Oakville, Vaughn, and Richmond Hill, residential structures were destroyed and high-rises heavily damaged. Within ten minutes of the detonation, everything within 100 square kilometres was destroyed with fires burning as far away as the Michigan border, Rochester New York, and Kingston, Ontario. The heat guaranteed no survivors, charring any skin left exposed if it hadn't already burned up the clothing a person was wearing. And from there, fires crept deeper, fingers of flame licking their way across the continent in a determined and pre-ordained execution as radioactive fallout was already beginning and long-silent volcanos—the sleeping giants of the underworld—began to wake, while space rocks rained from the sky like violent, murderous acid rain.

Labour Day | Leslieville

There was a click and the power went out. Ryan's heart beat like a hammer. A low rumble shook the floor and outside, car alarms started to sound. Peace fell over him. He stopped crying. He held the image of Aiya against his chest, wrapping it up in all the regret he could find. If she walked in, he'd kill her, but right now, he just wanted to hold her. Gwen, and all the other Gwen-like sluts he'd known during their eight year marriage, were distant memories; not mistakes, per se, but things/conquests/ whores that held no current value in the light of the rumbling earth. A loud roar sounded, the ground shook more. A crack appeared in the ceiling above him and he watched it move right through the crown moulding and down the wall. The windows shattered, he jumped at the sound and spilled the bourbon down his front. When the fire came, he had a moment to think that spill had been a blessing because it would go faster that way. The seconds it took for the flames to enter his lungs through a mouth stretched wide in a grotesque scream, were long enough for him to feel each blood cell melt, to notice the way skin will bubble and boil like a Shakespearian tragedy, to feel his scalp peel away from his skull, and to remember that once, he was lucky enough to taste summer.

Labour Day | The International Space Station

It had been all hands on deck since they lost communication with ground control over eight hours before. The crew was tired and grumpy and nervous. This was one of the longest radio silences on record and they couldn't find the problem, trusting that those on the ground would be able to troubleshoot before it went on much longer.

From Victor Korsakov's favourite window, the earth

looked normal. A blue, green, brown marble that held his family. He had a new baby girl—little Sofiya—he was going to meet in three short (long) months, and he blew a kiss at Russia as they orbited past it.

When he first saw the fire, he thought it was just one of the sixteen sunrises he saw every day, but this did not peek like a sunrise. No, it moved like rolling fingers crawling from both sides until they met in the middle and the earth looked like a new sun.

"*Bozhe moy*," Korsakov said, squinting against the excruciating brightness. *My God.*

Labour Day | Rabbit Mountain

Jude finished her beer and moved into the RV, shutting the door. She had waited for Brett but he hadn't returned, likely still waiting in line for one of the six porta-potties that were not sufficient to serve the crowd that had gathered. She shook four Ambien into her palm and kicked them back with a deep swing of water. It was enough to knock her out, not kill her. If Rajiv was wrong, she would wake up with one hell of a hangover.

After a moment of consideration, Jude spun the dial on the safe and pulled out the camera one last time. Rather than waste time with a tripod, she balanced it on the doghouse in the centre console and sat on the floor in front of it to record her final thoughts for the world.

"Hello, my name is Jude Abbott…" she began.

Labour Day | New Mexico

Belinda Carlisle sang her hymn on repeat.

The tabloid stations loved it—resurrecting the 1980s to mock a man who said they wouldn't make it to the 2030s. "Heaven is a Place on Earth." Penny wished for a glimpse into the heaven of Rajiv Montgomery Noah. She peered around their shelter, at the cement block walls and metal furniture and swaying bare bulbs. To her, heaven meant survival. To Rajiv it meant luxury box seats. To just have a peek inside one of those perfect little homes that lined one of his perfect little streets…

They heard a crash above their heads and on the television screens fires were erupting in the crowd gathered outside of Eden. "This is it," Penny said.

Pounding started on the outer door, insistent and desperate. "Wait here," Jessie said as if Penny had anywhere to go.

He rushed to the inner door and turned the lever, breaking the seal before running the cinderblock hall to the outer door. He could hear desperate cries from the other side. When he got the door open, a crowd pushed their way in, knocking him to the ground and bruising his ribs. He sealed the door again and followed them back to the large living area where Penny waited, wide-eyed.

The group lowered a man to the ground as Jessie limped back into the room, clutching his side.

Two of the women were crying and another worked to rip open the shirt of the man on the ground and assess his wounds.

"What happened?" Penny asked.

"Hell happened," one of them said—their neighbour from across the road. "Fire is just falling from the sky. It all happened so fast…That old bastard was right after all."

Penny counted the heads suddenly represented in their little bomb shelter. Thirteen. "Shit!" she said.

Another neighbour clapped her on the back. "Yeah," he said. "Shit."

Labour Day | Rabbit Mountain

Jude got into the driver's seat where she had a clear view of the sealed wall. The party raged around her and she felt herself grow heavy, the sweet arms of sleep ready to receive her as she smiled, remembering Brett's big hands on her body. It had been so long since she'd allowed someone in like that. Funny how the end of the world can remind you of what's important. Funny how human connection, in the end, is the only thing that truly matters. He had left his flannel behind and she put it on instead of her own, wanting to be wrapped up in his smell, unconcerned about the heat that continued to climb inside the RV. She said a prayer as she drifted. A word of thanks. Rajiv was right. Everything was a prayer. This was her church. She felt close to God in a way she hadn't before. All fear of angels had blissfully disappeared because, in the end, she chose love over fear.

Labour Day | Austin, Texas

Number 94 was rushing the goal line, on track to make the winning catch for the pennant. The stands were full of screaming students and proud parents. It happened so fast that no one saw, but the ball melted in mid-air, dripping steaming tears of leather onto the turf as 94's shoes began to melt and his jersey started to burn and the stands became writhing pillars of fire that quickly collapsed into a boiling mass of metal.

Labour Day | Ngong, Kenya

Dust billowed as Aasir Kamau ran a rural road just west of Nairobi. His pulse was on point and he was making better time than yesterday. A line of fire shot down in front of him and he skipped to a stop. His heart rate monitor screamed. He veered back the way he had come but a line of fire crossed the path. All around him, fire. He fell to his knees and lifted his palms to the sky. "*Mikononi mwako*," he yelled. *Into your hands.* Then he brought his own hands together and closed his eyes as the fire consumed him.

Labour Day | Washington, DC

A sinkhole on the north lawn opened up to receive the White House within moments of the first tremor. It took seven minutes for the massive structure to completely disappear into the chasm they claimed to have fixed in 2018. It took the president thirty-six minutes to suffocate when the systems designed to keep the bunker habitable were crushed by the fallen building. The vice president had been in the bathroom at the time and the extra walls kept her protected and alive for an additional four minutes. This was not a blessing.

Labour Day | Pyongyang, North Korea

There were 427 people aboard the Pyongyang Metro when the first wave hit. Though all power was knocked out, most of them survived for more than an hour. One woman suffered a heart attack when the train lurched to a stop. One man was trampled as people rushed the back door. An officer was stabbed when he tried to prevent someone from forcing a set of sliding doors open. It took the heat a while to make it down 110 metres, but like any oven, heat will travel where it is invited, and there was no seal to protect these tunnels from what went on over their heads. Though the flames didn't descend the whole way, the temperature rose, degree by degree, until blisters bubbled on flesh and the screams of 424 people being roasted alive echoed through that death chamber like the torture bells of hell.

Labour Day | Merritt Island, Florida

Jack Hammond was inside Circe31 at the Kennedy Space Centre VAB doing a full system's check beneath the front motherboard when everything lit up with a blinding white light. He hit his head as he pulled out from under the board and tried to make sense of what had happened. Through the front panels, a wicked fire raged. He tried to raise his crew on the walkie-talkie but was only met with static.

He remembered the radio DJ on his way into work that morning, mocking the predictions of that strange Noah character. "Guess this is the last time you'll ever hear me say it, so let's make it count. Good morning, Cape Canaveral!" he had said.

So then it was true. Jack sank to the floor and checked his watch. The shuttle held him like a capsule. Like a coffin. It was built to withstand the 5000° Fahrenheit temperature upon reentry into Earth's atmosphere, so he was fine for the time being. Had the ECLSS air system been turned on and recycling oxygen, he might have been fine for a while, but they weren't scheduled to be tested until the next day. By his calculation, he had seven days of air in the sealed shuttle, but dehydration would likely take him first. He watched the flames through the window and fought to control his breathing, though why and for what, he didn't know.

Labour Day | New Mexico

The picture on the television wavered. The ground continued to shake. Penny imagined the sounds of millions of people being burned alive and she retreated into a corner, drawing her legs up against her chest, and squeezing her eyes shut.

They had prepared for this. They had known this was coming. They had believed. Or she thought she had. In those final moments, while the world beyond their shelter died, she realized that she hadn't. Not really. She had fun following the eccentric leader. It had been exciting to stock the shelter shelves. She even liked the way the neighbours talked. She thought it made her interesting. What she realized now was that she had hoped it had all been a big joke, a hoax, the ravings of a madman.

"He was right," she whispered, holding her hand out for her husband to grasp. His eyes were lit with a strange fire of excitement. He took her hand and sat beside her, pulling her into his arms, and together they watched the neighbours working on the injured man. "It will all be over soon," Jessie said.

The television died and they were in darkness.

Labour Day | Svalbard, aboard the M/S Quest

Geraldine stood on the deck of the ship gazing at the glacier horizon that stood before her. A trip to the Arctic had always been on her bucket list and she'd saved it for the end because she found it beautifully poetic to think she'd be in the coldest place on Earth the day the fires came. Even through her sunglasses, she had to squint as she absorbed the blinding landscape, breathtaking in its stark beauty.

In her hand she held a small, palm-sized capsule, rated to withstand incredible heat. Within it she had placed the ring Rajiv had given her and a letter for the children. A prayer for the future of Daniel and Moriah. It would never reach them, she was wise enough to know that, but the act of writing it and sealing it within a capsule that had the capacity for survival brought her a peace that, in itself, was like a prayer.

There were two words for fear in Hebrew. *Yirah*, which was exhilaration and awe; and *pachad*, which expressed threat and panic and now, while the whole world was wrapped in *pachad*, she welcomed the rush of *yirah*. What a beautiful life she had lived.

She stepped up on the first rung of the safety rail. Behind the glacier, a light bloomed unlike any sunrise she'd ever seen. She moved to the second rung. With a sound like thunder, the glacier split and one large piece collapsed into the ocean, creating a massive wave that rushed to the ship. When it hit, she had made it to the top rung and didn't resist or cry out as she toppled over the edge.

Hitting water that cold was a pain that she had not prepared for, but it only lasted an instant as she sank, her heavy coat sucking in the frigid water and making struggle impossible. She couldn't open her eyes against the pressure, but through her eyelids could see the red orange of fire overtaking the surface of the water. Darkness wrapped around her and she gave herself to it, even as one hand continued to reach for the surface. In the other she held the capsule, fingers frozen around it in a last embrace as her heart, shocked by the cold and lack of oxygen, ceased to beat.

She was too deep for the fires to reach her, even as the top few feet of water evaporated from the violent first wave of heat, not one morsel of that warmth reached her. As all the world burned, she lay as a ghostly statue, pale against the ocean floor.

Labour Day | Rabbit Mountain

There was no answer from the RV when Brett knocked on the door. Between the long trek to the toilets and the massive crowd that had reached a crescendo that even a fighter jet would have struggled to surpass, the journey back to Jude had taken far too long.

Her dark femininity, bold independence, and gentle spirit proved to be the balm he needed as he navigated feelings around his own mortality. He hadn't expected a connection of any kind when he loaded the van for Eden. He'd expected little but his own death, and yet, here he was, on the precipice of the end… the beginning?… looking at something that felt a whole lot like love, though he had nothing true to compare it to. Sure, there had been women in his past, women that he might have loved, but his sadness held him with a richer sense of purpose and ownership than anyone else ever could. Until now.

The door was unlocked and he popped his head inside after knocking.

"Jude?"

No answer.

He saw the bed, blankets and sheets in disarray, pillows on the floor, and he smiled. Why would anyone ever make a bed when it stood as a testament to the truest connection two people could ever know?

When he stepped inside, he saw her, leaned back in the driver's seat and wearing his shirt, head tilted up like a cat reaching for the sun, eyes closed, breathing deep in a peaceful sleep.

He sat opposite her in the passenger seat, turned so he could stare directly at her, tracing the curve of her cheek with his eyes, the sweet way her nose turned up just slightly, those lips…

In the centre console atop the doghouse he saw the typical accoutrement: loose coins, chapstick, phone charger, a 15 amp to 30 amp converter, and an orange plastic pill bottle. Shocked, his first thought was that she'd taken too many, but when he lifted the bottle he could tell it was nearly full. Relief flooded through him and he knocked some into his own hand. *Sleep through the chaos, a new life on the other side,* he thought, and he swallowed the pills.

He leaned over and touched her forehead with his own. "See you soon," he whispered.

She didn't respond audibly, but he felt her warmth in his chest as he leaned back in his own chair and matched her posture. The pills worked quickly and he sank into the darkness, no longer alone, no longer sad, no longer afraid.

Labour Day | Thunder Bay

An oil lamp flickered and the odd collection of humans looked like the eerie faces around an 80s horror movie campfire. But in this film, no one told a ghost story. They were living it. The stone groaned. The noise of the hotel toppling over them had been deafening, their screams and the collapsing history mingling into one extended cacophony of terror.

The ceiling cracked, just a hairline that jutted back from the sealed door to the kitchen area. Every time something else crashed overhead, a trickle of fine debris fell into the bunker, slowly building a small white pile, like an early dusting of snow.

Maxine couldn't stop trembling. She and Rochelle clung to one another, a little warmth in the midst of the biting cold of fear. She tried to picture Bonnie's face, and though she knew it better than she knew her own, she couldn't conjure it from her memory. There were only feelings. Bonnie's presence had helped the world make sense. Safety. Comfort. Home.

With a shaking hand, she dug into her pocket and pulled out her phone, its light cutting through the darkness with a smoothness the lamp couldn't produce. Her lock screen held a picture of her and Bonnie, taken a year before on the day they decided to ride the Staten Island ferry "just for fun" and stayed on it for five round trips "just because they could." They were on the upper deck, Bonnie's mouth wide open in a laugh, her head tipped back slightly but turned towards Maxine who stared right at the camera, the wind pushing her hair across Bonnie's lips. It was her favourite picture of them together. Safety. Comfort. Home.

She touched a finger to Bonnie's face. Her battery said 23%. There was no signal.

"Who's that?" Rochelle asked.

"My home," Maxine chocked.

Rochelle squeezed her and tried to place a light kiss on Maxine's cheek. Instead, her lips hit the soft spot just below her ear and it sent a confusing whisper of pleasure through Maxine's pain.

I'm down the rabbit hole now, she thought dryly.

The phone faded to black and Maxine immediately forgot what Bonnie's face looked like. She pressed the button to light it up again. 22% battery.

She laid her head on Rochelle's shoulder and wept.

Chapter Twenty-Eight

Labour Day | Eden, the mine

Forty-two minutes after the countdown for Lisimba ended, we all watched the screens as in the distance behind the protesters outside of Eden, an orange glow blossomed. A tree on the left side of the camera shot burst into flames. The faces of the crowd turned from mocking to concerned. Someone pointed into the sky and soon every face was turned to see a sun that seemed poised to react to something. Sparks began to fall like rain drops. One man's shirt started to burn and we watched, eyes wide and mouths agape, as he ripped it from his body, throwing it without looking, catching a woman's hair on fire.

Labour Day | Rabbit Mountain

When the fire hit the RV, Jude was blissfully floating through a vast ocean of darkness. As the heat consumed her body, she didn't feel the transition from this plain to the next. For her, it was the same. Peace. Bliss. Rest. She was inside a prayer.

Her Hey Jude keychain melted, dripping hissing aluminum to the floor of the RV and melting right through to the ground beneath. Her Saint Jude charm however, turned from silver to a deep ebony as it swung from the rear-view mirror, the reflective glass now bubbling. He had done as he compelled others to do: he had saved her from the fire.

Had she thought to look beside her before being consumed by peace, by fire, she might have seen Brett, as peacefully unaware as she, welcoming the flames with a willingness that almost looked like a smile. Had she thought to look out her side window before being disappeared into whips of smoke, her ghost weaving with others in a poetry of white and grey, she might have seen Brett's caravan, looking as it always looked, except that at the back, a plastic pipe lay on the ground, ripped from where it had been sealed to the exhaust, let go from its commissioning to complete Rajiv's prophesy, should it be proven wrong. Small strings of yellowed caulking curled against the sand as the pipe lay, rejected among Brett's big footprints. This too, was a prayer.

Labour Day | Eden

Even in sleep, Edgar's ears twitched with anticipation. He stretched and yawned and looked for Jude. The musky smell of Goat covered him. He lifted himself from his straw bed and stretched again, this time arching his back in the way that always made Jude laugh. "Halloween stretch," she would say. He only heard sounds but her tone told him she was happy. Her smell was long gone from his own fur and he suddenly hated the way Goat lingered against him. Where was Goat anyway? He poised himself to bathe when the earth beneath him shook violently. His pupils swelled to round balls and he dashed to the nearest tree, quickly changing his mind when another shudder made a piece of fruit fall like a bomb, splashing him with juice as it burst against the ground. He looked to the buildings and ran that way, seeing water splash out of the fountain as another shock rocked the earth. He dashed beneath a porch, a growl building in his throat though he didn't know where to direct it. With a great roar, the foundation he had tucked against cracked and a small stone hit his back. Every hair he had stood on end, his eyes remained wide, the porch above him held, and darkness suddenly flooded the world. "Jude!" he cried out, his meow dusty and pained. "Goat!"

He raced from his hiding place and ran toward the rock that had swallowed his friends. The place they had disappeared into was sealed shut, though he could smell them like they stood there even now.

"Jude!" Where was his mistress? She needed him now and she wasn't here.

There! A fissure in the rock! His whiskers told him it was just wide enough to accommodate him and he squeezed inside, going deeper and deeper, feeling the concussions of the earth, crying, suddenly thinking of his mother, warm warm mother, milk, joy, peace. He met a wall deep within and curled up against it. It was cold. He knew he had been moving down. He was inside the earth. He was the world now. The darkness was so total even his cat-eye night vision revealed nothing. He heard a beetle scurry somewhere deeper than he could fit.

He cried. "Jude! Goat!"

But he was alone at the end of the world.

Labour Day | Eden, the mine

Gasps spread through the tent. I sat, rigid, my hand over my mouth.

More flames. Too much fire. Hell had come to Earth. The cameras sputtered and cut out; but not before we saw a clear shot of people flinging their burning bodies against the walls of Eden, a sudden gesture of *I believe* that came far too late. They could knock as long as they had breath, but it would do no good. Faith can only purchase a ticket *before* the main act takes the stage.

A great rumble was felt beneath us, like the very heart of the earth was breaking, as if the whole mountain was preparing to tumble away into the fire. I squeezed my eyes and tried to erase the sight of the burning bodies. I tried to centre my thoughts on the hope promised by Rajiv Montgomery Noah.

How could he have been right?

And why had no one believed him?

This was exactly what he said would happen.

Was Ryan already dead? The baby kicked and a sob escaped my lips, so loud and wretched that it scared me. It didn't sound human. It sounded like dying. I tried to resist. I tried to hold back and hold it in but it exploded from me in a violent rush of raw terror. I shouldn't have worried.

The sound of it was lost in the emotional outbreak throughout the whole tent.

All around me people cried out or prayed or screamed. The woman across from me rocked back and forth, her head in her hands, saying, "No, no, no, no, no."

I heard rain falling on the top of the tent but knew that couldn't be true. I knew it had to be bits of the mountain falling down on us. First dust, then rocks.

I waited to die.

The lights flickered. The ground shook. The people wailed. The world died.

And finally, without fanfare, with a sound of a fizzling sparkler—the kind we'd run around with as children on Canada Day—the lights went out.

Chapter Twenty-Nine

All across the globe, the earth shared the most universal experience it had shared since the devastating pandemic of 2020. That outbreak claimed 1% of the population. This claimed 99.998%. Finally, the world was one.

Epilogue

The fires burned for six days. On the seventh day, the earth rested. Silence, unknown since before the industrial revolution, occupied space that hadn't made room for it in centuries. Smoke hissed up from the skeletons of buildings and wind uncovered and recovered human remains; a ribcage here, a leg burned black there, a hand, melted wedding ring like part of the bone. In downtown Toronto, a high-rise that hung on during the initial earthquake finally let go, toppling to the ground in cascades of dust and flying cement. A chunk of rebar hit a car, igniting the alarm system, pulsing red brake lights through the fog as it screamed its distress and would continue to do so until the battery died. Did it make a sound? There was no one there to know.

This new ash-covered planet greeted morning and evening with no fanfare, day nearly as dark as the night as the sun remained hidden by the hanging cloud of smoke and pollution and toxic gases. Temperatures dropped by degrees each day as the earth's only heat source was denied.

At Rabbit Mountain, a war zone spread out as far as the eye could see—if there were any eyes left to witness such a thing. The ash lay like snow. There was no wind. There was no sun. Just a constant dusk that faded to deep night that faded back into dusk as echoes of shockwaves continued to assault the land, growing fainter as hours passed.

The husks of vehicles lay scattered with no discernible pattern. With imagination one might understand that one shape was a sedan, another a minivan. There was a pickup and a fry truck. And there was an RV. All hidden beneath the ash like stoic dinosaur remains.

The mountain stood, wounded but not destroyed, a massive bubble standing firm but covered in the same thick ash as everything else. Were it not for the perfect shape of its curve, it could have been mistaken for stone, just another part of the mountain, so dense and heavy with rock that no life could have been sustained within.

Snow started to fall in the northern hemispheres by

day nine. It was not pristine and clean like one might expect, it was grey and ugly, a dirty blanket of shame as nature desperately tried to wash the atmosphere of filth. By day twelve, there was snow in Mexico. On day seventeen, the Caribbean was buried.

But why did it matter? Who was there to see it?

The earth became the surface of the moon. Darkness became its mistress. Cold leaked into the top layer of soil and crept its icy fingers down to the subsoil, questing for the bedrock where it might reimagine the planet's weights and measures.

Ice began to creep across the ocean. Creatures of the deep that had avoided the initial destruction sought safety in caves, already accustomed to a life without light, tapping into evolutionary instincts that allowed them to slow their metabolic rates and enter a state of near hibernation. Would they survive an earth without sun? Why did it matter? Who would be there to know?

Up in the International Space Station, Victor Korsakov continued trying to reach ground control even though he knew in his heart it was futile. He looked for a change in the earth's grey covering each time they passed over the motherland, but it was in vain. After the fires, the planet had moved from green and blue to a universal grey/black/

white as if drained of all colour, which, he supposed, was exactly what had happened. He had done his best to sketch the image of his wife and their new baby daughter—little Sofiya—but he was no artist. He had a photograph of his wife, but had only seen the baby in their one video chat since her birth, before the fires wiped out all communication. Staring down at the planet that had once been his home, he wondered if he was the last living being to know of its destruction. The capsule that held him would now be his forever home. The capsule that now held him would become his coffin, now that he knew a re-supply craft would not be coming to him as scheduled. By his estimation, he had sixty-two days.

Outside of Eden, the shells of vehicles slowly disappeared beneath layers of accumulating snow. Within the skeleton of an old RV, a Saint Jude pendant hung from a half-melted rearview mirror, stoic and stained a deep raven-black, standing guard over the sweetly resting bones of his mistress, the one who had been named for him, the one who might still get to tell the story of this armageddon to the world.

Had this been a scene in one of Jude's documentaries, the camera would have started tight on the pendant, capturing how it did not move in the stillness of the new world. It would pull back slowly, lowering so as not to allow her skull into the frame, instead seeing one burned hand—just slender bones—hanging over the side of the seat, palm out as if ready to receive something. The camera would pull back further, back to the closet where the door would open to reveal a fireproof safe, turned black like the pendant, but intact, its treasure protected. How long before the future found this past? No one could say. Only time would tell.

Something stirred on the ground. A minuscule bit of snow shifted. A sound, barely audible and yet reverberant in the silence, cut across the graveyard. Two antenna appeared first. Black. Shiny. Then a body appeared, little legs scurrying as a cockroach left a tiny trail in a vast wilderness.

Acknowledgments

This series began in late 2016 as a therapeutic exercise to help me navigate my feelings around the US election and what I thought it said about the world. Ironically, it is releasing on the heels of another election that is igniting feelings that are much the same; though, instead of crying on the way to work, I am not surprised by this outcome, and that is maybe the most disturbing part of it all. In many ways, I fear our systems and governments are so broken that the only way to rebuild is to tear them down. And though this is not something that is reasonable to do in a functional society, that is what I was able to do within the world of *When The Trees All Burned*. I was able to play in that space of "what if" and, essentially, burn it to the ground. I don't want this book to stand as a manifesto or a political statement, but it might, in its own way, offer a warning. Of what? That is for you to decide.

Which brings me to my words of thanks. *You* are the reason I wrote this book. It has a message that only you can interpret and I believe it will be different for every single person who reads it. Choosing this book from all the other stories fighting for your attention is a generous gift you have given me and I hope it gives you just as much as I received in the writing of it.

To my husband, Scott. For more than two decades you have given me space to first explore who I was and then to lean into that discovery with the kind of passion that made me quit a secure job to pursue a creative career. Your faith in me, and the way you proudly champion everything I do, is a gift I will never take for granted. And when I'm rich and famous and you can quit your job, you'll be able to tell people it's all because you believed in me.

To my children:

Zander, our brain-storming sessions on the long drives back and forth from your Northern Ontario university were invaluable, even if it was just you allowing me to vent through plot struggles. The way you put your massive brain to work to provide me with dome schematics, mind-melting mathematics, and 3D modelling as I struggled to envision the dimensions and layout of the dome, blew my mind. You are so smart and I am so proud of you.

Liam, your sense of humour and the loud way you love me are two things I will never stop cherishing. I don't remember the context in which we discovered the "Third Gear" but I do remember laughing—a lot—and telling you I was going to find a way to work it into my book… which I did (and for which Bonnie thanks you also). The times we have spent together in your 2007 Mazda 3 (which, ironically, no longer has a third gear), jamming to Eminem, bouncing to KB featuring Lecrae, or crying to Shawn Mendes (me, not you) are some of my favourites.

Noa, your appreciation for a good story and strong characters is a powerful motivator for me to write something that might inspire others to read my work again and again just like you revisit some of your favourites. Your willingness to dive into open discussions about the state of the world, the subtle nuances of identity, and token-free representation have been wildly helpful as I made intentional choices to showcase the world as it is today. Your heart for inclusion and your dedication to continued learning is truly aspirational. Fear or love, bebe—the Moondance Diner bit was just for you.

To my parents, who nurtured a love of books and story in me before I even have memory of you doing so. You have cheered me on since I was a little girl, and allowed me to play in imaginative spaces without snuffing out my spark. Thank you for your love and support, even when I write in places that challenge your worldview or make you uncomfortable. Much of my confidence is because you gave me eighteen years of stability and then trusted me to face the world—though even then, I knew you'd always be there.

To Jeff Wardell, who (along with my husband) helped me bring Pocket Rochelle to life in the recording studio through an understanding of my vision and great skills in the areas of musicianship and production.

To Michael from the Prince Arthur Hotel in Thunder Bay, who provided an enthusiastic tour of the hotel basement, gifting me a first-hand look at where the old prohibition tunnels once stood. And to Janet from Portside Steak and Seafood, the attached restaurant, who eagerly shared the Prince Arthur ghost stories and rumours that will certainly receive screen time in the next book in the series.

To Steven King who taught me the value of world-building and the fact that long-windedness is reserved for those with literary fame.

To The Beatles, Belinda Carlisle, Fleetwood Mac, Madonna, and the Eurythmics, all of whom informed different parts of this story and made fun little cameos throughout.

To the stand-up comedians who helped me develop the character of Bonnie and find her voice. Specifically Taylor Tomlinson, Iliza Shleshinger, Fortune Feimster, and Jenny Slate. And to the comedians (whom I will not name) who taught me exactly who I didn't want Bonnie to be. And in this same vein, I need to thank Netflix, Amazon Prime, and YouTube for providing me hours of entertainment that I got to call research.

To Jerry Seinfeld for the Muffin Tops episode.

To Tiffany Allen, Dawn Edgcumbe, Brianne Lilly, E. Yvonne Pelletier, and Michael Werden for providing rich insight and constructive criticism in your role as a beta reader.

To everyone who is working to make the world a better place. Maybe we can save it. Maybe nothing has to burn. Thanks for being one of the reasons this is all worth it.

And to Heidi, who was right when she said haters should go lick a goat.

About the Author

Alanna Rusnak lives on a little patch of untamable land in small town Ontario with her husband (of more than two decades), children (two of which still live at home), a rude cat (who thinks he is a bird), and a vintage van she's far too excited about.

Her debut novel was a finalist for the 2018 Kobo Emerging Writer Prize and named one of the top reader-recommended titles of 2017 by cbcbooks.ca.

She writes fiction in her office, an old chicken coop that has been renovated into a beautiful work space, where she also runs an award-winning publishing company (for which she was named Most Influential Ontario Indie Publishing Businesswoman of 2024 by Acquisition International) and a literary arts magazine called *Blank Spaces*.

Soundtrack

Heaven Is A Place on Earth | Belinda Carlisle

Home Again | Michael Kiwanuka

No Rest - Acoustic | Dry the River

Courage | Villagers

Lost On The River #20 | The New Basement Tapes

Hot Scary Summer | Villagers

Heartbeats | José González

The Healing Day | Bill Fay

Cucurucu | Nick Mulvery

The Lion's Roar | First Aid Kit

The Great Escape | Patrick Watson

Naked As We Came | Iron & Wine

Untitled #4 | The Avett Brothers

The Longer the Waiting | Anna Ternheim

Daylight | David Kushner

Love Language | Connor Price, Evelyne Brochu

The Other Side | Clever Hopes

I'm Gonna Be | Najwajean

This Time Tomorrow (In The Canyon Haze) |
          Brandi Carlile

Dust to Dust | The Civil Wars

If I Go, I'm Goin | Gregory Alan Isakov

O Siem | Susan Aglukark

Rivers and Roads | The Head and the Heart

Dead for You | Najwajean

More To This | Marc Scibilia

Ordinary World | Duran Duran

Corner of the Universe | Creed Bratton

Life In My Bones | Mac Scibilia

Follow You Down to the Red Oak Tree |
          James Vincent McMorrow

Roar | Pocket Rochelle

We Meant to Say Amen | Pocket Rochelle

The Path That Takes Us Home | Pocket Rochelle

Get your free Pocket Rochelle tracks by visiting the shop at **alannarusnak.ca**. Put the EP in your cart and use the code MUSICFAN to download it for free.

Book Club

Welcome to the discussion guide for *When The Trees All Burned.* These twenty questions are designed to spark engaging conversations about the major themes, characters, and implications of the novel. While ambitious book clubs might tackle all these questions in one marathon session (don't forget the drinks and snacks!), you might find deeper discussions emerge by spreading them across two or three meetings. This allows time to really explore the novel's layers —from its lighter moments to its profound observations about human nature and survival.

The questions are arranged to flow from lighter "warm-up" discussions through deeper thematic explorations, before ending with some fun speculative questions. Feel free to jump around or focus on the topics that most interest your group.

Remember, there are no wrong interpretations—the best book club discussions often emerge from differing perspectives and experiences. Happy reading, and may your discussions be as rich and layered as Eden itself!

1. Let's play "Smuggle It Into Eden." If you were chosen and could secretly bring one item with you (assuming you could somehow hide it from the lions), what would you choose and why? Remember—you'll be living in a small house with minimal possessions, sharing communal meals, and potentially never seeing the outside world again. Would you pick something practical, sentimental, or maybe something to trade? What does your choice reveal about what you value most?

2. In Eden, each tiny house comes with a carefully curated collection of books built into the staircase —chosen specifically for each resident based on their interests and personality. We see books like *The God of Small Things* and *Utopia* on Rajiv's own shelf. If you were chosen for Eden, what books do you imagine would be waiting for you on your shelf? What would these selections reveal about who you are and what your role in the new society might be?

3. Throughout the novel, the author weaves in numerous pop culture references—from Pocket Rochelle's music to Belinda Carlisle's "Heaven is a Place on Earth" becoming an ironic anthem, from

Jude's love of The Beatles (shown in her naming of the Roombas) to mentions of everything from Michael Bay movies to Staten Island Ferry rides. How do these familiar references affect your experience of the story? Consider especially:

- The way Bonnie's comedy routines reference contemporary culture
- The contrast between current pop culture and what might be preserved in Eden's library
- How these references help anchor the story in our present moment while pointing toward an uncertain future
- The use of social media, viral videos, and memes in spreading both Rajiv's message and skepticism about it
- How different characters use cultural touchstones to process their experiences

4. Many characters demonstrate different responses to impending doom—denial, acceptance, preparation, celebration, etc. Which reactions felt most authentic to you? How do you think you would respond in a similar situation?

5. Technology plays a complex and sometimes contradictory role in the story. Rajiv bans the

internet from Eden while simultaneously using advanced tech to select and track his chosen ones. Meanwhile, Jude deliberately chooses analog equipment for her documentary work, believing it captures something more "honest" than digital technology. How do these different approaches to technology reflect larger themes in the novel? What commentary do you think the author is making about humanity's relationship with progress and authenticity? Consider especially how the "old" and "new" technologies serve different purposes in preserving human history and memory.

6.   The novel explores different types of faith—religious faith, faith in science, faith in humanity, and faith in love. How do different characters demonstrate or struggle with faith throughout the story? What statement do you think the author is making about the role of faith in times of crisis?

7.   The concept of consent is a major theme. From Rajiv's Kool-Aid program to Aiya's abusive marriage. How does the novel explore the complexities around choice, consent, and control? Were Rajiv's actions ethical given what he knew was coming?

8.   Several key relationships in the novel (Aiya and Ryan, Bonnie and Maxine, Jude and Brett) represent very different kinds of love. How does each relationship illuminate different aspects of human connection? What do you think the author is saying about love's power to both heal and harm?

9.   The novel explores various political ideologies and power structures—from Rajiv's self-described "communist utopia" to the world governments' dismissal of his warnings. How do different characters' political beliefs shape their actions? What commentary might the author be making about political systems' ability (or inability) to address existential threats? Consider especially how Rajiv's vision of a classless society in Eden contrasts with his unilateral power to choose who lives and dies?

10.   Eden's architecture is rich with symbolism, particularly the central fountain. Its androgynous figure, with feminine collarbones but masculine shoulders, holds an open book bearing Rajiv's lion insignia while water pours through its fingers. Hidden in the robes are chains and rings for restraining wrongdoers. How does this fountain's design reflect the complexities and potential

contradictions of Rajiv's vision? Consider other symbolic elements of Eden:

- The semi-circles of identical homes radiating out from the fountain
- The library housed in what appears from outside to be Rajiv's mansion
- The transparent dome itself
- The underground growing spaces carved from the old mine

What might each of these design choices suggest about power, equality, transparency, and control in this "perfect" society? How do these architectural elements reinforce or sometimes contradict Rajiv's stated values? What does the blending of natural and artificial elements tell us about his vision for humanity's relationship with nature?

11. Rajiv deliberately adopts the loaded imagery of "drinking the Kool-aid"—a phrase that emerged from the Jonestown massacre—but subverts it by being completely transparent about his intentions and the technology involved. He even seems to have a sense of humour about it as memes and social media trends emerge around "Kool-aid parties." How does his open acknowledgment of

this dark cultural reference affect your perception of him and his mission? Consider:

- The difference between his approach and traditional cult leaders who operate in secrecy
- His use of viral marketing and social trends to spread his message
- The irony of people treating his "Kool-aid" as a joke while simultaneously giving consent to be chosen
- The contrast between the playful delivery method and the serious technology it contains
- How he turns a symbol of blind faith into one of informed choice

What does this tell us about Rajiv's character? Is he genuinely playful, cleverly manipulative, or something else entirely? How does his approach to recruitment differ from historical doomsday prophets?

12. The novel includes multiple perspectives on survival—physical, emotional, cultural. What does the story suggest about what's truly worth preserving when civilization faces extinction?

13. Several characters grapple with whether they are "worthy" of survival. How does the novel explore ideas of human worth? Do you agree with Rajiv's selection criteria?

14. Throughout the novel, we see different styles of leadership and authority—from Rajiv's benevolent dictatorship to the world governments' bureaucratic paralysis to the potential of local community organizing in places like the Peters' bunker. Which approaches seem most effective in the face of catastrophe? What might this suggest about political systems' capacity to handle large-scale disasters?

15. Animals like Edgar the cat and the canaries in the mine serve interesting symbolic roles. How do these creatures contribute to the larger themes of the novel? What might they represent?

16. The novel can be read as a commentary on climate change, social inequality, or humanity's capacity for both destruction and renewal. Which interpretations resonated most with you and why?

17. Music plays a significant role in the story, from Pocket Rochelle's performances to the ironic use of "Heaven is a Place on Earth." How does the author

use music to develop themes and atmosphere? What does music represent in the larger context of human culture and what's worth preserving?

18. The ending leaves several questions unanswered about humanity's future. What do you imagine happens to the survivors in Eden? The bunker dwellers? Those few who might have survived elsewhere? What kind of world do you think emerges?

19. How does the author use physical spaces (Eden, the mine, the bunkers, the RV) to explore themes of safety, imprisonment, and freedom? What might these different spaces represent symbolically?

20. Would you rather: try to get into Eden, attempt to reach the Prince Arthur Hotel bunker with Rasmus and his group, or join the Peters in their DIY shelter in New Mexico. Which would you choose and why? Consider:

   • The different chances of long-term survival
   • Whether you'd rather be chosen or make your own fate
   • If you'd prefer to face the end with strangers or find your way to loved ones
   • How much freedom versus security matters to you

- The different leadership styles in each location
- The varying levels of comfort and community

— 367 —

Alanna would love to join your book club discussion! If you're located near Durham, Ontario, she's happy to attend in person. For clubs further afield, she's available for Zoom sessions to share insights about the story's development and answer your questions. Reach out through her website (alannarusnak.ca) or connect on social media to arrange a visit.

HAVE YOU TAKEN
THE ALGORITHM
QUIZ TO FIND OUT
IF YOU HAVE WHAT
IT TAKES TO BE
CHOSEN FOR THE
DOME?

READY TO DRINK
THE KOOL-AID?

Rabbit Mountain Dome - Eden

$\pi \times (d/2)^2 = 35\ acres$

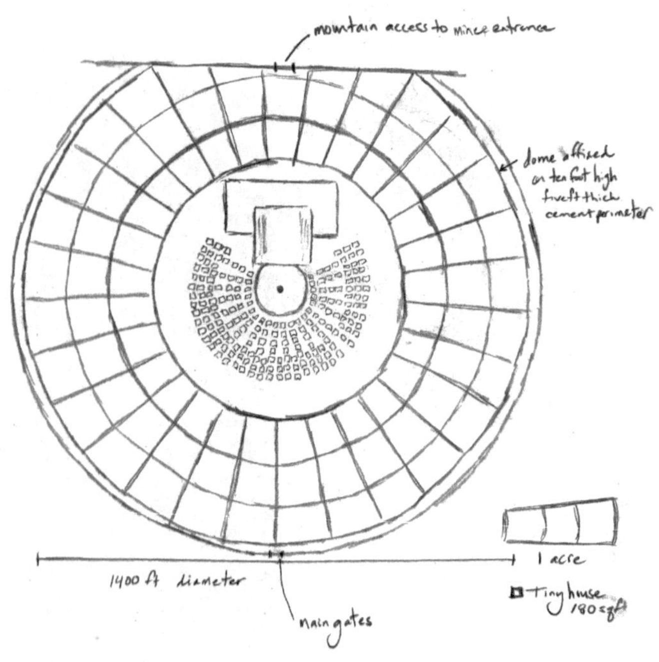

Also by the Author

The Church in the Wildwood (2017)
The Ghost of Iris Carver (2018)
Black Bird (2020)

www.ingramcontent.com/pod-product-compliance
Lightning Source LLC
Chambersburg PA
CBHW030735310726
48969CB00005B/1224